EVERYTHING
YOU NEED

Michael Marshall Smith

EVERYTHING YOU NEED

Michael Marshall Smith

EARTHLING PUBLICATIONS - 2013

FIRST EDITION, FIRST PRINTING
September 2013

ISBN-13: 978-0-9838071-4-8

EARTHLING PUBLICATIONS
P.O. Box 413
Northborough, MA 01532 USA
Email: earthlingpub@yahoo.com
Website: www.earthlingpub.com

Author's website: http://www.michaelmarshallsmith.com/

Printed in the U.S.A.

Contents

This Is Now

"OKAY," HENRY SAID. "SO NOW WE'RE HERE."

He was using his "So entertain me" voice, and he was cold but trying not to show it. Pete and I were cold too. We were trying not to show it either. Being cold is not cool, and it is not manly. So you look at your condensing breath as if it's a total surprise to you, what with it being so balmy and all. Even when you've known each other for over thirty years, you do these things.

Why? I don't know.

"Yep," I agreed. It wasn't my job to entertain Henry.

Pete walked up to the thick wire fence. He tilted his head back until he was looking at the top, four feet above his head. A ten-foot wall of tautly criss-crossed wire. "Who's going to test it?"

"Well, hey, you're closest." Like the others, I was speaking quietly, though we were half a mile from the nearest road or house or person.

7

This side of the fence, anyhow.

"I did it last time."

"Long while ago."

"Still," he said, stepping back. "Your turn, Dave."

I held up my hands. "These are my tools, man."

Henry sniggered. "*You're* a tool, that's for sure."

Pete laughed, too. I had to smile, and for a moment it was like it *was* the last time. Hey presto — time travel on a budget. You don't need a machine, it turns out; you just need a friend to laugh like a teenager. Chronology shivers.

And so — quickly, before I could think about it — I flipped my hand out and touched the fence. My whole arm jolted, as if every bone in it had been tapped with a hammer. Tapped *hard*, and in different directions.

"Christ," I hissed, spinning away, shaking my hand like I was trying to rid myself of it. "Goddamn *Christ* that hurts."

Henry nodded sagely. "This stretch has current, then. Also, didn't we use a stick last time?"

"Always been the brains of the operation, right, Hank?"

Pete snickered again. I was annoyed, but the shock had pushed me over a line. It had brought it all back much more strongly.

I nodded up the line of the fence as it marched off into the trees. "Further," I said, and pointed at Henry. "And you're testing the next section, bro."

It was one of those things you do, one of those stupid, drunken things, that afterward seem impossible to understand. You ask yourself why, feeling confused and sad, like the ghost of a man killed through a careless step in front of a car. But then it's too late.

We could have *not* gone to The Junction, for a start, though it was a Thursday and the Thursday session is a winter tradition with us, a way of making January and February seem less like a living death.

The two young guys could have given up the pool table, though, instead of bogarting it all night (by virtue of being better than us, and efficiently dismissing each of our challenges in turn): in which case we would have played a dozen slow frames and gone home around eleven, like usual — ready to get up the following morning feeling no more than a little fusty. This time of year it hardly matters if Henry yawns over the gas pump, or Pete zones out behind the counter in the Massaqua Mart, and I can sling a morning's worth of home fries and sausage in my sleep. We've been doing these things so long that we barely have to be present. Maybe that's the point. Maybe that's the real problem right there.

Anyway, by quarter after eight, proven pool-fools, we were sitting at the corner table. We always have, since back when it was Bill's Bar and beer tasted new and strange and metallic in our mouths. We were talking back and forth, laughing once in a while, none of us bothered about the pool but yes, a little bit bothered all the same. It wasn't some macho thing. I don't care about being beat by some guys who are passing through. I don't much care about being beat by anyone. Henry and Pete and I tend to win games about equally. If it weren't that way then probably we wouldn't play together. It's never been about winning. It was more that I simply wished I was better at it. Had *assumed* I'd be better, one day, like I expected to wind up being something other than a short-order cook. Don't get me wrong: you eat one of my breakfasts you'll be set up for the day and tomorrow you'll come back and order the same thing. I'm okay at what I do — it just wasn't what I had in mind when I was young. Not sure what I *did* have in mind — I used to think maybe I'd go over the mountains to Seattle, be in a band or something, but the thought got vague and lost direction after that — but it certainly wasn't being first in command at a hot griddle. None of our jobs are bad jobs, but they're the kind held by people in the background. People who are getting by. People who don't play pool that well.

It also struck me, as I watched Pete banter with Nicole when she brought us round number four or five, that I was still smoking. I'd been assuming I would have given it up by now. Tried, once or twice. Didn't take. Would it ever happen? Probably not. Would it give me cancer sooner or later? Most likely. Better try again, then. At some point.

Henry watched Nicole's ass as it accompanied her back to the counter. "Cute as hell," he noted, approvingly, not for the first time.

Pete and I grunted, in the way we would have if he'd observed that the moon was smaller than the earth. Henry's observation was both true and something that had very little bearing on our lives. Nicole was twenty-three. We could give her fifteen years each. That's not the kind of gift that cute girls covet.

So we sat and talked, and smoked, and didn't listen to the sound of balls being efficiently slotted into pockets by people who weren't us.

You walk for long enough in the woods at night, you'll start getting jittery. Forests have a way of making civilization seem less inevitable. In sunlight they may make you want to build yourself a cabin and get back to nature, get that whole Davy Crockett vibe going on. In the dark they remind you what a good thing chairs and hot meals and electric lights really are, and you thank God that you live now, instead of then.

Every once in a while we'd test the fence — using a stick. The current was on each time we tried. So we kept walking. We followed the line of the wire as it cut up the rise, then down into a shallow streambed, then up again steeply on the other side.

If you were seeing the fence for the first time you'd likely wonder at the straightness of it, the way the concrete posts had been planted at ten yard intervals deep into the rock. You might ask yourself if national forests normally went to these lengths to protect their boundaries, and you'd soon remember they didn't; that for the most part a cheerful little wooden sign by the side of the road was judged to be all that was needed.

If you kept on walking deeper, intrigued, sooner or later you'd see a notice attached to one of the posts. The notices are small, designed to convey authority rather than draw attention.

"NO TRESPASSING," they say. "MILITARY LAND."

That could strike you as a little strange, perhaps, because you might have believed that most of the marked-off military areas were down over in the moonscapes of Nevada rather than up here in a quiet northeast corner of Washington State. But who knows what the military's up to, right? Apart from protecting us from foreign aggressors, of course, and The Ongoing Terrorist Threat, and if that means they need a few acres to themselves then that's actually kind of comforting. The army moves in mysterious ways, our freedoms to defend. Good for them, you'd think, and you'd likely turn and head back for town, having had enough of tramping through snow for the day. In the evening you'd come into Ruby's and eat hearty, some of my wings or a burger or the brisket — which, though I say so myself, isn't half bad. Next morning you'd drive back south and forget about it, and us.

I remember when the fences went up, though. Thirty years ago. 1985. Our parents knew what they were for. Hell, we were only eight and *we* knew.

There was a danger, and it was getting worse: the last decade had proved that. Four people had disappeared in the last year alone. One came back and was sick for a week, in an odd and dangerous kind of way, and then died. The others were never seen again. My aunt Jean was one of those. But there's danger to going in abandoned mine shafts, too, or talking to strangers, or juggling knives when you're drunk.

So…you don't do it. You walk the town in pairs at night, and you observe the unspoken curfew. You keep an eye out for men who don't blink, for slim women whose strides are too short — or so people say.

There was never that much passing trade in town. Massaqua isn't on the way to anywhere. Massaqua is a single guy who keeps his yard tidy and doesn't bother anyone. The tourist season up here is short and not exactly intense. There is no ski lodge or health spa and the motel frankly isn't up to much.

The fence seemed to keep the danger contained and out of town, and within a few years its existence was part of life. It wasn't like it was right there on our doorstep. No big-city reporter heard about it and came up looking to make a sensation — or, if they did, they didn't make it all the way here.

Life went on. Years passed.

Sometimes small signs work better than great big ones.

As we climbed deeper into the forest, Pete was in front. I was more-or-less beside him, and Henry lagged a few steps behind. It had been that way the last time, too, but then we hadn't had hip flasks to keep us fuelled in our intentions. We hadn't needed to stop to catch our breath quite so often either.

"We just going to keep on walking?"

It was Henry asked the question, of course. Pete and I didn't even answer.

At quarter after ten we still were in the bar. The two guys remained at the pool table. When one leaned down, the other stood judiciously sipping from a bottled beer. They weren't talking to each other, just slotting the balls down. Looked like they were having a whale of a time.

We were drinking steadily, and the conversation was often a two-way while one or other of us trekked back and forth to empty our bladder. By then we were resigned to just sitting around. We were a little too drunk to start playing pool, even if the table became free. There was no news to catch up on. We felt aimless. We already knew Pete was ten years married, that they had no children and it was likely going to stay that way. His wife is fine, and still pleasant to be with, though her collection of dolls is getting exponentially bigger. We knew Henry was married once too, had a little boy, and that, though the kid and his mother now lived forty miles away, relations between them remained cordial. Neither Pete nor I are much surprised that he has achieved this. Henry can be a royal pain in the ass at times, but he wouldn't still be our friend if that's all he was.

"Same again, boys? You're thirsty tonight."

It was Pete's turn in the restrooms so it was Henry and me who looked up to see Nicole smiling down at us, thumb hovering over the REPEAT button on her pad. Deprived of Pete's easy manner (partly genetic, also honed over years of chatting to the public while totting and bagging groceries), our response was cluttered and vague.

Quick nods and smiles; I said thanks, and Henry got out a "Hell, yes!" that sounded a little loud.

Nicole winked at me and went away again, as she has done many times over the last three years. When she got to the bar I saw one of the pool-players looking at her, and felt a strange twist of something in my stomach. It wasn't because they were strangers, or because I suspected they might be something else, something that shouldn't be here. They were just younger guys, that's all. Of course they're going to look at her.

She's probably going to want them to.

I lit another cigarette and wondered why I still didn't really know how to deal with women. They've always seemed so different from guys, somehow. So confident, so powerful, so in themselves. Kind of scary, even. Most teenage boys feel that way, I guess, but I'd assumed age would help. That being older might make a difference. Apparently not. The opposite, if anything.

"Cute just really doesn't cover it," Henry said, again not for the first time. "Going to have to come up with a whole new word. Super-cute, how's that. Hyperhot. Ultra —"

How about just beautiful?

For a horrible moment I thought I'd said this out loud. I guess in a way I did, because what pronouncements ring louder than the ones you make only in your own head?

Pete returned to the table at the same time as the new beers arrived, and with him around it was easier to come across like grown-ups. He came back looking thoughtful, too.

He waited until the three of us were alone again, and then reached across and took one of my Marlboro: like he used to, back in the day, when he couldn't afford his own. He didn't seem to be aware he'd done it. He looked pretty drunk, in fact, and I realized I was too. Henry is generally at least a *little* drunk.

Pete lit the cigarette, took a long mouthful of beer, and then he said:

"You remember that time we went over the fence?"

The stick touched the wire, and nothing happened.

I did it again. Same result. We stopped walking. My legs ached and I was glad for the break.

Pete hesitated, then reached out and brushed the thick black wire with his hand. When we were kids he might have pretended it was charged, and jiggered back and forth, eyes rolling and tongue sticking out.

He didn't now. He just curled his fingers around it, gave it a light tug.

"Power's down," he said, quietly.

Henry and I stepped up close. Even with Pete standing there grasping it, you still had to gird yourself to do the same.

Then all three of us were holding the fence, holding it with both hands, looking in.

That close up, the wire fuzzed out of focus and it was almost as if it wasn't there. You just saw the forest beyond it: moonlit trunks, snow; you heard the quietness. If you stood on the other side and looked out, the view would be exactly the same, I guess. With a fence that long, it could be difficult to tell which side was in, which was out.

This, too, was what had happened the previous time, when we were fifteen. We'd heard that sometimes a section of the fence went down for a brief period, and so we went looking. What with animals, snowfall, the random impacts of falling branches, and a mountain wind that could blow hard and cold at most times of year, once in a while a cable stopped supplying the juice to one ten-yard stretch. The power was never down for more than a day. There was a computer that kept track, and — somewhere, nobody knew where — a small station from which a couple of military engineers would quickly be dispatched to come to repair the outage.

But for now, a section was down.

We stood, a silent row of older men, and remembered what had happened back then.

Pete had gone up first. He shuffled along to one of the concrete posts so the wire wouldn't bag out, and started pulling himself up. As soon as his feet left the ground, I didn't want to be left behind, so I went to the other post and went up just as quickly.

We reached the top at around the same time. Soon as we started down the other side — lowering ourselves at first, then just dropping, Henry started his own climb.

We all landed silently in the snow, with bent knees.

We were on the other side, and we stood very still. As far as we knew, no one had ever done this before.

To some people, this might have been enough.

Not to three fifteen-year-old boys.

Moving very quietly, hearts beating hard — just from the exertion, none of us were scared, not *exactly*, not enough to admit it anyway — we moved away from the fence.

After about twenty yards I stopped and looked back.

"You chickening out?"

"No, Henry," I said. His voice had been quiet and shaky. I took pains that mine sound firm. "Memorizing. We want to be able to find that dead section again."

He'd nodded. "Good thinking, smart boy."

Pete looked back with us. Stand of three trees close together there. Unusually big tree over on the right. Kind of a semi-clearing, on a crest. Shouldn't be hard to find again.

We glanced at each other, judged it logged in our heads, then turned and headed away, into a place no one had been for nearly ten years.

The forest floor led away gently. There was enough moonlight to show the ground panning down toward a kind of high valley lined with thick trees.

As we walked, bent over a little with unconscious caution, part of me was already relishing how we'd remember this in the future, leaping over the event into its retrospection. Not that we'd talk about it, outside the three of us. It was the kind of thing that might attract attention to the town, including maybe attention from this side of the fence.

There was one person I thought I might mention it to, though. Her name was Lauren and she was very cute, the kind of beautiful that doesn't have to open its mouth to call your name from across the street. I had talked to her a couple times, summoning bravery I hadn't known I possessed. It was she who had talked about Seattle, said she'd like to go hang out there some day. That sounded good to me, good and exciting and strange. What I didn't know, that long-ago night in the forest, was she would go on to do this, and I would not, and that she would leave without our ever having kissed.

I just assumed...I assumed a lot back then.

After a couple hundred yards we stopped, huddled together, shared one of my cigarettes. Our hearts were beating heavily, even though we'd been coming downhill. The forest is hard work whatever direction it slopes. But it wasn't just that. It felt a little colder here. There was also something about the light. It seemed to hold more shadows. You found your eyes flicking from side to side, checking things out, wanting to be reassured, but not being confident that you had been after all.

I bent down to put the cigarette out in the snow. It was extinguished in a hiss that seemed very loud.

We continued in the direction we'd been heading. We walked maybe another five, six hundred yards.

It was Henry who stopped.

Keyed up as we were, Pete and I halted immediately, too. Henry was leaning forward a little, squinting ahead.

"What?"

He pointed. Down at the bottom of the rocky valley was a shape. A big shape.

After a moment I could make out it was a building. Two wooden storeys high, and slanting.

You saw that kind of thing, sometimes. The sagging remnant of some pioneer's attempt to claim an area of this wilderness, and pretend it could be a home.

Pete nudged me and pointed in a slightly different direction. There were the remnants of another house further down. A little fancier, with a fallen-down porch.

And thirty yards further, another. Smaller, with a false front.

"Cool," Henry said, and briefly I admired him.

We sidled now, a lot more slowly and heading along the rise instead of down it. Ruined houses look very interesting during the day. At night they seem different, especially when lost high up in the forest. They sit at angles that do not seem quite right. Trees grow too close to them, pressing in. The lack of a road, long overgrown, can make the houses look like they were never built but instead made their own way to this forgotten place, in which you have now disturbed them.

I was beginning to wonder if maybe we'd done enough, come far enough, and I doubt I was the only one.

Then we saw the light.

* * *

After Pete asked his question in the bar, there was silence for a moment. Of course we remembered that night. It wasn't something you'd forget. It was a dumb question unless you were really asking something else, and we both knew Pete wasn't dumb.

Behind us, on the other side of the room, came the quiet, reproachful sound of pool balls hitting each other and then one of them going neatly down a pocket.

We could hear what each other was thinking. Thinking it was a very cold evening, and that there was thick snow on the ground, as there had been on that other night, when we were fifteen. That the rest of the town had pretty much gone to bed. That we could get in Henry's truck and be at the head of a hiking trail in twenty minutes, even driving drunkard slow.

I didn't hear anyone thinking a reason, though.

I didn't hear anyone think *why* we might do such a thing, or what might happen if we did.

By the time Pete had finished his cigarette, our glasses were empty. We put on our coats and left the bar and crunched across the lot to Henry's truck.

Back *then,* on that long-ago night, suddenly my young heart hadn't seemed to be beating at all. When we saw the light in the second house, a faint and curdled glow in one of the downstairs windows, my whole body suddenly felt light and insubstantial.

One of us tried to speak. It came out like a dry click. I realized there was a light in the other house, too, faint and golden.

Had I missed it before, or had it just come on?

I took a step backward. The forest was silent but for the sound of my friends' breathing.

"Oh, no," Pete said. He started moving backward, stumbling.

Then I saw it too.

A figure, standing in front of the first house.

It was tall and slim, like a rake's shadow. It was a hundred yards away, but still it seemed as though you could make out an oval shape on its shoulders, the color of milk diluted with water.

It was looking in our direction.

Then another was standing near the other house.

No, two.

Henry moaned softly, and we three boys turned as one, and I have never run like that before or since.

The first ten yards were fast but then the slope cut in and our feet started to slip, and after that we were down on our hands half the time, scrabbling and pulling — every muscle working together in a headlong attempt to be somewhere else.

I heard a crash behind and flicked my head around to see Pete had gone down hard, banging his knee, falling on his side.

Henry kept on going but I made myself turn around to grab Pete's hand, not really helping but just pulling, trying to yank him back to his feet or at least away.

Over his shoulder I glimpsed the valley below, and I saw that the figures were down at the bottom of the rise, heading our way in jerky blurred-black movements, like half-seen spiders darting across an icy window pane.

Pete's face jerked up and I saw in it what I felt in myself, and it was not a cold fear but a hot one, a red-hot meltdown as if you were going to rattle and break apart.

Then he was on his feet again, moving past me, and I followed on after him toward the disappearing shape of Henry's back. It seemed so much further than we'd walked. It was uphill, and the trees no longer formed a path and even the wind seemed to be pushing us back.

We caught up with Henry and passed him, streaking up the last hundred yards toward the fence. None of us turned around again.

You didn't have to. You could feel them coming, feel them getting closer like rocks thrown at your head, rocks only to be glimpsed at the last minute, when there is time to flinch but not to turn.

I was sprinting straight at the fence when Henry called out. I was going too fast and didn't want to know what his problem was. I leapt up at the wire.

It was like a truck hit me from the side.

I crashed to the ground fizzing, arms sparking and with no idea which way was up. Then two pairs of hands were on me, pulling at my coat.

I thought the fingers would be long and pale and strong but then I realized it was my friends and they were pulling me away from the wrong section of the fence, dragging me to the side, to the right part, when they could have just left me where I fell and made their own escape.

The three of us jumped up at the wire at once, scrabbling like monkeys, stretching out for the top. I rolled over wildly, grunting as I scored deep scratches across my back that would earn me a long, hard look from my mother when she happened to glimpse them a week later.

We landed heavily on the other side, still moving forward, having realized as one that we'd just given away the location of a portion of dead fence.

But now we *had* to look back, and what I saw — though my head was still vibrating from the electric shock I'd received, so I cannot swear to this — was at least three, maybe five, figures on the other side of the fence. Not right up against it, but a few yards back.

Black hair whipped up around their faces in the wind, and they looked like absences ill-lit.

Then they were gone.

We moved fast. We didn't know why they'd stopped, but we didn't hang around. We didn't stick too close to the fence, either, in case they changed their minds.

We half-walked, half-ran, and at first we were quiet but as we got further away and nothing came after us, we began to laugh and then to shout, punching the air, boys who had come triumphantly out the other side.

The forest felt like some huge football field, applauding its heroes with whispering leaves.

We got back to town a little after two in the morning. We walked down the middle of the deserted main street, slowly, untouchable, knowing the world had changed: that we were no longer the boys who had started the evening together, but men, and that the stars were there to be touched.

That was then.

As older men, we stood together at the fence for a long time, recalling that night.

Parts of it are fuzzy now, of course, and it's reduced to snapshots: Pete's terrified face when he slipped, the first glimpse of light at the houses, Henry's shout as he tried to warn me, narrow faces the color of moonlight. The other guys most likely remembered other things, defined that night in different ways, and were the center of their own recollections. As I looked now through the fence at the other forest I was thinking how long a decade had seemed back then, and how you could learn that it was no time at all.

Henry stepped away first. I wasn't far behind. Pete stayed a moment longer, then took a couple of steps back. Nobody said anything. We just looked at the fence a little longer, and then we turned and walked away.

Took us forty minutes to get back to the truck.

The next Thursday, Henry couldn't make it, so it was just me and Pete at the pool table. Late in the evening, with many beers drunk, I mentioned the fence.

Not looking at me, chalking his cue, Pete said that if Henry hadn't stepped back when he did the week before, he'd have climbed it.

"And gone over?"

"Yeah," he said.

This was bullshit, and I knew it. "Really?"

There was a pause. "No," he said, eventually, and I wished I hadn't asked the second time. I could have left him with something, left *us* with it. Calling an ass cute isn't much, but it's better than just coming right out and admitting you'll never cup it in your hand.

The next week it was the three of us again, and our walk in the woods wasn't even mentioned. We've never brought it up since, and we can't talk about the first time any more, either. We killed it.

I think about it sometimes, though. I know I could go out walking there myself some night, and there have been slow afternoons and dry, sleepless small hours when I think I might do it: when I tell myself such a thing isn't impossible now, that I am still who I once was.

But I have learned a little since I was fifteen, and in the end I just go smoke another cigarette on the porch, or out back of the diner, because in my heart of hearts I know that was then, and this is now.

Unbelief

IT HAPPENED IN BRYANT PARK, a little after six o'clock in the evening. He was sitting by himself in lamp shadow amongst the trees, at one of the rickety green metal tables along the north side, close to where the Barnes & Noble library area is during the day. He was warmly dressed in nondescript, casual clothing and sipping a Starbucks in a seasonally red cup, acquired from the outlet on the corner of Sixth, opposite one of the entrances to the park. He queued, like any normal person. Watching through the window you'd have got no idea who he was, or the power he wielded over this and other neighborhoods.

He had done exactly the same on the preceding two evenings. I'd followed him down from Times Square both times, watched him buy the same drink from the same place and then spend half an hour sitting in the same chair in the park, or close enough, watching the world go by. Evidently, as I had been assured, it was what this man always did at this time of day and this time of year. Habit and ritual are some of our greatest comforts, but they're a gift to people like me.

He might as well have tied himself up with a bow.

* * *

On the previous occasions I had merely observed, logged his actions, and walked on by. The thing had been booked for a specific date, for reasons I neither knew nor cared about. That day had now come, and so I entered the park by the next entrance along, strolling into the park casually and without evident intent.

I paused for a moment on the steps. He didn't appear to be there with protection. There were other people sparsely spread around the park, perched at tables or walking in the very last of the twilight, but there was no indication they were anything more than standard-issue New Yorkers, taking a little time before battling the subway or bridges and tunnels or airports, heading home to their family or friends or partner for the holidays. Grabbing a last few seconds' blessed solitude, an unwitnessed cigarette, or an illicit kiss and a promise not to forget, before entering a day or two of enforced incarceration with the people who populated their real lives.

Their presence in the park did not concern me. They were either absorbed with their companions or something within themselves, and none would notice me until it was too late. I have done harder jobs in more difficult conditions. I could have just taken the shot from twenty feet away, and kept on walking, but I found I didn't want it to happen like that.

Not with this guy. He deserved less than that.

I watched him covertly as I approached his position. He appeared relaxed, at ease, as if savoring his own few private moments of peace before tackling some great enterprise. I knew what he thought that was going to be. I also knew it wasn't going to happen.

There was an empty chair on the other side of his table. I sat down in it.

He ignored me for a couple minutes, peering in a vaguely benign way at the skeletal branches of the tall trees that stand all around the park's central area: at them, or perhaps at all the buildings around the square revealed by the season's dearth of leaves. Being able to see these monoliths makes the park seem both bigger and yet more intimate, stripped.

Defenseless.

"Hello, Kane," he said, finally.

I'd never actually seen him before — not in the flesh at least, only pictures — so I have no idea how he'd managed to make me straight away. I guess it's his job to know things about people.

"You don't seem surprised," I said.

He glanced at me, finally, then away again, seemingly to watch a young couple perched at a table twenty yards away. They were bundled up in thick coats and scarves and necking with cautious optimism. After a few minutes they separated, tentatively smiling, still with their arms around each other's shoulders, and turned to look at the lights strung in the trees, to listen to the sound of cars honking, to savor being where they were. A recent liaison, the legacy of an office party, perhaps, destined to be a source of embarrassed silences in the office by Valentine's Day. Either that or pregnancy and marriage and all the far longer silences afterward.

"I knew it could happen," the man said, taking the lid off his coffee and peering inside, as if gauging how long he had left. "I'm not surprised that it's you sitting there."

"Why's that?"

"Accepting a job for this evening? That's cold. Takes a certain kind of person. Who else they going to call?"

"That supposed to be a compliment? You think if you butter me up then I won't do it?"

The man looked calmly at me through the steam of what smelled like a gingerbread latte. "Oh, you'll do it. I have no doubt of that."

I didn't like his tone, and I felt the thing start to uncurl inside me. If you've ever tried to give up smoking, you'll have felt something like it — the sudden, lurid desire to lay waste to the world and everything in it, starting right here, right now, and with the person physically closest to you.

I don't know what this thing is. It doesn't have a name. I just know it's there, and I feel when it wakes. It has always been a very light sleeper.

"No, really," I said. "Just because I live in a big house these days and I got a wife and a child, you think I can't do what I do?"

"You've still got it. You'll always have it."

"Fucking right I will."

"And that's something to be proud of?" He shook his head. "Shame of it is, you were a good kid."

"Isn't everyone?"

"No. Some people come out of the womb broken. You can nurture all you want, but sooner or later they're going to pass the damage on. With you, it could have been different. That makes it worse, somehow."

"I am who I chose to be."

"Really? Everyone in the neighborhood knows the kind of person your father was."

My hands twitched involuntarily.

"He had no faith in anything," the man said. "He was a hater. And a hurter. I remember watching him when he was young, too, knowing how he'd grow up to be. Either dead inside or affectionate in inappropriate ways. Maybe both. Am I right?"

"If you'd like this to play out in a civilized fashion," I said, my voice tight, "you would do well to drop this line of discussion."

"Forgive me. But you've come here to kill me, Kane. That's pretty personal, too, wouldn't you say?"

I knew I should get on with it. But I was also aware this was the biggest job of my career, and when it was done, it would be over. I was also simply curious.

"What the fuck makes you think you're better than me?" I said. "What you do isn't so different."

"You think so?"

"You put yourself in a position of power; you made it so you get to choose who gets what. Who prospers, who gets nothing. And then you point the finger and lives get fucked up forever. Same as me."

"I don't see it that way." He looked into his cup again. The habit was beginning to get on my nerves.

"Yeah, drink up," I said. "Time's running out."

"One question."

"How'd I find you?"

He nodded.

"People talk."

"My people?"

I shook my head, irritably. The truth was his own soldiers had held the line. I'd tracked down a couple of them (one slurping pho in a noodle bar under a bridge in Queens, the other sleeping in a tree in Central Park) and leaned on them hard — to the point where one of them would not be working for him, or anyone else, ever again. Both had merely looked up at me with their cold, strange eyes and waited for whatever I was going to do. It was not them who'd told me to go and stand in Times Square at the end of any December afternoon, and wait there until this man appeared, arriving there from directions unknown.

"So, who, then?"

"It's too late for you to be taking names," I said, with some satisfaction. "That's all over now."

He smiled again, but coldly, and I saw something in his face that had not been there before — not on the surface, at least. I saw the steady calm of a man who was used to making judgment calls, decisions upon which the lives of others had hung. A man who had measured, assayed, and who was now about to pay the price, at the behest of people who had fallen on the wrong side of the line he had believed it was his God-given right to draw.

"You think you're this big, bountiful guy," I said. "Everybody's old man. But some understand the real truth. They realize it's all bullshit."

"Have I not made my rules clear? Have I not looked out for the people who deserved it?"

"Only to make them do what you want."

"And what do *you* want? Why are you really here tonight, Kane?"

"Someone paid me to be. More than one, in fact. A syndicate. People saying that enough is enough. Getting back for what you did to them."

"I know about that," he interrupted, as if bored. "I can even guess who these people are. But I asked why *you're* here."

"For the money."

"No. Otherwise you'd have done it from ten yards away and be on your way home by now."

"So you tell me why, if you're so fucking wise."

"It's personal," he said. "And that's a mistake. You've made a good living out of what you do, and have something of a life. In your terms. That's because you've merely been for hire. But you want this one for yourself. Admit it. You hate me on your own account."

This man was smart enough to know a lie when he heard it, so I said nothing.

"Why, Kane? Did something happen, some night, when there was snow on the ground outside and everything should have been carols and fairy lights? Did your Christmas presents come with conditions, or costs? Payments that came due in the middle of the night, when Mom was asleep?"

"That's enough."

"How many people have you killed, Kane? Can you even remember?"

"I remember," I said, though I could not.

"When you let it get personal, the cost becomes personal, too.

You're opening your own heart here. You sure you want to do that?"

"I'd do it for free. For the bullshit you are, and have always been."

"Disbelief is easy, Kane. It's faith that takes courage, and character."

"You're out of time," I said.

He sighed. Then he tipped the cup, drained the last of his coffee, and set it down on the table between us.

"I'm done," he said.

In the fifteen minutes we'd been talking, nearly half the people had left the park. The necking couple had been amongst them, departing hand in hand. The nearest person was now sixty yards away. I stood up, reached in my jacket.

"Anything you want to say?" I asked, looking down at his mild, rosy face. "People do, sometimes."

"Not to you," he said.

I pulled out the gun and placed the silenced end in the middle of his forehead. He didn't try to move. I took hold of his right shoulder with my other hand, and pulled the trigger once.

With all the traffic around the square, I barely even heard the sound. His head jerked back.

I let go of his shoulder and he sagged slowly around the waist, until the weight of his big, barrel chest pulled his body down off the chair to slump heavily onto the path, nearly face-first.

A portion of the back of his head was gone, but his eyes were still open. His beard scratched against the pavement as he tried to say something. After a couple of times I realized it was not words he was forcing out, but a series of sounds. I put the barrel to his temple and pulled the trigger again. A portion of the opposite temple splatted out onto the stones.

Yet still he was trying to push out those three short syllables, each the same.

I pulled the trigger a final time, and he was quiet. I bent down close to make sure, and to whisper in the remains of his ear.

"Check it twice, right, asshole?"

I walked out of the park. A few blocks away I found a cab, and started the long, slow journey home to New Jersey.

I woke early the next morning, like most fathers, to the sound of my son hurrying past our bedroom and down the stairs. On his way to the fireplace, no doubt.

Good luck with that, I thought, though I knew his stocking would be full nonetheless.

A few minutes later, Lauren levered herself into a sitting position. She pulled on her robe and went to the window, yanking aside the drapes.

She smiled at something she saw out there, then turned and quickly left the room.

By the time I'd got my own robe on and headed down to the kitchen to make coffee, I knew what she'd seen through the window. It had snowed heavily overnight, covering the yard and hanging off the trees. The whole nine yards of Winter Wonderland set-dressing. Probably I would have to help build a snowman later, whether I felt like it or not.

In the living room, my wife and child were sitting together Indian-style in the middle of the floor, cooing over the stockings they'd already taken down from the fireplace. Candy, little gifts, pieces of junk that were supposed to mean something just because they'd been found in a sock. I noticed that the cookie left on the table near the hearth had a large bite taken out of it. Lauren has always been good with detail.

"Happy Christmas, guys," I said, but neither of them seemed to hear.

I stepped around them and went to the fireplace. I took down the remaining stocking. I knew something was different before it was even in my hand.

It was empty.

"Lauren?"

She looked up at me. "Ho, ho, ho," she said.

Three short syllables, each the same.

There was nothing in her face.

Then she smiled, briefly, before going back to chattering with our son, watching for the third or fifth time as he excitably re-packed and then unpacked his stocking. Her smile went straight through me, but then they always have. I left the stocking on the arm of one of the chairs and walked out into the kitchen.

I opened the back door and went to stand outside in the snow.

It was very quiet, and it was nothing but cold.

Walking Wounded

WHEN AFTER TWO DAYS THE DISCOMFORT in his side had not lessened, merely mutated, Richard finally began to get mildly concerned. It didn't hurt as often as it had at first, and he could make a wider range of movements without triggering epic discomfort, but when the pain did come it was somehow deeper, as if settled into the bone.

Christine's solution to the problem was straightforward in its logic and strident in delivery. He should go to the casualty department of the nearest hospital, or at the very least to the doctor's surgery just down the street from their new flat in Kingsley Road.

Richard's view, though unspoken, was just as definite: bollocks to that. There were more than enough dull post-move tasks to be endured without traipsing up to the Royal Free Hospital and sitting amongst stoic old women and bleeding youths in a purgatory of peeling linoleum. As they were now condemned to living on a different branch of the Northern line to Hampstead, it would require two dogleg trips down to Camden and back out again — together with a potentially limitless spell on a waiting room bench — and burn up a whole afternoon. Even less appealing was the prospect of going down the road to the nearest GP and explaining in front of an audience of whey-faced locals that he had been living somewhere else, now lived nearby, and wished both to register with the surgery and have the doctor's apathetic opinion on a rather unspecific pain in Richard's side. And that he was very sorry for being middle-class and would they please not beat him up.

He couldn't be bothered, in other words, and instead decided to dedicate Monday to taking a variety of objects out of cardboard boxes and trying to work out where they could be least unattractively placed. Christine had returned to work, at least, which meant she couldn't see his winces or hear the swearing that greeted every new object for which there simply wasn't room.

The weekend had been hell, and not just because Richard hadn't been a hundred percent behind the move in the first place. He *had* wanted to, kind of; or at least he'd believed they *should* do. It had come to him one night while lying in bed in the flat in Belsize Park, listening to the even cadence of Chris's breathing and wondering at what point in the last couple of months they had stopped falling asleep together. At first they'd drifted off simultaneously, facing each other, four hands clasped into a declaration, determined not to leave each other even for the hours they spent in another realm. Richard half-remembered a poem by someone long dead — Herrick, possibly? — the gist of which had been that though we all inhabit the same place during the day, at night each one of us is hurled into a several world. Well, it hadn't been that way with them, not at first. Yet after nine months there he was, lying awake, happy to be in the same bed as Chris but wondering where she was.

Eventually he'd got up and wandered through into the sitting room. In the half-light it looked the same as always. You couldn't see which pictures had been taken down, which objects had been removed from shelves and hidden in boxes at the bottom of cupboards. You couldn't tell that for three years he had lived there with someone else.

But Richard knew that he had, and so did Christine. As he gazed out over the garden in which Susan's attempts as horticulture still struggled for life in the face of his indifference, Richard finally realized that they should move. Understood, suddenly and with cold guilt, that Chris probably didn't like living here. It was a lovely flat with huge rooms and high ceilings. It was on Belsize Avenue, which meant not only was it within three minutes walk of Haverstock Hill, with its cafés, stores, and tube station, but also Belsize "village" just around the corner. A small enclave of shops specifically designed to cater to the needs of the local well-heeled, the village was so comprehensively stocked with patés, wines, videos, and magazines that you hardly ever needed to go up to Hampstead, itself only a pleasant ten minutes' stroll. The view from the front of the flat was onto the Avenue, wide and spaced with ancient trees. The back was onto a garden neatly bordered by an old brick wall, and although only a few plants grew with any real enthusiasm, the overall effect remained pleasing.

The view through Christine's eyes was probably different, however. She perhaps saw the local pubs and restaurants in which Richard and Susan had spent years of happy evenings. She maybe felt the tightness with which her predecessor had held Richard's hand as they walked down to the village, past the gnarled Mulberry tree which was the sole survivor of the garden of the country house that had originally stood there.

She certainly wondered which particular patches of carpet within the flat had provided arenas for cheerful, drunken sex. This had come out one night after they'd come back from an unsuccessful dinner party at one of Christine's friends', drunk themselves, but irritably drunk. Richard had been bored enough by the evening to respond angrily to her question, and the matter had been dropped.

Standing there in the middle of the night, staring around a room stripped of its familiarity by darkness, he remembered the conversation, the nearest thing they'd yet had to a full-blown row. For a moment he saw the flat as she did, and almost believed he could hear the rustling of gifts from another woman, condemned to storage but stirring in their boxes, remembering the places where they had once stood.

The next morning, over cappuccinos on Haverstock Hill, he'd suggested they move. At the eagerness of her response he felt a band loosen in his chest that he hadn't even realized was there, and the rest of the day was wonderful.

Not so the move.

Three years' worth of flotsam, fifty boxes full of stuff. Possessions and belongings, which he'd believed to be individual objects, somehow metamorphosed into a mass of generic crap to be manhandled and sorted through. The flat they'd finally found was tiny. Well, not *tiny*; the living room and kitchen were big enough, and there was a roof garden — but a good deal smaller than Belsize Avenue, and nearly twenty boxes of Richard's stuff had to go into storage. Books that he seldom looked at but would have preferred to have around; DVDs that he didn't want to watch next week, but might in a couple of months; old clothes that he never wore but that had too much sentimental value to be thrown away.

And, of course, The Susan Collection. Objects in boxes, rounded up and buried deeper by putting in further boxes, then sent off to be hidden in some warehouse in King's Cross.

At a cost of fifteen pounds a week this was going to make living in the new flat even more expensive than the old one — despite the fact it was in Kentish Town and you couldn't buy a decent chicken liver and hazelnut paté locally for love or money.

On Friday night, the two of them huddled baffled and exhausted together in the huge living room in Belsize Avenue, surrounded by mountains of cardboard. They drank cups of coffee and tried to watch television, but the flat had already taken its leave of them. When they went to bed it was if they were lying on a cold hillside in some country where their visa had expired.

The next morning, two affable Australians arrived with a van the size of Denmark, and Richard watched, vicariously exhausted, as they trotted up and down the stairs, taking his life away. Chris bristled with cleaning know-how in the kitchen, periodically sweeping past him with a damp cloth in her hand, humming to herself. As the final pieces of furniture were dragged away, Richard tried to say goodbye to the flat, but the walls stared back at him with vacant indifference, and offered nothing more than dust in corners which had previously been hidden. Dust, some particles of which were probably Susan's skin — and his and Chris', of course. He left to the sound of a vacuum cleaner and followed the van to their new home.

Where, it transpired, his main bookcase could not be taken up the stairs. The two Australians, by now bedraggled and hot, struggled gamely in the dying light but eventually had to confess themselves beaten. Richard, rather depressed, allowed them to put the bookcase back in the van, to be taken off with the other storage items.

Much later he held out ten pounds to each of them, watched the van squeeze off down the narrow road, and then turned and walked into his new home.

Chris was still at Belsize Avenue, putting finishing touches to the cleaning and negotiating with the old twonk who owned the place. Richard moved a few boxes around while he waited for her to arrive, not wanting to do anything significant before she was there to share it with him, but too tired to just sit still. The lower hallway was almost completely impassable, and he resolved to carry a couple of boxes up to the living room.

It was while he was struggling up the stairs with one of them that he hurt himself.

He was about halfway up, panting under a box that seemed to weigh more than the house itself, when he slipped on a cushion lying on the stairs. Muscles that he hadn't used since his athletic glory days at school kicked into action, and he managed to avoid falling, colliding heavily with the wall instead. The corner of the box he was carrying crunched solidly into his ribs.

For a moment the pain was truly startling, and a small voice in his head said, "Well, that's done it."

He let the box slide to the floor and stood panting for a while, fingers tentatively feeling for what he was sure must be at least one broken rib. He half-expected it to be protruding from his chest. He couldn't find anything that yielded more than usual, however, and after a recuperative cigarette he carefully pushed the box the remainder of the journey up the stairs.

Half an hour later Chris arrived, cheerfully cross about their previous landlord's attempts to whittle money off their deposit, and set to work on the kitchen.

They fell asleep together that night, three of their hands together; one of Richard's unconsciously guarding his side.

The next morning his side hurt like hell, but as a fully-fledged male human, Richard knew exactly how to deal with the situation: he ignored it. After four days of looking at the cardboard boxes cheerfully emblazoned with the logo of the removal firm, he had begun to hate the sight of them, and concentrated first on unpacking everything so he could be rid of the boxes.

In the morning he worked in the living room, unpacking to the sound of Chris's whistling in the kitchen and bathroom. He discovered that two of the boxes shouldn't even have been there at all, but were supposed to have been taken with the others and put in storage.

One was full of manuals for software he either never used or knew back to front; the other was a box of Susan Objects. As he opened it, Richard realized why it had hurt quite so much when making contact with his ribs. It contained, amongst other things, a heavy and angular bronze she had made and presented to him. He was lucky it hadn't impaled him to the wall.

It wasn't worth calling the removal men out to collect the misplaced boxes, and so they ended up in his microscopic study, squatting on top of the filing cabinet. More precious space taken up by stuff that shouldn't be there; either in the flat or in his life.

The rest of the weekend disappeared in a blur of tidal movement and pizza. Objects migrated from room to room in smaller and slower circles before finally finding new resting places. Chris efficiently unpacked all their clothes and put them in the fitted wardrobes, cooing over the increase in hanging opportunities. Richard tried to organize his books into his *decreased* shelving space, eventually having to lay many on their side and pile them up verti-cally. He tried to tell himself this looked funky and less anal, but couldn't get the idea to take. He set up his desk and computer.

By Monday most of it was done, and Richard spent the morning trying to make his study habitable by clearing the few remaining boxes. At eleven Chris called from work, cheerful and full of vim, and he was glad to sense that the move had made her happy. As they were chatting, he realized that he at some point during the morning he must have scraped his left hand, because there were a series of shallow scratches, like paper cuts, over the palm and underside of the fingers.

They hardly seemed significant against the pain in his side, and aside from washing his hands when the conversation was over, he ignored them.

In the afternoon he took a break and walked down to the local corner store for cigarettes. It was only his second visit but he knew he'd already seen all it had to offer. The equivalent establishment in

Belsize Village had stocked fresh-baked bread, the *New York Times* and three different types of handmade pesto. Next door had stood the delicatessen with homemade duck's liver and port paté. "Raj's EZShop" sold none of these things, having elected instead to focus single-mindedly on the pot noodle and cheap toilet paper end of the market.

After he left — empty handed but for the cigarettes, which had never happened in Belsize Park — Richard went and peered dispiritedly at the grubby menu hanging in the window of the restaurant opposite. Eritrean food, whatever the hell that was. One of the dishes was described as "three pieces of cooked meat," which seemed both strangely specific and discomfortingly vague.

He turned and walked for home, huddling into his jacket against the cold and feeling — he imagined — like a deposed Russian aristocrat, allowed against all odds to remain alive after the revolution, but condemned to lack everything that he had once held dear. The sight of a small white dog scuttling by only seemed to underline his isolation.

When Chris returned at six, she couldn't understand his quietness, and he didn't have the heart to try to explain it to her.

"What's that?"

The answer, Richard saw, appeared to be "a scratch." About four inches long, it ran across his chest, directly over his heart. He hadn't noticed it before, but it seemed to have healed and so must have been there for a day or two.

"Another souvenir from the move," he guessed. It was after midnight and they were lying in bed, having just abandoned an attempt to make love. This wasn't from any lack of enthusiasm — far from it — simply that the pain in Richard's ribs was too bracing to ignore. He was fine so long as he kept his chest facing directly forwards. Any twisting and it felt as if someone was stoving in his rib cage with a well-aimed boot. "And no, I'm not going to the doctor about that either."

Chris smiled, started to tickle him, and then realized she shouldn't. Instead she sighed theatrically, and kissed him on the nose before turning to lie on her side.

"You'd better get well soon," she said, "Or I'm going to have to buy a do-it-yourself book."

"You'll go blind," he whispered, turning off the bedside light, and she giggled quietly in the dark. He rolled gingerly so that he was snuggled into her back, and lightly stroked her shoulder, waiting for sleep.

After a moment he noticed a wetness under his hand, and pulled his hand out from under the duvet.

In the threadbare moonlight he confirmed what he'd already suspected. Earlier in the evening he'd noticed that the little cuts on his hand seemed to be exuding tiny amounts of blood. It was happening again, or still. Constantly being reopened when he lugged boxes around, presumably.

"S'nice," Chris murmured sleepily. "Don't stop."

Richard slid his hand back under the duvet and moved it gently against her shoulder again, using the back of his fingers, cupping his palm away from her.

The bathroom was tiny, but very adequately equipped with mirrors. Richard couldn't help noticing the change as soon as he took off his dressing gown the next morning.

There was still no sign of bruising over his ribs, which worried him. Something which hurt that much ought to have some external manifestation, he believed, unless it indicated internal damage. The pain was a little different this morning, less like a kicking, more as if two of the ribs were grating tightly against each other. A kind of cartilaginous twisting.

There were also a number of new scratches.

Mostly short, they were primarily congregated over his stomach and chest. It looked as though a cat with its claws out had run over him in the night. As they didn't have a cat this seemed unlikely, and Richard frowned as he regarded himself in the mirror.

Also odd was the mark on his chest. Perhaps it was merely seeing it in proper light, but this morning it looked like more than just a scratch. By spreading his fingers out on either side, he found he could pull the edges of the cut slightly apart, and that it was a millimeter or so deep. When he allowed it to close again it did so with a faint liquidity, the sides tacky with lymph. It wasn't healing properly. In fact — and Richard held up his left hand to confirm this — it was doing the same as the cuts on his palm. They too seemed as fresh as the day before — maybe even a little fresher.

Glad that Chris had left the house before he'd made it out of bed, Richard quickly showered, patted himself dry around the cuts, and covered them with clothes.

By lunchtime the flat was finally in order, and Richard had to admit parts of it looked pretty good. The kitchen was the sole room bigger than he'd been used to in the previous flat, and in slanting light in the late morning, it was actually very attractive. The table was a little larger than would have been ideal, but at least you could get at the fridge without performing contortions.

The living room upstairs also looked pretty bijou, if you ignored the way half his books were crammed sideways into the bookcases. Chris had already established a nest on the larger of the two sofas; her book, ashtray, and an empty coffee mug placed within easy reach. Richard perched on the other sofa for a while, eyes running vaguely over his books, and realized he ought to make an effort to colonize a corner of the room for his own, too.

Human, All Too Human.

The title brought Richard out of his reverie. A second-hand volume of Nietzsche, bought for him as a joke by Susan. It shouldn't have been on the shelf, but in one of the storage boxes. Chris didn't know it had been a present from Susan, but then it hadn't been Chris who'd insisted he take the other stuff down. It had simply seemed to be the right thing to do, and Richard had methodically worked around the old flat hiding things the day before Chris moved in. Hiding them from whom, he hadn't been sure. It had been six months by then since he and Susan had split up, and she wasn't even seeing the man she'd left him for any more. To have the old mementos still out didn't cause him any pain, and he'd thought he'd put them away purely out of consideration for Chris. As he looked over the bookcase, however, he realized how much the book of Nietzsche stood out in their new flat. It smelled of Susan. Some tiny part of her, a speck of skin or smear of oil, must surely still be on it somewhere.

If he could sense that, then surely Chris could too. He walked across the room, took the book from the shelf, and walked downstairs to put it in the box on top of his filing cabinet in the study.

On the way he diverted into the bathroom. As he absently opened his fly, he noticed an unexpected sensation at his fingertips. He brushed them around inside his trousers again, trying to work out what he'd felt. Then very slowly he removed them, and held his hand up.

His fingers were spotted with blood.

Richard stared coldly at them for a while, and then calmly undid the button of his trousers. he lowered them carefully and then pushed down his boxer shorts. More cuts.

A long red line ran from the middle of his right thigh to within a couple of inches of his testicles. A similar one lay across the very bottom of his stomach. A much shorter but deeper slit lay across the base of his penis, and it was from this that the majority of the blood was flowing.

It wasn't a bad cut. It hardly put one in mind of the *Texas Chainsaw Massacre*. But Richard would still have much preferred it not be there.

Looking up at the mirror above the toilet, he undid the buttons on his shirt. The scratches on his stomach now looked more like cuts, and a small thin line of blood rolled down from the cut on his chest.

Like many people — men especially — Richard wasn't fond of doctors. It wasn't the sepulchral gloom of waiting rooms, or the grim pleasure their receptionists took in patronizing you. It was the boredom and the sense of potential catastrophe, combined with the knowledge that there probably wasn't a great deal they could actually do. If you had something really bad, then they sent you to a hospital. If it was trivial, it would go away of its own accord.

It was partly for these reasons that Richard did his shirt and trousers back up again, after patting at some of the cuts with pieces of toilet tissue. It was partly also because he was afraid. He didn't know where the scratches were coming from, but the fact that, instead of healing, they seemed to be getting worse was disquieting. With his vague semi-understanding of such things, he wondered if his blood had stopped clotting, and if so, what that meant in turn. He didn't think you could suddenly develop hemophilia. It didn't seem likely. But what then? Perhaps he was tired, run-down after the move. Would that make a difference?

In the end he resolved to go on ignoring it for a little longer, like the mole that keeps growing but you don't wish to believe might be malignant.

He spent the afternoon sitting carefully at his desk, trying to work and resisting the urge to peek at parts of his body. It was almost certainly his imagination, which made it feel as if a warm, plump drop of blood had sweated from the cut on his chest and rolled slowly down beneath his shirt; and the dampness he felt around his crotch must only be a result of his having turned the heating up very high.

Absolutely.

* * *

He took care to shower well before Chris was due back. The cuts were still there, and had been joined by another on his upper arm. When he was dry he took some surgical dressing and micropore tape from the bathroom cabinet and covered the ones that were bleeding most. He then put on his darkest shirt and sat in the kitchen, waiting for Chris to come home. He would have gone upstairs, but didn't really feel comfortable up there by himself yet. Although most of the objects in the room were his, Chris had arranged them, and the room seemed a little forlorn without her to fill in their structure.

That evening they went out to a pub in Soho, a birthday drink for one of Chris's mates. Richard had discovered that Chris had several different groups of friends. He had also discovered that the ones she regarded as her closest were the ones he found hardest to like. It wasn't because of anything intrinsically unpleasant, more an insufferable air of having known each other since before the dawn of time, like some heroic group, the Knights of the Pine Table. Unless you could remember the hilarious occasion when they all went down to the Dangling Cock in Mulchester and good old "Kipper" Philips sang "Bohemian Rhapsody" straight through while lying on the bar with a pint on his head before going on to amusingly prang his father's car on the steps of the village church, you were no more than one of life's spear carriers — even after you'd been going out with one of them for nearly a year. In their terms God was a bit of a Johnny-come-lately, and the Devil, even had he turned up to dinner with a hostess gift and a bottle of very good wine, would have been treated with the cloying indulgence reserved for friends' younger siblings.

Luckily that evening they were seeing a different and more recent group, some of whom were certified human beings. Richard stood at the bar affably enough, slowly downing a series of Kronenbourgs while Chris alternately went to talk to people or brought them to talk to him. One of the latter, a doctor whom Richard believed to be called Kate, peered hard at him as soon as she hove into view.

"What's that?" she asked, bluntly.

Richard was about to tell her that what he was holding was called a "pint," that it consisted of the liquid alcoholic byproducts of the soaking, boiling, and fermenting of certain natural vegetative species, and that he had every intention — regardless of any objections she or anyone else might have — of drinking it, when he realized she was looking at his left hand. Too late, he tried to slip it into his pocket, but she reached out and snatched it up.

"Been in a fight, have you?" she asked. Chris turned from the man she was talking to, and looked over Kate's shoulder at Richard's hand.

"No," he said. "Just a bizarre flat relocation accident."

"Hmm," Kate said, her mouth pursed into a moue of consideration. "Looks like someone's come at you with a knife, if you ask me."

Chris looked at Richard, eyes wide, and he groaned inwardly.

"Well, things between Chris and me haven't been so good lately…" he tried, and got a laugh from both of them. Kate wasn't to be deflected, however.

"I'm serious," she said, holding up her own hand to demonstrate. "Someone tries to attack you with a knife, what do you do? You hold your hands up. And so what happens is the blade will nick the defending hands a couple of times before the knife gets through. See it all the time in Casualty. Little cuts, just like those."

Richard pretended to examine the cuts on his hand, and shrugged.

"Maybe Kate could look at your ribs," Chris said.

"I'm sure there's nothing she'd like better," he said, quickly. "After a hard day at the coal face there's probably nothing she'd like more than to look at another piece of fossilized wood."

"What's wrong with your ribs?" Kate asked, squinting at him closely.

"Nothing," he said. "Just banged them."

"Does this hurt?" she asked, and suddenly cuffed him around the back of the head.

"No," he said, laughing.

"Then you're probably all right," she winked, and disappeared to get a drink. Chris frowned for a moment, caught between irritation at not having got the bottom of Richard's rib problem and happiness at seeing him get on well with one of her friends. Just then a fresh influx of people arrived at the door, and Richard was saved from having to watch her choose which emotion to go with.

Mid-evening he went to the gents and shut himself into one of the cubicles. He changed the dressings on his penis and chest, and noted that some of the cuts on his stomach were now slick with blood. He didn't have enough micropore to dress them. He would have to hope that they stayed manageable until he got home. The cuts on his hands didn't seem to be getting any deeper.

Obviously they were just nicks. Almost, as Kate had said, as if someone had come at him with a knife.

They got home well after midnight. Chris was more drunk than Richard, but he didn't mind. She was one of those rare people who got even cuter when she was plastered, instead of maudlin or argumentative.

She staggered straight into the bathroom to do whatever the hell it was she spent all that time in there doing. Richard made his way into the study to check the answer phone, gently banging into walls whose positions he still hadn't internalized yet.

One message.

Richard pressed the play button. Without even noticing he was doing so, he turned down the volume so only he would hear what was on the tape. This was a habit born of the first weeks of his relationship with Chris, when Susan was still calling regularly.

Her messages, though generally short and uncontroversial, had not been things he wanted Chris to hear. Again, a program of protection, now no longer needed.

Feeling self-righteous, and burping gently, Richard turned the volume back up.

He almost jumped out of his skin when he realized the message actually *was* from Susan, and quickly turned the volume back down.

She said hello, in the diffident way she had, and went on to observe that they hadn't seen each other that year yet. There was no reproach, simply a statement of fact. She asked him to call her soon, to arrange a drink.

The message had just finished when Chris caromed out of the bathroom smelling of toothpaste and moisturizer.

"Any messages?"

"Just a wrong number," he said.

She shook her head slightly, apparently to clear it, rather than in negation. "Coming to bed then?" she asked, slyly. Waggling her eyebrows, she performed a slow grind with her pelvis, managing both not to fall over and not to look silly, which was a hell of a trick. Richard made his "sex life in ancient Rome" face, inspired by a book he'd read many years before.

"Too right," he said. "Be there in a minute."

But he stayed in the study for a quarter of an hour, long enough to ensure that Chris would have fallen asleep. Wearing pajamas for the first time in years, he slipped quietly in beside her and waited for the morning.

As soon as Chris had dragged herself groaning out of the house, Richard got out of bed and went through to the bathroom. He knew what he was going to find before he took his night clothes off. He could feel parts of his pajama top sticking to areas on his chest and stomach, and his crotch felt warm and wet.

The marks on his stomach now looked like proper cuts, and the gash on his chest had opened still further. His penis was covered in dark blood, and the gashes around it were nasty. He looked as if he had collided with a threshing machine. His ribs still hurt a great deal, though the pain seemed to be constricting, concentrating around a specific point rather than applying to the whole of his side.

He stood for ten minutes, staring at himself in the mirror. So much damage. As he watched, he saw a faint line slowly draw itself down three inches of his forearm, a thin raised scab. He knew that by the end of the day it would have reverted into a cut.

Mid-morning he called Susan at her office. As always he was surprised by how official she sounded when he spoke to her there. She had always been languid of voice, in complete contrast to her physical and emotional vivacity — but when you talked to her at work, she sounded like a headmistress.

Her tone mellowed when she realized who it was. She tried to pin him down to a date for a drink, but he avoided the issue. They'd seen each other twice since she'd left him for John Ayer; once while he'd been living with Chris. Chris had been relaxed about the meetings, but Richard hadn't. On both occasions, he and Susan had spent a lot of time talking about Ayer; the first time focusing on why Susan had left Richard for him; the second on how unhappy she was about the fact that Ayer had in turn left her, without even saying goodbye. Either she hadn't realized how much the conversations would hurt Richard, or she hadn't even thought about it. Most likely she had just taken comfort from talking to him, in the way she always had.

"You're avoiding it, aren't you?" Susan said, eventually.

"What?"

"Naming a day. Why?"

"I'm not," he protested, feebly. "I'm just…busy, you know. I don't want to say a date and then have to cancel."

"I really want to see you," she said. "I miss you."

Don't say that, Richard thought, miserably. *Please don't say that.*

"And there's something else," she added. "It was a year today when…"

"When what?" Richard asked, confused. He knew that they'd split up at least eighteen months ago.

"The last time I saw John," she said, and finally Richard understood.

That afternoon he took a long walk to kill time, trolling up and down the surrounding streets, trying to find something to like. He discovered another corner store, but it didn't stock paté either. Little dusty bags of fuses hung behind the counter, and the plastic strips of the cold cabinet were completely opaque. A little further afield he found a local video store but he'd seen every thriller they had, most more than once. The storekeeper seemed to stare at him as he left, as if wondering what he was doing there.

After a while he simply walked, not looking for anything. Slab-faced women clumped by, screaming at children already getting into method for their five minutes of fame on *CrimeWatch*. Pipe-cleaner men stalked the streets in brown trousers and zip-up jackets, heads fizzing with horseracing results. The pavements seemed unnaturally grey, as if waiting for a second coat of reality, and hard green leaves spiraled down to join brown ashes already fallen.

And yet as he started to head back toward Kingsley Road, he noticed a small dog standing on a corner, different to the one he'd seen before. White with a black head and lolling tongue, the dog stood still and looked at him, big brown eyes rolling with good humor. It didn't bark, merely panted, ready to play some game he didn't know.

Richard stared at the dog, suddenly sensing that some other life was possible here, that he was occluding something from himself.

The dog skittered on the spot slightly, keeping his eyes on

Richard, and then abruptly sat down. Ready to wait. Ready to still be there.

Richard watched him a moment longer and then set off for the tube station. On the way he called and left a message at the house phone on Kingsley Road, telling Chris he'd gone out, and might be back late.

At eleven he left The George pub and walked down Belsize Avenue. He didn't know how important the precise time was, and he couldn't actually remember it, but this felt about right. Earlier in the evening he had walked past the old flat and established that the "To Let" sign was still outside. Probably the landlord had jacked the rent up so high he couldn't find any takers.

During the hours he'd spent in the pub he had checked the cuts only twice. Then he'd ignored them, his only concession being to roll down the sleeve of his shirt to hide what had become a deep gash on his forearm. When he looked at himself in the mirror of the gents', his face seemed pale; whether from the lighting or blood loss he didn't know. As he could now push his fingers deep enough into the slash on his chest to feel his sternum, he suspected it was probably the latter. When he used the toilet, he did so with his eyes closed. He didn't want to know what it looked like down there now: the sensation of his fingers on ragged and sliced flesh was more than enough. The pain in his side had continued to condense, and was now restricted to a circle about four inches in diameter.

It was time to go.

He slowed as he approached the flat, trying to time it so he drew outside when there was no one else in sight. As he waited, he marveled quietly at how different the sounds were to those in Kentish Town. There was no shouting, no roar of maniac traffic or young bloods prowling the streets looking for damage. All you could hear was distant laughter, the sound of people having dinner, braving the cold and sitting outside Café Pasta or the Pizza Express. This area was different, and it wasn't his home anymore.

It was time to say goodbye.

When the street was empty he walked quietly along the side of the building to the wall. Only about six feet tall, it held a gate through to the garden. Both sets of keys had been yielded, but Richard knew from experience that he could climb over. More than once he or Susan had forgotten their keys on the way out to get drunk, and he'd had to let them back in this way.

He jumped up, arms extended, and grabbed the top of the wall. His side tore at him, but he ignored the pain and scrabbled up. He slid over the top without pausing and dropped silently onto the other side, leaving a few slithers of blood behind.

The window to the kitchen was there in the wall, dark and cold. Chris had left a dishcloth neatly folded over the tap in the sink. Other than that, the room looked as if it had been molded in an alien's mind. Richard turned away and walked out into the garden.

He limped toward the middle of it, trying to recall how it had gone. In some ways it felt as if he could remember everything; but in others it was as though the sequence of events had never happened to him, but was a tale told by someone else:

A phone call to an office number he'd copied from Susan's Filofax before she left.

An agreement to meet for a drink, on a night Richard knew that Susan would be out of town.

Two men, meeting to sort things out in a gentlemanly fashion.

The stalks of Susan's abandoned plants nodded suddenly in a faint breeze, and an eddy of leaves chased each other slowly around the walls. Richard glanced toward the living room window. Inside, it was empty, a couple of pieces of furniture stark against walls painted with dark triangular shadows. It was too dark to see and he was too far away, but he knew all the dust was gone. Even that little part of the past had been sucked up and buried away.

He felt a strange sensation on his forearm, and looked down in time to see the gash there disappearing, from bottom to top, from finish to start. It went quickly, as quickly as it had been made.

He turned to look at the verdant patch of grass, expecting to see it move, but it was still. Then he felt a warm sensation in his crotch, and realized it too would soon be whole. He had hacked at Ayer there long after he knew he was dead; hacked symbolically and pointlessly until the penis which had slipped into Susan had been reduced to a scrap of offal.

The leaves moved again, faster this time, and the garden grew darker, as if a huge cloud had moved into position overhead. It was now difficult to see as far as the end wall of the garden, and when he heard the distant sounds from there, Richard realized the ground was not going to open up. No, first the wound in his chest, the fatal wound, would disappear. Then the cuts on his stomach, and the nicks on his hands from where Ayer had resisted, trying to be angry but so scared he had pissed his designer jeans.

Finally the pain in his side would go; the first pain, the pain caused by Richard's initial vicious kick after he had pushed his drunken rival over. A spasm of hate, flashes of violence, wipe pans of memory.

Then they would be back to that moment, or a few seconds before. Something would come toward him, out of the dry, rasping shadows, and they would talk again. How it would go Richard didn't know, but he knew he could win, that he could walk away back to Christine and never come back here again.

It was time. Time to go.

Time to move on.

The Seventeenth Kind

HI. I'M JAMES RICHARD. No, not "Richards," but "Richard." Dumb name, I think you'll agree. No, it's okay. Really. Enjoy yourself. I've had many years to savor the name, to laboriously spell it out over the phone and find parcels arriving at my door marked for Richard James anyhow. I didn't even make it up. It's not a stage name. My parents gave it to me when I was born, bless them — along with a very straight nose, nice wavy brown hair, and next to no talent at all.

"Why," I asked my father one time, back when I was young in years and full of hope, "why in the name of sweet Jesus did you call me James Richard?"

He stared down at me, confused, and I belatedly realized he was in the same predicament. His name was David. David Richard. Maybe when he was young his peers also snarled "Hey, shithead — why have you got two first names?" For a moment I felt a strange and poignant affinity with my dad, as if we were holding hands down the years, two small boys a generation apart who'd shouldered a similar burden.

Then I kicked him in the shin.

Anyway. This isn't about my name. This is about what I do, and what I do is I'm a presenter on a shopping channel. No, go ahead. Laugh all you like. Just the stupidest job in the whole damned universe, right? Well, you know, screw you. If I hear one more person say a chimp could do my job then I'm going to take some innovative and durable kitchen implement — retailing in stores for $19.99 but available for this hour only at the low-low price of $11.99 plus postage and packing — and shove it up their ass.

This is a skill. It really is.

And it saved my life.

I wound up in home shopping via a circuitous route. Everyone does. Nobody wakes up one morning thinking, "Hey, I want to be on live cable selling people shit they don't need." Or perhaps they do, in which case they genuinely *are* stupid. Maybe they think it counts as television, and is therefore glamorous. It's not. The point of being on the tube is first, to earn big bucks; second, to be recognized in the street. Anyone who tells you different is a moron. What — they instead want the unsociable hours, the threat of being sacked at any moment, the ever-present danger of exposure and embarrassment — not to mention the joy of standing under hot lights while hairy-backed yahoos point cameras at you and swap impenetrable jokes behind your back? The money in cable really isn't that great, and the people you actually *want* to recognize you are pretty young things of the opposite sex. Or of the same sex, whatever. You work a shopping channel then these are not the people who are going to being recognizing you. They're going to be…well, I'll come to that.

I was an actor originally. I was profoundly average, and there's only so many times you can emote your heart out to scraggly-bearded directors to then be told you're insufficiently tall or Turkish-looking or female or frankly even any *good*. So I switched to stand-up as a kind of holding pattern. Easier to get gigs, but the money stinks like fish, and I couldn't write my own material so I was going nowhere fast. Finally there was a spell on a local radio news station for which cattle made up the main demographic. That was *really* grim. It was while I was there, reading out the weather and listening to the neurons in my brain popping one by one, that I saw a trade ad for a presenter on a cable channel. I combed the straw out of my hair, jumped on a plane and went and did my thing. I dug deep, gave it everything I had. I was desperate.

I got the gig.

Now. If you don't do any home shopping then I'm going to have to explain the deal to you. (If you do, then just skip-read or have a sandwich or something. I'll be back in a minute.) How it works is this: The channels basically have a pile of goods which they want to sell. Pots and pans. Jewelry. Gardening implements. Technical gizmos for the home. Limited Edition *Star Trek*® bathmats. The buy-me inducements they offer are severalfold. First, the goods are cheap. No store overheads, plus the advantages of buying in bulk. Two, you just pick up the phone and give a credit card number (hell, just your *name,* if you're a returning customer) and the thing will be with you in a couple days — without you even having to get up off your couch. I assume when it drops through your mailbox you have to get up and go fetch it, or maybe these people have someone who does that for them, too.

The third inducement is people like me. The presenters. Your friend on the screen.

As the audience, this is what you see. A live picture of the object in question with a panel at one side telling you the cost and the product code and just how beguilingly cheap it is compared to normal in-store prices. You listen to a voice-over, with cutaways to the presenter's face and upper body as he or she tells you how much the thing costs (in case you can't read), how many are left to buy ("Only three-quarters of our stock left now — this one's moving *incredibly* quickly everybody, so hurry, hurry, pick up your phone and make that call, operators are standing by ..."), and also explains to the hard-of-thinking why they should want the damn thing in the first place. If it's a ring, for example, my job would be to remind you that you could put it on your finger and wear it for cosmetic purposes, in order to enhance your attractiveness and/or perceived status. You think I'm kidding. I'm really not.

Sounds easy, but wait. Sometimes you may have to fill twenty minutes with this crap. You try talking for *half* that time, non-stop — with no help, no cues, and moreover with people pointing cameras at you and some fool chattering in your earpiece — explaining why someone would want to buy an enormous cookie jar shaped like a chicken, and you'll begin to see it's not as easy as it sounds. Most of the presenters cheat. They'll repeat themselves endlessly, rehearsing the remaining stock levels time and again just to give themselves something extra to say. I never did that. I never dried. I also never said anything like "Today's special value today is really special," as one of my colleagues once did; nor "In the sixteenth century was the Renaissance, and garnet was a stone," another of my personal favorites.

I didn't do these things because when I found myself in this weird job it was like I'd come home. I knew it was worthless, but on the other hand I thought: "Hey — perhaps this is something I could be *good* at. Maybe this was a corner of an ill-regarded field which I could make forever James Richard." Most of the stuff the channel pushed was skull-crushingly dull, but that didn't mean you couldn't talk about it. Okay, so it might be a frankly hideous hexagonal pendant in faux gold with a minuscule pseudo-emerald in the middle: but you could point out how *delightfully* hexagonal it was, and how neatly the "emeraldite" sat in its exact center. You could measure it with the special Home Mall ruler, just in case someone in the audience didn't understand perspective and was worried that the pendant was as big as a house. You could tell them how *many* different occasions they'd find to wear it, and list them, and generally evoke just how unspeakably lovely their lives would become — all because of this twenty-dollar piece of costume jewelry.

The whole time you're working, you have the director talking at you, relaying sales information through a plug in your ear. But I mentioned availability twice, three times in each hour. At *most*. Just enough to keep people on their toes, to convince them they ought to get working that phone. And you can believe this — when I was doing the selling, the units started shifting. That sounds arrogant, I guess. Well, maybe; and so what? For all the times some shithead casting agent dumped on me; for all the times I died on a small stage because the jokes I wrote weren't funny; for all the times I was shown that I couldn't do a job well enough to be proud of myself — now I had Home Mall to demonstrate that I could do *something*.

So what if no one respected it? I could *do it*. That's what counts.

Which is why, after a couple of months with the station, I found myself handling a lot of the Specials. Every evening there'd be some product the station had a particular deal on. They'd wheel on the manufacturer or other front person with the promise of shifting extra units, and stick him or her on the screen to demonstrate the product. These slots lasted a whole hour, and of course needed a professional to guide the civilian through the live television experience, to keep things running smoothly. And increasingly that professional was me.

Talking about something for ten minutes is one thing. An hour is a *whole* different kettle of ballgames. The big factor you have in your favour is that you aren't just a talking torso in these slots. You're there, live on camera, standing next to some guy demonstrating a CD player or salad shooter or car wrench. You can use everything about yourself, not just your voice. Employ your body to suggest things, use hand movements, shrug; if you weren't too proud, you could even pout winsomely. God knows I've pouted on occasion, winsomely and otherwise.

All that helped, but the Specials were still tough, and I enjoyed the challenge. As the months went on I might resort to a little cocaine on occasion to keep myself humming along; but my main juice was pure adrenaline. That, and a genuine drive to dance the jig of semi-relevance, to keep the balls in the air when they didn't deserve to be up there in the first place — to *just keep talking.*

To communicate with the viewer at home.

Once the products were shifting nicely, you see, we'd start taking calls from people who were buying the merchandise. Initially this was the part of the job that most freaked me out. I mean, who the hell *were* these people? What were they doing, calling a shopping channel at 1:30 A.M. on a Wednesday night to tell us why they'd bought some neo-bosnium trinket? Didn't they have beds to go to? Didn't they have *lives?* Ninety five percent of the callers were middle-aged women, too, which I found especially hard to get my head around. I could have understood guys in their twenties, maybe, too stoned to change the channel, or thinking they were being ironic. I even suggested to Rod that we should institute a Stoner Hour, where we sold big bags of candy and potato chips along with small glittering baubles which might appeal to the chemically enhanced mind. People would call up in droves, collapse in bed later and forget all about it, and then be completely bemused when boxes of munchies arrived a couple days after. We could probably get away with not sending out the product at all, which would be a big fat profit all round. (The idea wasn't taken up, which I think reveals commercial timidity.)

I quickly realized that taking the calls was a crucial part of the selling process, however, and made it my specialty. Nobody called in to say that something they'd bought was a piece of shit — they rang in to say it was fabulous. They wanted to say something nice, which meant everyone else listening in got a ringing product endorsement from *someone who was just like them.* I would imagine these callers, dumpy and dough-faced, sitting in darkened rooms around the country, their faces lit by the flicker of the selling screen. Just occasionally I believed that once they'd finished talking to us, they abruptly switched off, like abandoned robots, their heads tilting forward onto their chests, hands folded in their laps — and that they would remain that way until the following night, when they got a chance to talk about their obsessions again. Sometimes this impression was stronger, and I felt I could imagine them all at once, all sitting in their rooms, bathed in the twinkling eeriness of television light, eyes focused on the screen, their loneliness and need pouring back through the cables toward me.

God bless cocaine.

The job settled into a rhythm. I'd do a couple of sessions late afternoon or early evening, standard stuff — then at the beginning of the late shift, somewhere between 10 P.M. and 1 A.M., I'd do a Special. The late shift is when the real action begins, the time when the heavy hitters of couch potato purchasing settle down with their buckets of soda and sacks of potato chips and get into their stride. The products varied wildly but that was part of the fun. The manufacturers were also mixed, from a monosyllabic sauté pan dude who said maybe three words all hour, to a woman I worked with selling a home organ who was damned nearly as good as me. *Christ* did that woman know a lot about organs. I thought she'd never shut up.

Then…okay: here we go.

The night in question, I was doing a Special for a cleaning product called Supa Shine. Some dude from Texas had spent ten years working on polishes and had finally come up with a real humdinger. The stuff had been on the channel once before, but this was the first time it had gotten its own segment. When I heard what the Special was that evening I thought even *I* was going to have trouble. Metal polish: it's useful, it may even be essential to some people. But say what you like, it's really just not very exciting.

An hour before we were due to go on air, I dropped by the green room to meet the guy. Rusty, his name was. He was about fifty, grey-haired, bearded, and kind of heavy round the gut, but affable enough in a good-old-boy kind of way — and wow, did he like his job. I'm not kidding. Polishing was this guy's *life*. He'd got into town early that morning and straightaway gone trawling junk stores and antiqueries picking up old bits of silver and copper to use on the show. He showed me how to use the product. The polish was a silvery paste which came in a very small tin. You put a subliminal amount on a rag, wiped it over your metal in a desultory way and then rubbed it off. And it worked. It worked to a freakish degree. I was genuinely impressed. He took an old coin, so dirty and corroded it looked more like a disk of wood, and after about ten seconds it was better than the day it popped out of the mint.

I relaxed. Okay, so polish was dull. But this stuff worked, by Jesus. Selling something that works is never too hard. I hung out for a while longer, took a couple of minutes in the john to tip my chemical balance in the direction of enthusiasm, then got the five-minute call.

I murmured encouraging things to Rusty — who'd begun to shake slightly — and strode out under the lights. I don't know why I did that, because we weren't on air. They always cut in with you already in position. But I always stride on anyway. Call it profes-sional pride.

Then the floor manager counts you down, the light on Camera One goes red, and you're on. It's showtime. Suddenly it's not just you and some perspiring Southerner — it's you and the rest of the world. Well, the world that's up and watching a shopping channel at 12:02 A.M., anyway.

I started the hour with a searching but light-hearted meditation on the amount of old metalware in people's houses, and went on to muse about how folks would get a lot more fun out of antique stores and yard sales if it weren't for the prospect of having to *clean* their prizes when they got them home. I didn't mention the other metal in people's houses — the silverware, furniture, even the fascias of DVD players. Not yet. Throw out all your ideas in the first minute on a Special and by twenty after the hour you're going to be treading water until you drown.

I segued direct from this into Rusty doing his thing. He was okay, even pretty good. There was something so down-home about him that you couldn't help watching. "Christ," you were soon thinking, "this guy's fucking *obsessed*. If he gets off this much on polishing, there's *got* to be something in it. Let me have a try."

He took a pair of old candlesticks, equally tarnished. Talking slowly, he described the process of using his wonder-polish, demonstrating as he went. I didn't do much more than provide an echo every now and then — "Okay, so you put it on a *cloth*, right?" — because I knew as the hour progressed he'd run out of steam. A minute later one of the candlesticks was looking brighter than the day it was made. I'd kind of preferred it with the tarnish, to be honest: for me, taking an antique and making it look new was like sprucing up Stonehenge with fiberglass. But I knew that the audience would feel differently, and Rod the director was already chattering happily in my earpiece. The calls had started right away, and Supa Shine was out of the starting blocks.

For the next fifteen minutes Rusty tirelessly polished and buffed. I tried it myself, of course, affably pouring the full weight of my personality into restoring the shine to a variety of pieces of old trash — while being careful to make it clear that James Richard, like the viewer at home, had no previous expertise in the field. We did gold, we did silver, we did copper, we did chrome. They all worked spectacularly. We actually had to start being careful about the way we held the pieces, because the glitter was throwing the cameras off.

Twenty-five minutes in, I took over from Rusty, helping him out of a circuitous ramble he'd trapped himself into. The calls were really flooding in by now; Supa Shine was shifting big time.

It was time to start talking to people.

Our first call was typical. Lori from Black Falls rang to say that she'd bought Supa Shine when it'd been on before and it had changed her life. She described in detail how she'd polished everything in her street and how happy that had made her. She'd called that evening to buy stocks for her sisters, daughters, and friends. She was so patently sincere that I let her run on for quite some while, knowing she was doing our job for us. Rusty nodded benignly, dislodging a small droplet of sweat from his hairline, which rolled slowly onto his forehead. I covertly signaled the director to switch to a close-up product shot, and Mandy the make-up girl darted on to powder us both. No more than six seconds, then back to a medium shot of the two of us, and all the while I kept the banter going with the caller until she'd said all she had to say.

Lori finally stopped yakking and went off to polish her dog's head, and we took a call from Ann in Raenord. Ann had called because she was concerned that Supa Shine might harm her gold-plated jewelry. Rusty whipped a piece of plated stuff off the pile and polished it there and then. It came up beautifully, and Ann was mollified. She thanked us for talking to her and was transferred to the purchase operators.

It was a natural point to take five, and so I signaled to Rod and talked us into a short break…giving just a hint of some of the exciting polishing action still to come.

As soon as the ident was on the screen, I winked at Rusty and disappeared behind the set and into the green room. None of the production staff batted an eyelid. I'd left a line chopped and ready on the one table that wasn't covered with crap from previous shows, and so it was the matter of a moment to get the marching dust into my bloodstream.

I strode back into the studio — taking care to grab a glass of water for cover — and stood next to Rusty. "Going great," I enthused. "Just had a word with the guys — you're selling by the *shit*load."

Rusty smiled shyly, and I noticed that another droplet of sweat was already forming. Mandy swabbed, Rod counted us back in. and we were on air less than three minutes after I'd left the room.

The next five minutes were fine. Rusty told us how it would only take two cans of Supa Shine to clean an entire 747, and it didn't seem hard to believe. I must admit that by this time I was kind of wondering what was actually *in* the stuff: the pile of metal in front of us was gleaming so much it was starting to hurt my eyes. I got Rusty to tell his story about working in his mother's garage for ten years coming up with the formula, then decided it was time to take another call.

And that's where the evening went a little weird.

"Hi," I said, smiling direct to Camera One. "So, who do we have come to talk with us now?"

The normal response to this question is the caller's name and location, utterly promptly and clearly. They've been briefed by an operator and most of them blurt the information out super-fast, as if eager to prove they can follow instructions properly and will make a great addition to the programme.

This time, however, there was a silence.

Which is fine — sometimes people get overawed once they realize they're really on air. The tactic then is to ask them a *very simple question* to start them off.

"Have you already experienced Supa Shine's cleaning miracles, caller?" I asked. "Or do you have a question for friend Rusty here before you try it?"

Usually that'll do it. The silence continued, however, and I began to let my right hand wander up toward my neck — in preparation for the agreed code for cutting a caller off. But then the caller spoke.

"He's not Rusty."

The voice was deep and ragged and wet and rough. My heart sank. Every now and then one of the directors, Rod in particular, would let a weird one slip through. The stated intention was "keeping it real," but as Rod wouldn't know real if it slapped him upside the head, I believed it was more likely to be about fucking up the presenter for the delight of the assembled spear carriers. Kind of irresponsible when the product was shifting so well, but that's assholes for you. They're assholey.

"Well, not literally, of course," I pouted (winsomely). "But you know what? It wouldn't surprise me one bit to find that Supa Shine wasn't only great with stains and tarnish — but could handle a little spot of rust as well. In fact, I was just going to ask…"

"His name isn't Rusty," the voice said. It sounded like the guy had the world's worst ever cold. Or flu. Or maybe the plague.

"Well, no, it's kind of a nickname, isn't it?" I chuckled. "No one gets called Rusty right off the bat, do they? Just like some of my friends call me Jim. And so, caller, while we're talking, what's *your* name?"

There was no reply.

Screw this, I thought. I very obviously scratched my Adam's apple. In other words, *get this loser off the air.*

Meanwhile I turned to Rusty, who was starting to look nervous. It's often the way with the guests. When things start well they can get lulled into forgetting they're on live television — but it's a perilous relaxation. The smallest upset can unsettle them for good.

"So how *about* that, Rusty?" I asked, holding his eyes to lock him back into where he was, and what he was doing. "Obviously Supa Shine isn't going to be able to cope if something's totally *covered* in rust, kind of falling apart, but how about a little spot or two?"

Rusty opened his mouth to speak, but then a very bizarre noise came over the studio monitor. It sounded like a loud, liquid cough, mixed up with the sound of a handful of nails being dropped on a metal surface.

"Whoa! I apologize for that, viewers," I laughed. "Little technical glitch here in the studio, don't know if you heard it at home — just goes to show that we really are *live* tonight in your living room, live and *a*live, bringing you the very best in bargains 24/7. So…"

Then the noise happened again.

I laughed once more, throwing my hands up in the air for good measure — as if helpless with mirth at the hilarious events which tumbled through life: not just my life, you understand, but also the lives of the viewers at home.

Then something else came over the speakers. The deep, broken voice said: "That's my name."

"What?" I said, momentarily thrown.

"That's my name," the voice repeated. Then the strange liquid noise rumbled through the speakers again. "That's it."

"That…noise is your name?"

"Yes."

"Well make sure you spell it out when you talk to our purchase operators…" I said, with a wink directly into camera — to the normal man and woman on the couch, "…because I'm not sure they'll have come across that one before. Eastern European, is it?"

"No."

"Well okay then. I know that we have many, many other viewers out there who really want to share their experiences with Rusty's Supa Shine polish with us, so maybe if…"

"It's not his."

By now I was finally beginning to get pissed off. The entire exchange had probably only taken forty seconds, but that's a *long* time on live television. Rusty was looking extremely wary again, and a whole army of perspiration drops were massed at the hair line, ready to roll down his face. That could not happen, not on my watch. Nobody wants to buy something from a guy who's sweating like a pig.

I made the cut sign again, even more clearly.

"Jim, there's something odd going on."

This voice didn't come out over the speakers, but only into my earpiece. It was Rod.

I turned to Rusty and cheerfully suggested he show us his polish working magic on the second candlestick, which was weak, but I needed a few seconds' cover.

As I watched him get to this, I raised my eyebrows quickly, just about the only way I could communicate to the box that I needed to hear more.

Rod spoke again, and what he said was strange. "We can't get this joker off the air."

I risked a glance off. Normally you never do this. You look direct to the camera, at the object you're selling, or at your civilian co-host. Anywhere else looks weird to the viewer at home, reminding them that they're watching a guy in a studio. But I swept my eyes quickly over the window to the director's booth — their lair was sealed from the studio so chatter and techspeak didn't leak onto the live microphones — and saw Rod standing looking directly at me, his hands held up in professional mime-quality "I have no fucking clue what is going on" pose.

Behind him a couple of techs were moving quickly about the room, fiddling with wires. By this point in my life I had done many, many hours of live television. I'd never seen something like that before. I realized there and then that I was entering new and uncharted territory.

"He has stolen it," said the speaker voice, loudly.

"Stolen what?" I said.

"His so-called polish. It is not his. It belongs to us."

I was still trying conjure a response to this when I heard Rod's voice in my ear once more. He wasn't speaking directly to me this time, but what he said was so weird I decided from then on I was just going to ignore everything except what was happening in front of me.

Rod's voice was on the edge of cracking. "What the fuck do you mean?" he was shouting, to someone, "Time is slowing *down?*"

I assumed he was ragging out some technician and it was a geek wires-and-sockets thing. Whatever. Their problem, not mine. If they couldn't get this idiot off the air I'd have to plough on regardless. The show must go on, always. This was precisely what I got paid the big bucks for, Well, the bucks, anyway.

I smiled at Camera Two, the one currently showing a red light. "Well, *thank* you caller, it's been great to hear your own special perspective on this. But just right now I want to ask Rusty here something."

I turned to my co-host, the first time I'd looked directly at him for maybe a minute or two. I should have checked back before. He'd got stressed, nervous, a big old dose of stage fright. The line of sweat droplets I'd seen forming earlier had decided to all go over the top at once, and fresh ranks were following in their wake — taking with them what appeared to be a thick layer of make-up. Every guest gets some pancake, to smooth out blotches and variations and make everyone look nice under the lights. This make-up was a lot thicker than that, though. And, I noticed, looked kind of like…latex.

I stared at Rusty. Rusty looked back at me.

I noticed then that his eyes were perhaps suspiciously blue, too, like they were contacts. And that where the make-up was running or melting or whatever it was doing, the skin underneath seemed to be both rough and warty and also a unusual color.

"Rusty," I said, suspiciously, "are you…green?"

He turned away suddenly, tilting his head toward the speaker hanging above us, out of shot. He barked something angrily at it, and now his voice didn't sound like it had before. It didn't sound like he was from the South. It sounded like a large bucket of nuts and bolts dropped down an old drain pipe. Then he made another sound, even louder. The force of the utterance caused a whole strip of skin to fall off one side of his face, revealing something that looked like a piece of steak that had being lying in a parking lot for a couple weeks.

"Okay," I said, into the silence. "So I'm guessing maybe you're not from East Texas after all?"

The voice from the speaker spoke once again.

"No, he is not," it said, "and his polish belongs to us. In reality it is a foodstuff. And we are running perilously low. It must be returned."

"Whoa," I said. "Back up. Who's 'us'? Who am I talking to?"

All around me, cameramen and production assistants and random techs were frozen like statues. No one was doing anything anymore. They were just staring up at the speaker from which the voice was coming, and all looked like they'd never move again, as if their minds so wanted to be somewhere else that their bodies had been left to their own devices for a while.

But I'm different. I'm used to the challenges of going live. And a goddamned professional, too.

"We are from a planet you do not have a name for," the voice said. "In our tongue it is called..." And he made a sound I'm not even going to try to describe. You wouldn't want to hear it outside your house late at night, that's for sure. "The being you call 'Rusty' is one of us. We are allowed to leave the ship every now and then on a strict rotation basis. But he has outstayed his leave. And he is selling what belongs to us alone."

"Wait there a second," I said, holding my hand up. "Ship? What kind of ship?"

"A scout ship."

"From where? Okay, right, the unpronounceable place." I turned to the being that I had previously been introduced to as Rusty. "But what are you *doing* here?"

"We have been experiencing some technical difficulties," Rusty/it muttered, his voice now halfway between Southern drawl and hacking flu-cough. "Because the captain is a complete..."

And then suddenly he/it vanished.

The thing that had been Rusty was gone, leaving only a small pile of clothes, two vivid blue contact lenses, and a head and beard wig lying on the floor.

And over the speaker came the sound of something very bad and physical and permanent happening.

Suddenly there *was* movement amongst the assembled people in the studio. Some running, a little shrieking, a lot of men and women crying out. But it didn't amount to much. I heard someone in back shouting that all the doors had mysteriously become locked. I glanced over at the window to the control booth once more and saw everyone in there was standing frozen, watching me through the glass. I think Rod was still shouting things in my ear, too, but I wasn't listening. He was never any help.

"If you're some kind of scout ship," I said, talking directly to the disembodied voice again, "how come you can't just phone home? Contact the mothership or whatever, tell them you've got issues and to send help?"

There was a pause, then something that sounded a little like a human cough.

"We're not supposed to be here," the voice said.

"Why?"

"Long story," the voice said.

"You got lost?"

"No," the voice said, irritably, as if I'd opened a big can of worms. "We were going to invade. But there was some last-minute discussion on board about the ethics of the thing. Your world is protected, theoretically, and there was some…heated discussion. A small amount of equipment damage ensued. The remote control for the radial neo-transponder matrix got stepped on, and without it the ship doesn't work."

"So you're *stuck?*"

"Yes."

"For how long?"

There was something like a sigh, a sound that reverberated

through the studio like a gust of wind wandering alone through the Grand Canyon in the dead of night.

"Eleven-point-five thousand of your years."

"Jesus," I said. "That's quite a layover."

"Yes. To be honest, the time's beginning to drag."

"I'm not surprised. Holy cow. Where are you, exactly?"

"In a mountain."

"In a…"

"I don't want to talk about it."

"And you're completely alone here?"

"There's a crew down in Key West. But not our kind. They're spindly. And assholes, actually. And they won't help."

"Have you tried changing the batteries?"

There was a pause. "Excuse me?"

"Well," I said, "this radial neo-transponder matrix widget or whatever sounds like the kind of thing that's going to need some juice, right? Couldn't it just be the batteries went flat? Have you checked?"

There was a long, long pause. I mean — really, *really* long. Another cough. Then a further pause.

Finally: "I don't believe our technicians have explicitly evaluated that possibility, no."

"You think maybe they…should?"

"Even if your suggestion had merit, the batteries of our kind are completely different from yours. Actually…do you say different 'from' or different 'to'?"

"Whichever," I said. "You're the boss."

"They are both different from and different to your batteries. They are transquantum piso-structures one mile square in five dimensions. And not available here."

"Have you tried a universal remote?"

"Universal remote?"

"Sure," I said. "In fact…wait here."

I ran out of the studio, back into the green room, and searched through the various piles of crap spread all over it. Spare jackets and ties, bits and pieces left from other random segments, free samples from previous Special hours. After a minute — thank god — I found what I was looking for and which I *thought* I'd remembered seeing a couple nights before.

Then I strode back out into the studio, already talking direct to camera as I hit the floor.

"Do *you* suffer from 'remote proliferation'?" I asked. "Is *your* den deluged under a pile of remotes, your sitting room swamped with switches and kitchen ka-flumped with kontrols, each one designed to work with only one piece of equipment? Do you have one for the television, one for the cable, one for DVD, CD…maybe even one for the cat? You do, right? So do I. Or I *did*, that is, until I discovered the Relco Universal OmniRemote."

I triumphantly held up the remote I'd found. It caught one of the big lights overhead, and glittered like a chalice.

"Truly, my friends, this is a leap forward in both technology and tidiness, a breakthrough in convenience and style. I'll tell you right now — and regular viewers know I don't say this often — I've even got one of these babies myself at home. I'd have two, but…" — and here I paused for a trademark winsome smile to camera: I was back in the zone — "…you'll only ever *need* one, right?"

"We don't have a den," said the voice over the speaker. "This is a spaceship."

"I get that," I said. "My point is you could maybe use one of these things. Reprogram it to work a radial neo-transponder gizmo, or whatever it is you said."

"Hmm," said the voice. "Hold on a minute."

There was a brief humming sound, followed by utter silence. Then the voice came back.

"Put it in the middle of the floor."

"What?"

"The device of which you speak. Put it in the middle of the floor with a minimum of two Trajelian Nippits of clear space all around it. That's approximately a 'yard,' in your currency."

I walked out from behind the counter and placed the remote carefully in the middle of the floor. Then I stepped back, shooing the cameramen and production flunkies away, so there was a lot of space around it.

"You got it," I said. "Now what?"

There was a sudden rushing sound, followed by a brief whir. Both sounded as if they came from inside my own head. Then a simple and very loud *ping*.

And the remote on the floor had disappeared.

And everything was silent.

There was not a sound in the studio. Everyone stood, waiting. It was as if the world outside had disappeared.

Then, from over the speaker, came a noise that sounded like distant and somewhat relieved cheering.

Everyone in the studio looked at each other.

"Well, who knew?" said the rough, liquid voice, coming back. "So the monkey-people finally came up with something useful. Point to you."

"You're welcome," I said. "So now you're free to go?"

"Our engines are coming up to speed as we speak. We are going to need that tin of 'polish' on the counter there, though. Leave no man behind. Or evidence, I mean."

I picked up the tin of Supa Shine and went around to put it in the cleared space in the floor. Wind/whir/*ping* — and it was gone.

"Remain right where you are," the voice said.

I stayed put, frozen in the middle of the floor.

"You have been helpful, people of Earth. We are grateful. Now… we're going to have to destroy you all."

"*What?*"

"You know too much."

"We know shit," I protested. "Really. Zip. Nada. Especially me."

"Sorry," the voice said. "Health and safety."

People began to break down in earnest then. They knew this was the end. They understood suddenly that this was irrevocable, that no argument, however cogent, well-argued or frankly even *right,* would ever make a difference once the twin godhead of health and safety had been invoked.

"Well, look, Christ," I spluttered, regardless, knowing I had to keep talking until the very end. "That seems kind of harsh, you know? We fixed your, you know, that thing that was broken. We helped you out, right?"

"No," the voice said. "*You* did. Say goodbye."

I looked around the studio, at the people all terrified and flinching, the tear-running faces and trembling shoulders. I glanced at Max and Clive and Jeff, the camera and lights crew, not looking so tough now. At Mandy from makeup, and Trix and Pinky the PA girls, and finally through the window at Rod and his open-mouthed producers and other familiars: at these people, my colleagues and acquaintances, the people I had worked with, these fellow-toilers at the sharp end of retail.

These humans. Every single one of them remains burned into my mind. They're the last ones I ever saw.

"Goodby —" was all I got out.

Then my mind went white, and there was the sound of wind, and then a whir, and then a *ping.*

The viewers at home never saw me vanish, or what happened to Rusty. They never even heard the strange voice over the speakers — all they saw was a whacky few seconds where James Richard seemed to be going very seriously off message…before the Home Mall signal went fuzzy for a couple minutes.

Then the channel abruptly left the air forever, as the studio, warehouse, and surrounding city block was vaporized — by what was later explained, I gather, as an unexpected meteorite. I guess the CIA or NSA or some other bunch of spooks covered the whole thing up somehow. Clearly *someone* back at home knows where Earth stands in the bigger picture — since I've been away I discovered there's even a secret website at www…oh, I guess I shouldn't say. But that's how I know the official U.S. government classification for what happened to me: a close encounter of the seventeenth kind, one involving "a commercial transaction conducted over some form of mass telecommunication (including but not limited to television, radio, or particle net sub-rotation) and involving individual items valued at one hundred dollars or less." It's kind of rare. In fact I think I may have been the first. To survive, anyhow.

So — there's the scoop on how I came to be here, like you asked. Edit as you see fit, of course — I know it's kind of long for a press release. I'm sure my new agent will want some tweaks, too: the stuff about my name won't mean a lot to a guy called fLKccHL±±sgdo273-fx2, I guess.

Anyhoo. Got to go, bro. The bright lights call, the roar of the greasepaint, and the smell of the crowd. I'm five minutes away from a two-hour pan-galactic Special for a massive consignment of mesquite-roasted Alpha Centaurian pengulnuts and their associated serving dishes and cookware. Yum yum. The buying public awaits eagerly, always, and James Richard is their friend, advisor, and honest guide through the retail jungle…

…whatever damned planet they're from.

A Place for Everything

AT LAST, METCALFE SAW IT. It was very hard to concentrate by then, and the speck was extremely small. But in the end he spotted it, and knew where it should be.

Careful not to alter his own position, he reached out to it.

The book on feng shui had not been the beginning; more the beginning of the end. He'd known for years that his environment, and the positioning of the objects within it, could affect his state of mind. He couldn't seem to settle if a room was untidy. The newspapers strewn on the table or the mug left on top of the television set would impinge on his field of vision and affect his ability to work. He had to get up and move them. It was one of the reasons that he'd had to stop living with Diane. Her tendency to leave things where they lay meant countless wasted minutes tidying up before he could get down to work. Not just work, in fact: he couldn't relax properly, either, unless everything was just right.

He came across the book by accident when browsing in a second-hand bookshop off Charing Cross road. Metcalfe had pulled down the volume almost at random and had been inclined to dismiss it without another glance: Feng Shui, so far as he'd gathered, seemed a mechanism for charlatans to relieve the gullible middle classes of their money. He soon saw he was holding no gaudy pamphlet, however, but a well-produced old book, and after perusing the text on the back cover he bought it and hurried home.

The ancient Chinese, the book reminded him, had developed a science around the relative placing of natural land formations and man-made objects. Originally applied to the positioning of graves, it had come to be an all-encompassing system that issued guidelines on where best to place a house, or business, and how to arrange furniture and other internal objects to best direct the flow of "ch'i." The life force.

Although he was not terribly convinced of the existence of a life force, Metcalfe quickly saw there were parallels between the habitual tidiness he'd developed and the advice given in the book. A lot of it was common sense, of course, and possibly no more. A carefully placed plant brought a corner into a room; a wind chime or mobile broke up empty space and seemed to bring the air to life. Some of the remedies, however, were less easy to discount. Metcalfe moved the position of his bed to bring it into better conjunction with the shape of the room and the location of the door, and immediately found that not only did he feel more at home in his rather bleak bedroom, but he seemed to sleep better, too. He rearranged the furniture in the living room too, again working from guidelines in the book, and hung a mirror on the wall to counter the building opposite, the corner of which pointed aggressively through his window and directly toward where he usually sat.

He even made such changes as were possible to his office at work, and while the slightly eccentric layout caused some of the others to look at him oddly, they seemed to make the long days spent selling his time easier to bear.

* * *

The shaft of light coming through the window was obscured for a moment by a passing cloud, making the speck of dust harder to see. Metcalfe paused, bided his time, waiting for it to come back into clear view again.

He'd quickly learned all he could from the book, and outgrew it. He knew where it was — he knew the position of every object in the flat now — but hadn't referred to it in weeks. It had been useful as a source of rough principles, but Metcalfe soon realized that "close enough" wasn't sufficient. Although he was less distracted in his rearranged room, it still wasn't perfect. Now that the major objects were in the right places, and the disturbing influences from the outside world were deflected or absorbed, it became easier to discern the small imperfections that remained.

His desk was in the correct position relative to the wall, and his armchair angled properly to the table, but as long as the books on the bookcase weren't right, and the curtains were slightly too long, the overall effect was marred. Not only that, but while an ashtray could be positioned correctly so as not to jar with the table it rested on, it might be out of alignment with a mug on the desk on the other side of the room. There was more than one level, more than one set of relationships.

It would have been easier if straight lines and consistent angles were involved, but they weren't. It was often, at least to start with, a matter of trial and error, distance and angle and bearing and height all needing to be experimented with. Although Metcalfe found that he was getting even less work done in the evenings, now that he was spending hours fine-tuning the positions of everything in his room, it was worth it. The new relations created a much better atmosphere, and he found himself feeling more and more relaxed, less distracted, less prone to anxiety and doubt.

Leaving the house in the morning started to become difficult. Giving up the serenity and calm of his carefully arranged room, and having to undergo the jumbled chaos of the outside world, increasingly made him almost cry out in discomfort. Fighting the noise and unreason of London, of the office and its endless meaningless demands, eventually became too unpleasant to contemplate — and one morning Metcalfe simply failed to put himself through the trauma of leaving the front door.

He didn't know if the office had ever tried to contact him. The phone's irregular shape had proved impossible to align satisfactorily with the rest of the objects in the living room, and Metcalfe had thrown it away with little regret.

The sun came out from behind the cloud, and he reached slowly toward the speck. It was very hard to move his arm now, and he could feel its correct position crying out to it, but he persevered, believing the effort — and temporary misalignment — would be worth it.

The breakthrough had come less than a week ago.

Sitting in his armchair one evening, facing across the room, Metcalfe had forced himself to concentrate. He knew he still had more to do, but was finding it increasingly hard to puzzle out what it might be.

The initial position he'd found for the desk, though an improvement, had turned out to be wrong. Now it stood on its end, partially obscuring the door to the hall, and that was perfect. He could feel the utter correctness of that corner of the room, as he could of all the others. The pile in the carpet was brushed in the correct directions, and the thin white line he had drawn at a certain angle on one wall had been, he was sure, a conclusive touch. After painting it he'd had what he could only describe as a blackout. For half an hour he'd lost all sense of time and place, even of self. Everyday thoughts and worries had left him, and for that brief period it was almost as if he'd become simply an object.

Coming to, taking back his customary relationship to the world, had felt like an unwanted weight settling back onto his mind. It was while remembering this feeling that Metcalfe realized it was not enough simply to arrange objects in relation to each other. Harmony between them was most of the work, but not all. They were not the only things in the room.

There was one more, and its positioning was just as important.

Carefully, Metcalfe wiped his finger on the carpet to pick up the speck of dust. As he moved his arm closer to where he knew the mote should go, he felt the proof of what was coming, the quiet joy of knowing he'd been right.

He dropped the speck.

An easy thing to forget, his body. Thirty years of believing that the thing he lived in was somehow different, somehow special, had blinded him to its essential similarity to everything else in the world, to all the other things that took up space. As he experimented over the following days, first finding his ideal position within the room and then readjusting other objects in line with the altered relationships this caused, he came to realize what a sham the body's individuality was.

As he fine-tuned and got closer to the truth, it became harder and harder to think of himself as different. It became difficult to think at all, in fact. His mind relaxed, relinquishing its accustomed difference to the outside world and slowly feeling its way toward dissolution. If he could have brought himself to believe it still important, he would have liked to tell someone what he'd discovered.

That all things have a place, and that a man is just a thing.

* * *

Metcalfe watched with wonder as the speck fell into position, everything becoming white before his eyes.

His breath slowed, the movement of his lungs and other organs ceasing to beat a rhythm.

As the mote came to rest, he stopped, became still; merely one object among many, in an untidy room.

The Last Barbecue

ARCHIVAL RECORD: CA/6857F
MEDIUM: digitized CCTV
DATE: [Labor Day, 2017]

Contextualizing statement:

Following is a transcript of CCTV footage recovered from the LakeView Resort & Spa, 3534 Lake Tahoe Boulevard, South Lake Tahoe, CA 96150, United States (hereinafter designated "LVRS"). LVRS was a popular hotel and condominium resort on the shore of this key vacation and recreation destination until its desertion. Founded in 1962 and regularly upgraded, in its final form LVRS consisted of twenty-two blocks, each holding four small wooden townhouses, arranged around paths in pine woods leading down to the lake. Six additional one-story beach houses flanked a facility at

83

the shore consisting of a pool, children's paddling pool, and hot tub, formerly serviced by a small café and surrounded by a terraced area. From this a wooden jetty reaches eighty feet out into the lake. On either side of the foot of the jetty were arranged a number of informal barbecuing facilities, along with picnic tables on a small grassy area leading to a narrow sandy beach.

LVRS remained sparsely inhabited for several months after The Death, primarily by former staff members, people either aware that their homes elsewhere in the state had already been over-run, or those who believed that the resort would provide an easily defensible location. This hope proved unfounded. The second major wave of No Longer Living Individuals exiting the Bay Area over-ran LVRS during the weekend of October 13-15. All remaining inhabitants of the resort perished during that two-day period.

Since this time the LakeView Resort & Spa, along with all other previous habitations and businesses along the south shore of Lake Tahoe, has remained deserted. A few generator-supported functions such as motion-sensitive lights and low-voltage digital CCTV security imaging remain active; otherwise the resort is a dead facility.

TRANSCRIPT:

Footage is in black and white, with sound. Camera shows a fixed viewpoint of the edge of the terraced area associated with the spa café, a portion of the grassed area on the other side, and the beach, which is approximately twenty feet in depth. A basic cinderblock barbecue facility stands on the grass. The beginning of the jetty is also visible, stretching out into darkness. Initial sound consists of lapping sounds of water against the jetty supports. Visibility is limited.

Recorded events commence at 20:38, according to time code, though there is evidence that the motion-sensitive CCTV camera failed to trigger at some earlier point, as a FIRST MAN is already in vision at the start of the recording. He is visible from behind, sitting against the edge of the terrace.

At 20:38 a SECOND MAN enters the field of view. He is bulky, wearing denim jeans and a plaid shirt, and in middle age. He is carrying a supermarket paper sack under each arm, with some difficulty. When he gets close to the barbecue one of these starts to slip. He elects to place both hurriedly on the ground.

MAN 2: Fuck *me* that's some heavy shit. I never realized how heavy all this shit *is*. You could have helped, man.

The FIRST MAN grunts.

MAN 2: Yeah, right. Wear the young ones out first, huh? Like Dad always said. I get why, now.

Man 2 puts his hands on his hips and looks out into the darkness over the lake.

MAN 2: Fuck, bro. How long has it been? I mean…how long? Seriously. I was trying to work it out on the way here. But it's like, I'm driving, and it's dark and actually I'm pretty fucking drunk. 'Course we don't have to worry about traffic on the roads, right? That's one thing. But let's work it out. I'm forty-seven, which is a fucking joke in itself. How did *that* happen? And the last time I remember us all being here, the entire family and cousins and dah dah dah, is…it was the year before I moved to Chicago, right? I was twenty-nine. Which is like…a zillion years ago. No, hang on, come on. Forty-seven. Twenty-nine. Twenty-eight? No way. It can't be nearly thirty fucking years. Oh. *Eighteen* years, duh. Shit. That's still long, man. That's still really fucking *long*. Seems like it was, okay not yesterday, but, you know, not…*that* long.

Man 2 is silent for a few moments, swaying slightly.

MAN 2: That's some pretty easy math I was fucking up there. I'm amazed we got here in one piece.

Man 1 grunts again. Man 2 turns back to look at him.

MAN 2: Right. Whatever. Let's do this.

He squats down and starts removing things from the bags he put on the ground. He takes out a large bag. He takes out a smaller bag wrapped in white plastic.

MAN 2: Burgers, plain and simple. Steak? Ha. No fucking chance. When's the last time you saw a steak? Right. Steak would have not been... *realistic*. Suits me fine. I always thought burgers kicked steak's ass on a barbecue anyway.

He peers down at the barbecue.

MAN 2: Basic fucking grill this is, man. Guess you got to make the best of what you got, though, right? If it was enough for Dad to work his magic, it's good enough for us.

He takes out another, lighter bag.

MAN 2: Buns. Uh, right. Yeah. Buns. Fuck — did I remember mustard?

He leans down to rootle through the second bag. Loses his balance and keels over until he is lying on the grass.

MAN 2 [MUFFLED]: Crap.

After a moment he moves his head, peering.

MAN 2: Ha. Found the mustard, though. And the JD, halle-fucking-lujah.

He pushes himself up to a sitting position and pulls a bottle of Jack Daniels from the nearest bag. He takes a large gulp, and holds it out toward Man 1. No response.

MAN 2: Good call, man. You're wasted enough. Okay. Let's get these burgers rock-and-rolling.

He gets up, surprisingly fluently, and starts unpacking bags onto the support area around the barbecue.

MAN 2: Duh. Might want to start the fire, right?

He picks up one of the larger bags, tears vaguely at one end, and eventually opens it. He pours charcoal into the grill. Then brings up a small tin, which he up-ends and squirts liberally over the coals. He pulls a box of matches from his pocket. Lights one, tosses it in. The fuel ignites noisily, momentarily whiting out the image onscreen.

MAN 2: Whoops.

The image settles and the sound of flames dies down, to show Man 2 lighting a cigarette off another match. Man 1 grunts again, louder this time.

Man 2: Are you kidding? You're giving me a hard time about *smoking* — when the world's fucked to shit? Fuck it. Not to mention we're in the fucking out*doors*, dude. Lake fucking Tahoe, man. First cigarette I ever *had* was by this lake, matter of fact. Your eighteenth birthday, did you ever know that? I remember…I remember you were standing with Mom and Dad, must have been pretty much right *here,* and I'd got this half-pack of smokes somebody had given me at school, who was it: yeah, Jimmy Garwhen, fucking asshole he turned out to be. And I'm fifteen and Dad's let me have two beers because it's a *special* special occasion and I'm thinking fuckin'-A, this is the life. *This* is the grown-up thing, right here. And I went around the back of…

He indicates vaguely with his hand toward beach houses outside our FOV.

MAN 2: …and lit one up. Coughed like a fucking maniac. Had two more later, though. I worked at it. You've got to work at that shit, right? Even bad habits don't come easy.

He regards the fire for a moment.

MAN 2: You know what? I'm just going to put these babies right on there now. Going to take forever otherwise. I'm hungry. You hungry?

MAN 1 grunts, louder this time.

MAN 2: Right. Bet you are.

He opens the white plastic bag and takes out a couple of patties. Dithers for a moment, then holds both in one hand.

MAN 2: Dude…the *barbecue sauce*. Dad's special blend, the secret recipe, made by my own good self. But you got to *remind* me of this shit. If we're relying on me to get this thing done right, we'd be better off chewing on twigs.

He picks up a plastic bottle. He squirts the contents onto the burgers. And his hands, by accident. And his jeans. He slaps the burgers on the grill portion of the barbecue. There is a hissing sound and flames leap up, whiting out the screen again. He rears back, staggering slightly.

MAN 2: Guess they're going to be pretty fucking chargrilled, huh.

He picks up the bottle of Jack Daniel's and comes to sit on the wall fairly near Man 1. He takes a drag of his cigarette and flicks it out toward the lake. Thinks a moment.

MAN 2: Ah, shit.

He gets up, trudges into the darkness out of sight. There's a faint splashing sound. Then he trudges back into vision, holding something, slumps back down near to the other man.

MAN 2: Still can't do it. Nobody here, whole world's gone to shit, and I can't flick a butt in the lake. Not *this* lake. You know, in my whole life, I never smoked in front of Mom and Dad? Not once. Even at Dad's funeral, I'm shaking and totally fucked up and I still went and hid behind a tree so Mom wouldn't even see, though I was forty-two years old. But *you,* you used to do it right there at the table. And then you gave up smoking and they're all "You rock, son." Though of course I didn't give it up. Ha. Looking back, I really do *not* regret the decision not to give up. That turned out okay for me. But I still remember you smoking the first time some year, you were like seventeen or something, right at that picnic table over there, and it's Thanksgiving as usual and everyone's hanging out and you just pull out the Marlboros and light up like it ain't no thing. And nobody bats an eyelid. That was cool, man. You're good at that shit. Seen you pull that all your life but I never learned the lesson. And now...nobody... gives...a...damn. I could drop my pants and fuck a dog in the middle of the street and nobody...would...care.

Man 2 takes another pull off the bottle of alcohol — holds it out to Man 1, who grunts, but doesn't take it.

MAN 2: Burgers starting to smell good, though, right?

He laboriously get to his feet and lurches toward the barbecue. He picks up a burger with his fingers and turns it over.

MAN 2: Holy FUCK that's hot.

Nonetheless, he does the same with the second. Then flaps his hand about, before slowly stopping. He is quiet for a full minute before speaking more quietly.

MAN 2: You know what I regret? Not coming that one year. When I was twenty-fucking-nine. I don't even know what the fuck that was *about*. Okay, I'd gone to Chicago and it would have been a lot further to come, but…I still don't actually know why I didn't do it. I could have got on a plane, whatever. I guess it was an age thing, maybe. You think you're getting too old for the family-all-together shit. Plus Julie didn't get why I'd do it and she didn't want to come and…I really wish I'd come, man. And the next year, too. I remember you calling me that second time, you were standing here with Mom and Dad and eating burgers and I was…I don't know, in a bar, I think, drinking away the fact the dumb bitch Julie had then left me, I guess, and you called and I didn't pick up because I was wasted and I figured you'd be wanting to give me a hard time for not making it to the big rah-rah family event…and in fact you just left a message saying "Wish you were here."

He turns back to look at the seated man.

MAN 2: I got back into it after that but then Paul started skipping every other year and Marie did the same the other way around and the cousins stopped bothering and it just seemed like it was never the same as it had been when we were kids, except for Mom and Dad were always here. Feels sometimes like it was my fault it went that way. Like I fucked the whole thing up. Did I? Was it down to me? If I hadn't skipped those two years, would it have kept…shit. Whatever. I don't know. You think you know every damned thing when you're young. You think, great, thanks for all the years and I love you still but I'm out here on my own now. Big fucking mistake. If you got a family and it likes getting together once a year…*just fucking do it*. Bite the bullet and get on the fucking plane. There's plenty of time and a million different ways to be an asshole. Don't feel you got to get them all done at once.

He leans forward and peers at the barbecue.

MAN 2: Getting there, bro. Getting there. Better get the rest of the road on the show. And at least we're here *now*, right? That's something. And that's down to me. If I hadn't come got you, it wouldn't have happened. Score one to me. 'Course getting there *earlier* would have been even better, but that'd have meant getting my shit together and not being a fucking asshole, and it's too late for that now.

He starts pulling stuff out of the bags on the ground. Buns, a bag of lettuce, tomato, ketchup, mustard, two paper plates. Lays them out on the side. He starts moving things around, trying to things in a particular order.

MAN 2: You not going to do this? You *always* did this part. Me, I'd've probably just picked the meat up in my fingers, left to myself. You were always up in it with the got-to-be-just-so and do-it-right. And you were right, as I came to appreciate in the fullness of fucking time. And you know what? You know…what?

His hands stop moving. He has started to cry.

MAN 2: This shit changes nothing. You were right. Do everything just so. Do it *right*. If the rest of the world can't be fucked, then fuck 'em. Do your thing. *Do it right.*

He stands, no longer trying to do anything, shoulders heaving. Then he sniffs, pulls his sleeve across his face.

MAN 2: Okay then. Glad we got that straight.

Then suddenly he looks off to his right. Stands absolutely still, and silent, for twenty seconds.

MAN 2 (quietly): You hear that?

He's silent again, staring off into the darkness.

MAN 2: You hear your buddies? Off down along the shore. Seems like maybe there's braindeads still in these woods after all. I knew there would be. Told you so. I never thought those things were as dumb as everybody makes out — and they're getting smarter now, too. *Lots* smarter. And they gotta be loving that smell, right? Burgers cooking in the open air. Cooked by someone you know, in a place you've been to so many times it feels like home. There is no food in the fucking *world* tastes like a burger eaten with people you've known your whole life. That, my friends, is the word of God.

He grabs the bottle of alcohol and takes another big gulp, before shouting into the darkness.

MAN 2: You *like* that smell? 'Course you do. That's *meat* cooking, and it's meat done right. Old Man Stegnaro's special sauce. Fucking shitheads just gnawing dead shit. That's not how it's *done,* don't you fucking get it?

He's quiet for a moment, looking off along the shore.

MAN 2: Fuck, dude. There's a *lot* of them. Not sure we got enough to go 'round all these fuckers. 'Course you probably won't be eating your burger and, to be honest with you, I don't really want mine, what with the ground round having come out of your actual fucking *leg,* but that's the kind of joke you would have loved, bro — say it ain't so. You make do with what you got, right? You were always telling me that. *And* you'd have made me bring all this other shit if you'd been alive to have a say-so, and so that's what I done. Standards must be maintained. You can turn the Stegnaro brothers' world to crap, but we ain't coming down to your level. Still here, still standing, still doing it right.

He looks off along the shore and cackles triumphantly — gesturing toward himself as if instigating a fight. He addresses people out of frame.

MAN 2: You want some? You fucking *want* some? If you're going to eat, you dead fucking *assholes,* then do it *right.*

He holds the barbecue sauce bottle above his head and squirts it liberally over himself.

MAN 2: Fucking deadheads.

At the left and right extremities of the screen, we can make out shadows of human size, lurching toward Man 2. The fire is unsettling them, but they are neither retreating nor halting their progress.

MAN 2: Yeah, yeah — "Oh, look at us, we just keep on coming." Assholes. And don't forget the mustard.

The encroaching shapes are now within yards of him. He picks something else up from the ground. He holds it, flips the cap, looking over at the slumped other man.

MAN 2: Sorry I didn't get there sooner, bro.

He holds the thing in his hand up and squeezes, squirting something else all over his clothes and head and body. Then pulls something else out of his pocket, as he squirts the fuel over the shapes now closing in on him.

MAN 2: I love you, man.

He lights a match and holds it to his chest. The flare of the flames whites out the screen. Dark shapes surround him, also burning, grunting.

MAN 2: Gonna be pretty fucking chargrilled, huh.

A shape reaches out toward the camera.

TAPE ENDS.

The Stuff That Goes On in Their Heads

I FIRST HEARD THE NAME on Monday night, when I was putting him to bed. Kathy was out for an early dinner and catch-up with a friend, and so it had been the Ethan-and-Daddy Show from late afternoon. The recurring plot of this regular series boils down to my preparing one of the pasta dishes which have gained my son's tacit approval (and getting him to focus on eating it before it turns into a congealed mass), and the two of us then watching his allotted one-per-day ration of *Ben 10: Alien Force*. After its conclusion I coax him up to the bathroom and into the bath — against sustained and imaginative resistance — followed by the even more protracted process of getting him to *leave* the bath, Ethan having in the interim realized that the nice, warm tub is the best place in the world to be, and an environment he is not prepared to leave at any cost. Then there's the putting-on-of-pajamas and the brushing-of-the-teeth and various other tasks which sound (and should be) simple and quick but always seem to end up taking *forever* — little tranches of time, which add up to really *quite a lot of time* when taken together, time that I'll never get back. We had Ethan relatively late in life (he's six, making me exactly forty years his senior) but what the older parent may lack in energy and vim is hopefully tempered by what they bring in terms of perspective, and so I understand that it won't be so very long before my presence in the bathroom (or anywhere else) will not be enjoyed or even tolerated by a child who'll grow up faster than seems possible. Two more lots of six years, and he'll be leaving home. I get that. I try, therefore, to take all these little tribulations in good spirit, and to enjoy their fleeting presence in my life. But still, at the end of a long day, you do kind of wish they'd just brush their bloody teeth, by themselves, without all the stalling and prevarication.

For *the love of God*.

Eventually we got clear of the bathroom and proceeded in state to Ethan's bedroom — him leading the way, regal in pint-sized dressing gown, chattering about this and that. He resisted getting into bed for a while, but without any real purpose and in a pro forma manner, as if he knew this section of the evening was merely part of a ritual and he was doing it for my sake more than for himself. Eventually he yawned massively and headed toward the bed. He was tired. He always is on Mondays and Wednesdays because of after-school club. The trick with tired children is to resist in a passive, judo-style fashion, putting up no specific barriers for them to kick against, instead letting them use their own strength against themselves. This, at least, I have learned.

When he was finally tucked under the covers I asked him how his day had been. I'd meant to do this earlier, but forgot, which meant the inquiry was doomed to failure. Ethan appears to blank his working day within minutes of leaving the school gates, as if what happens there has no more reality than a dream, and melts like ice under the fierce sun of The Outside World. Or perhaps the opposite is true, and there's a fundamental reality about the universe of the school that is impossible to convey to we shades who live in the unconvincing hinterland outside.

Either way, he appeared as usual to have zero recollection of what had occurred between nine A.M. and four P.M. that day. When pushed for a definitive account, however, he issued a brief statement saying that it had been "fine."

"And how was after-school club?"

Many of the kids who go to The Reynolds School have parents who both work. This means the school runs a slick and profitable range of activities to tide tots over from the end of actual school to the point where their stressed-out handlers can pick them up. Ethan's after-school diversion on Mondays is swimming. This is a bit pointless, I can't help thinking. Partly because Monday happens also to be when his class does swimming anyway — and so all his piscine endeavors are concentrated on the same day; mainly because said classes boil down to the children spending most of the half-hour shivering on the edge of the pool, waiting for their brief turn to splash about. Ethan's already pretty confident in the water — courtesy of a vacation in Florida last year — but untutored in terms of strokes, beyond a hectic doggy-paddle that is full of sound and fury but conveys little in the way of forward motion. We hoped the after-school club would help refine this. So far, he seems to be going backward.

"Terrible," Ethan said.

"Terrible?" This is strong for him. He usually confines pronouncements of quality to "fine" or "okay," occasionally peaking in a devil-may-care "good." I suspect the deployment of "great" would require the school suddenly deciding to hand out free chocolate. I'd never heard "terrible" before, either. "Why terrible?"

"Arthur Milford was mean to me again."

I snorted. "Arthur Milford? What the hell kind of name is that?"

Ethan turned his head in bed to look at me. "What?"

"How *old* is this kid?"

"Six," Ethan said, with gentle care, as if I was crazy. "He's *six*. Like me."

"Sorry, yes," I said. I tend to talk to my son as if he's a miniature adult for much of the time — too much of it, perhaps — but there was no way of explaining to him that the name "Arthur Milford," while theoretically acceptable, seemed more appropriate to a music-hall comedian of the 1930s than a six-year-old in 2011. "What do you mean, he was mean to you again?"

"He's always mean to me."

"Really? In what way?"

"Telling me I'm stupid."

"You're not stupid," I said, crossly. "*He's* stupid, if he goes around calling people names. Just ignore him."

"I can't ignore him." Ethan's voice was quiet. "He's always doing it. He pushes me in the corridor, too. Today he said he was going to throw me out of a window."

"*What?* He actually *said* that?"

Ethan looked up at me solemnly. After a moment he looked away. "He didn't actually say it. But he meant it."

"I see," I said, suddenly unsure how much of this entire story was true. "Well, look. If he says mean things to you, just ignore him. Mean boys say mean things. That's the way it is. But if he pushes you, tell a teacher about it. Immediately."

"I do. They don't do anything about it."

"Well, if it happens again, then tell them again. And tell me, too, okay?"

"Okay, Daddy."

And then, as so often in such conversations, the matter was dismissed as if it had never been of import to him — and instead merely something that I'd been rather tediously insisting on discussing — and my son asked me a series of apparently random questions about the world, which I did my best to answer, and I read him a story and filled up his water cup and read more story, and eventually he went to sleep.

We tend to alternate in picking Ethan up (as with most parenting duties), and so Tuesday was Kathy's turn. I had a deadline to chase and so — barring his dashing into my study to say hello when they got back — I barely saw Ethan before I kissed him on the head and said goodnight when Kathy led him up toward bath and bedtime.

Fifty minutes later, by which time I'd made a start on cooking, my wife appeared in the kitchen with the cautiously relieved demeanor of someone who believes they've wrangled an unpredictable child into bed.

"Is he down?"

"I'm not enumerating any domesticated, egg-producing fowl," she said, reaching into the fridge for the open bottle of wine. "But he might be. God willing."

She poured herself a glass and took a long sip before turning to me. "God, I'm tired."

"Me too," I said, without a lot of sympathy.

"I know. I'm just saying. By the way — has Ethan mentioned some kid called Arthur to you?"

"Arthur Milford?"

"So he has?"

"Once. Last night. Why — did he come up again?"

"Mmm. And it's not the first time, either."

"Really?"

"Ethan mentioned him last week, and I think the week before, too. They're in after-school swimming together."

"I know. Last night he said this Arthur kid had been mean to him. In fact, he said he'd been mean 'again'."

"Mean in what way?"

"Pushed him in the corridor. Called him stupid." I thought about mentioning the threat to throw Ethan through a window, but decided not. I didn't think Kathy needed to hear that part, especially as the telling had subsequently made it unclear whether it had taken place in what Ethan called "real life."

"Pushed him *in the corridor?* That means it's not just happening during swimming class."

"I guess. If it's happening at all."

"You don't believe him?"

"No, no, I do. But you know what he's like, Kath. He's all about the baddies and the goodies. It just sounds to me a bit like this Arthur Milford kid is in the script as Ethan's dread Nemesis. And that maybe not all of his exploits are directly related to events in what we'd think of as reality."

"Doesn't mean there isn't a real problem there."

"I know," I said, a little irritated that Kathy seemed to be claiming ownership of the issue, or implying I wasn't taking it seriously enough. "I told him to talk to the teachers if this kid is mean to him again. And to tell me about it, too."

"Okay."

"But ultimately, that's the way children are. Boys especially. They give each other grief. They shove. Little girls form cliques and tell other girls they're not their friends. Boys call each other names and thump each other. It has been thus since we lived in caves. It will be so until the sun explodes."

"I know. It's just… Ethan's such a cute kid. He can be a total pain, of course, but he's…so sweet, really, underneath. He doesn't know about all the crap in life yet. I want to protect him from it. I don't want him being hit just because that's what happens. I don't want him being hurt in any way. I just want…everything to be nice."

"I know," I said, relenting. "Me, too."

I rubbed her shoulder on the way over to supervise the closing stages of cooking, and privately raised my State of Awareness of the

Arthur Milford situation from DefCon 4 to DefCon 3. Despite what everyone seems to think, the readiness-for-conflict index increases in severity from five to one, with *one* being the highest level. (The highest level ever officially recorded is DefCon 2, which obtained for a while during the Cuban Missile Crisis. I knew all this from some half-hearted research for an article I was drafting on Homeland Security.)

Be all that as it may, and despite my pompous such-is-life declaration, Kathy was right.

I didn't want anyone hassling my kid. Much more of it, and words would need to be spoken.

I picked Ethan up the following afternoon, and remembered to ask him about his day as soon as we got into the car. He proved surprisingly well-informed on his own doings, and filled me in on a variety of Montessori-structured activities he'd undertaken (neither Kathy nor I truly understand what Montessori is about, but we believe/hope that it's generally agreed to be A Good Thing, like lowering CO_2 levels, and being kind to dogs). There was no mention of Arthur Milford. I thought about asking a direct question but decided that if Ethan hadn't deemed him worth mentioning, there was probably nothing to say.

Ethan went to bed easily that night, in his unpredictable fashion. We had a laugh during bath-time, he brushed his own teeth without being asked, and then — after quite a short reading — he drifted off to sleep before I was even ready for it. I sat for five minutes afterward, enjoying the peace of quietly being in the same space as someone you love very much. There's usually a hidden edge to the observation that nothing's as beautiful as a sleeping child (the point being it's all too often nicer than them being awake), but the fact is... there really isn't. To watch your son, asleep in his comfortable bed with a tummy full of food that you made him and a head full of story you've just told, arm gripping a furry polar bear you bought him on

a whim but to which he's taken as if they'd been separated at birth…
that's why we're born. That's why everything else is worth it.

Yet sometimes I get so angry with him that I don't know what to
do with myself. And he knows it. He must.

About six hours later I woke in my own bed, dimly aware I could
hear a noise that shouldn't exist in a house in the middle of the night.
By the time I'd opened my eyes, it was quiet. But as I started to relax
back into oblivion, I heard it again.

A quiet sob.

I quickly hauled myself upright and staggered out of bed. Kathy
lay dead to the world, which was unusual. She generally sleeps on
far more of a hair trigger than me. She evidently was really tired, and
I blearily regretted my snipe before dinner the evening before.

I padded out into the hallway to stand outside Ethan's room and
listen. Nothing for a minute, but then I heard the sound again. I
opened the door.

Before I even got to the side of his bed, I could tell how hot he
was. Children beam their heat out in the night, like little suns. I
squatted down and put my hand on his head.

"Ethan," I said. "It's okay. It's just a dream."

He sobbed once more, very quietly.

"*Ethan*, it's okay."

He opened his eyes suddenly. He looked scared. Scared of me.

"It's Daddy," I said, disconcerted. "Just Daddy, okay?"

His eyes seemed to swim into focus. "Daddy?"

"Yes. It's okay. Everything's okay."

Ethan's eyes swiveled. "Is he still here?"

"Who?"

"Arthur Milford."

The back of my neck tickled. "No. Of course not."

"He was *here*. He came up the stairs and stood outside my room saying things. Then he came in. He stood by my bed and said he was going to…"

"No, he didn't," I said, firmly.

"He *did*."

"Ethan, it was just a dream. No one's in the house apart from you and me and Mummy. Nobody can get in. The doors are locked. The alarm system's on."

"Are you *sure?*"

"I'm sure," I said. "I did it myself. I promise you. It's just the three of us, and everything's okay."

Ethan's eyelids were already starting to drift downward. "Okay."

He was asleep five minutes later. I went back to bed and lay there for an hour before I could get under again. Once I've been woken, I find it hard to get back to sleep.

The next morning I was irritable, and snapped pretty badly at Ethan when he made a laboriously annoying job of putting on his school shoes. I shouldn't have, but I was tired, and for fuck's sake — he should be able to put on his own shoes.

But as I watched him and Kathy walk down the path toward the car, the wailing over and a new détente being hammered out between them, I realized that at some point after coming back to my bed in the night, I'd raised the Arthur Milford Awareness Level to DefCon 2.

On Thursday evening Kathy has yoga, and so The Ethan Going To Bed Show once again featured Daddy in a co-starring role (or supporting actor, more likely, my name below the title and in a notably smaller typeface), for the second night in a row.

Bedtime did not, however, follow the same course as the night before. That's not how the shorties roll. Like some snappy young boxer on the way up, they'll pull you in, fake like they're running out of steam, and then unleash a brutal combination that will leave you glancing desperately back at your corner as you take a standing eight count. I'm getting better at rolling with the punches, shifting the conflict to safer ground, and letting the passion defuse, but that night I went back at Ethan like some broken-down old scrapper who knew this was his last chance in the ring, and wanted to go out in a bare-knuckles slugfest.

He wouldn't eat his pasta, instead deliberately distributing it over the floor — meanwhile looking me steadily in the eye. He wouldn't come upstairs. He wouldn't get into the bath, and then wouldn't get out, and broke a soap dish. I had to brush his teeth for him, and I did it none too gently. He wouldn't get into his pajamas because they "always itched" — the very same pair that he'd cheerfully gone to sleep in the previous night. He wouldn't get into bed, instead breaking out of the room and stomping downstairs, wailing dismally for Kathy though he knew damned well she was out.

By the time I'd recaptured him, harsh words had been spoken on both sides. I had been designated an "idiot" and a "doofus" and been informed that I was no longer loved. I had likened his behavior to that of a significantly younger child, and had threatened to inform the world at large of this maturity shortfall: his friends, grandparents, and Father Christmas had all been invoked as potential recipients of this information. I'd said he was being childish and stupid, and had even called him the very worst word I (or you) know, though thankfully I'd managed to throttle my voice down into inaudibility at the last moment so he hadn't caught the word.

The anger had sure as hell made it through, though. The anger, and probably my pitiful level of powerlessness, too.

I did, however, finally manage to get him into bed.

He lay there silently. I sat equally silently in the chair, both of us breathing hard, wild-eyed with silent fury and sour adrenaline.

"Arthur Milford was mean to me today, too," Ethan muttered, suddenly.

I was still pretty close to the edge, and the "too" at the end of his pronouncement nearly pushed me over it into somewhere dark and bad.

I took a breath, and bit my tongue. "Mean in what way?" I managed, eventually.

"In the upstairs corridor. On the third floor."

"Okay — so now I know where the alleged event occurred. But *how* was he unpleasant? In what actual *way?*"

"Why are you being so *mean* to me tonight?"

"I'm…just tell me, okay? What did he *do?*"

"He pushed me again. *Really* hard. Into the wall. And then… against the window."

"Really?"

"*Yes.*"

"Did you tell a teacher? Like I told you?"

"No."

"*Why?* That's what you've got to do. You *have* to tell a teacher."

"He said…he said that if anyone told a teacher about what he was doing, he'd throw me out of the window for sure."

"Really? He actually *said* it this time?"

"*Yes.*"

"But you've just told *me* about it — so why not a teacher?"

"Arthur said telling you didn't matter. *You* can't do anything. Only the teachers can."

"I see. How interesting."

I decided then and there that I'd had quite enough of Arthur sodding Milford. I'd like to think this was solely because of the evident discomfort he was causing Ethan during both waking and sleeping hours, but I know some of it was due to pathetic outrage at hearing myself thus dismissed. As a parent you often encounter moments when you feel impotent, and may often be genuinely unable to affect events. I had to take crap from my own child, evidently: that didn't hold true for someone else's. It was time for Arthur, and his parents, if necessary, to learn that the world did *not* stop at the school gates.

As Ethan and I moved on to talking about other things, gradually opening the doors to each other once more, and calming down, I silently determined that the Arthur Milford situation had finally reached DefCon 1.

I got to the school a little after two o'clock. My appointment would mean I'd have time to kill in the area afterward before picking Ethan up, but it was the only time the headmistress/owner would deign to see me. It's a small school, privately owned, and to be fair, I imagine Ms. Reynolds is pretty busy. I was shown to a little office, part of the recent extension on the ground floor, and given a cup of coffee. I sat sipping it, looking up through the glass roof at the side of the building. Two further storeys, grey brick, with long bands of windows.

Schools, even small and bijou ones, all feel the same. They take you back. I knew that when Ms. Reynolds arrived I'd stand up too quickly and be excessively deferential, though she was ten years younger than me and effectively ran a service industry in which the customer should always be right. None of that matters. School is where you learn the primal things, the big spells, the place where you become versed in the eternal hierarchies and are appraised of our species's hopes and fears. Being back in one as an adult is like returning in waking hours to some epic battleground in the dream-scape — even if, like me, you had a pretty decent time during your formative years.

It was quiet as I waited, all the little animals corralled into class-rooms for now, having information and cultural norms stuffed into their wild and chaotic heads.

Eventually the door opened and the trim figure of Ms. Reynolds entered. "Sorry I'm late."

I stood. "No problem."

She smiled briefly, and perched at an angle on the chair on the other side of the desk. I tried hard not to take offense against her posture, the way it signaled a belief that this was going to be a short conversation. I sat back down, square-on to the table.

"So. How can I help?"

"I wanted a quick word. About Ethan."

"I'm sure it's temporary," she said, briskly. "I honestly don't think it's anything to worry about."

"What is?" I asked, thrown. "Worry about what?"

"Ah," she said, smoothly covering a moment of confusion. "I talked with your wife about this, yesterday, at the end of school. I assumed she'd mentioned it to you."

"Mentioned what?"

"Ethan's schoolwork. It's taken a dip recently, that's all. Nothing major. It happens with most of them, the boys. From time to time. But we're aware of it, and we're working with Ethan to lift things. I can appreciate your concern, but I really…"

"That's not why I'm here."

"Oh. So…"

"I *am* concerned if there's an issue with his work," I said. I was also a little ticked that Kathy hadn't mentioned it to me when she got back from yoga the night before. "But I wanted to talk about the bullying."

"*Bullying?*"

"For the last week, maybe two, Ethan's been talking about being bullied."

Ms. Reynolds swiveled to sit square in her chair. It was clear I'd got her full attention now. "If that's the case then it's a very serious matter," she said.

"It's the case."

She frowned. "One of the teachers did notice a mark on his arm this morning. Very minor. It looked as though someone had gripped his arm. Is that what you're referring to?"

Her eyes were on me. There was probably no way she could know that the mark, which I'd noticed myself when helping Ethan get dressed that morning, was the result of me shoving him into bed the night before. Not so very hard, but children's skins are sensitive.

And my own father raised me to tell the truth.

"No," I said. "That was me."

"You?"

"There was a disagreement over getting into bed last night. I ended up guiding him into it."

She nodded, a minimalist raise of the chin. "So then what *are* you referring to?"

"One of the other boys has been picking on him. Muttering things in after-school swimming class, calling him stupid. Shoving him in the corridors."

"Ethan told you this?"

"Yes. And this boy's even threatened to throw Ethan out of a window."

"Throw him out *of a window?*" Ms. Reynolds looked stricken. "When? When did this happen?"

"Last Monday. And again yesterday." I'd forgotten, for the moment, that this threat hadn't actually been made on Monday — only implied, intuited (or fabricated) by Ethan. It didn't matter. Yesterday it *had* been said. "I'm not happy about this. At all."

"Well, of course not," the headmistress said, putting her hands out flat on the table in front of her. "And who does Ethan say is doing all this?"

"Arthur Milford," I said, experiencing heavy satisfaction as I handed up the name. Not merely at finally stepping up to the plate on behalf of my son, but also through disproving what Arthur had told Ethan — that it was only teachers who could do anything about a situation.

Learn this, you little shit: stuff that happens in the outside world also counts.

"Arthur Milford?"

"Yes."

"It can't be," she said.

"I'm sure he behaves perfectly when teachers are around."

"No, that's not what I mean. I mean...we don't have an Arthur Milford at this school. Are you *sure* that's the name?"

"Absolutely sure. I've heard it every day this week, including in the middle of Wednesday night, when Ethan had a nightmare about this bloody boy coming into his room and threatening him. Kathy's heard the name too."

The teacher looked baffled. "We did have an Arthur Ely in the school, a few years ago, who was quite big, and boisterous, but he left well before Ethan joined us. And there was a Patrick Milford, I think...Yes. He was here even before Arthur. But again, he's moved on. There's no Milfords here now. No Arthurs either."

"That's the name Ethan used."

"I'm afraid...he may just have made it up. Or one of the other children did."

"What — and the fact there have been kids here with very similar names is just a coincidence?"

"No. Making something up doesn't mean it isn't real. I know this is hard to hear, but... Their parents, everything out there in the world... They're important, of course, you're important. But still not as real to the children as what happens in here."

I nodded, remembering the thoughts I'd had while sitting in the chair waiting, and how it had been when I was a child.

"Facts, too," she went on. "Children get them muddled up. Or half-hear things. Or add two and two and make twenty eleven and a half. Perhaps Ethan got shoved by accident. Or he and another boy really getting on — or perhaps he's having arguments with a someone who *is* his friend, really, and so Ethan doesn't want to use the child's real name. Children remember the names of those who have gone before. Perhaps they use them, too, sometimes. Like mythological figures. I spend all my working hours in this place, but it doesn't mean I understand everything that goes on."

"So you don't think anyone's actually bullying Ethan?"

"I sincerely doubt it — and not just because we do a lot to make sure that kind of thing doesn't happen. None of the other boys or girls have said anything. None of the teachers, either. But trust me, I'll look into it. The moment you've gone. And if there's anything — anything at all — to be concerned about, I'll call you right away. I promise."

"Thank you," I said. I didn't know what to feel. A little foolish, certainly.

She stood up, and reached out her hand. I did the same, and we shook. "I hope I haven't wasted your time."

"No time spent talking about a child is wasted," she said, and I felt a little less silly. "But do you mind if I offer a piece of advice?"

"Go ahead," I said, assuming it would be some way of helping Ethan move past this, or of helping him to get his schoolwork back on track.

"Do be careful about...the ways in which you have physical contact with your son."

I froze, indignation and guilt melting together. The room seemed suddenly larger, and very cold. "What do you mean?"

She looked steadily at me. Her eyes were clear, and kind, and for a moment she didn't looked like a teacher, or Ethan's headmistress, just like a woman who meant well and cared about her charges a great deal.

"I know what it's like," she said. "What *they* can be like. I don't have a child of my own, not yet, but I spend a *lot* of time with them. Which is why, every day after I leave here, I go to the gym and get it out of my system for an hour. I kickbox. I'm not very good, but boy do I give those punch bags a thump. And then I go home and have a gin and tonic that would make most people's eyes water. That information is not for general consumption, okay?"

"Okay," I said.

"Loving children can be hard work. But it's what we do. I know you love Ethan, very much. I'm just saying…be careful. Because of the assumptions others might make if they see a mark on him. And also because of how *you* feel, about yourself, and about how he'll feel too. Boys need strong fathers. Men who are strong, and kind, not full of anger and guilt."

I nodded, knowing she was right.

"There's evidently *something* going on in Ethan's universe, and it's good that I know. You did the right thing coming in to tell me about it."

"I hope so," I said, anxious now to lighten the mood. "Ethan said last night that's it was okay to tell *me* about it, but teachers couldn't know. Otherwise, Arthur would, you know."

Ms. Reynolds smiled, and rolled her eyes, as she started to lead me toward the door. "The stuff that goes on in their heads," she said, with just the right amount of irony and affection.

I realized that I'd started to like Ms. Reynolds, and respect her, and that perhaps I'd start to take a more active role in Ethan's schooling, and that would be good.

She walked with me out of the doors and to the waiting area outside. I had an hour to kill, and had decided to go find a coffee somewhere. To think through what had been said, to find a way of accessing a calm which must still exist somewhere inside me. To lighten up. To remember how to be strong, and kind.

"You did the right thing," she said, once more.

As we shook hands again there was the sound of glass breaking, somewhere high above. We looked up and saw the third floor, and the broken window there. Saw the small, boy-shaped figure that came out of it, and started to fall.

Unnoticed

THERE IS A HOMELESS MAN DOWNTOWN CALLED TONY. Unlike many places in California, Santa Cruz is pretty tolerant of people without fixed abode, and so long as they don't hassle passers-by or smoke on the main street (it's illegal for everyone, not just vagrants), the police tend to leave them be. Tony is in his early thirties, I guess, though it's hard to be sure. His hair is long and matted. His skin is tan and weathered. His clothes are battered and very worn, but he does not smell bad. You see him around. Like many of the wanderers in downtown, if he diffidently asks for spare change toward a cup of coffee, a cup of coffee is what he's got in mind. I gave him a dollar recently and later saw him on a side street, holding a Starbucks cup. He raised it to me in thanks. We wound up having a conversation, and after a while I went and bought him another coffee.

He told me his story. This is it.

* * *

One morning about three years ago Tony was over where he lived at the time, in a part of town called Live Oak, near Twin Lakes beach. Way back in the day the area had been agricultural land, smallholder chicken farms and tulip fields: now it's a higgledy concentration of single-story houses and tidy trailer parks, plus a few multi-family units, leavened with pine trees and eucalyptus and spriggy cypress and palms. It's like that on the inland side of East Cliff Drive, anyway; on the other, the block next to the ocean, you'll find more expensive two-story houses and vacation rentals and a few family-friendly restaurants, generally Mexican in tone. Though it's not as noticeably Latino as somewhere like Beach Flats down by the Board-walk, if a passing truck spills loud music out of its windows in Live Oak then it's almost certain to involve the enthusiastic use of trumpets.

On this particular morning Tony was returning to his house from the Windmill Cafe, the local coffee shop. He had his regular triple shot latte in one hand and was musing vaguely about what he had to do when he got home. Having recently lost a job in the coding mines over the hill, where he'd worked as a web programmer for a startup in Mountain View: the company's recent buy-out by a social networking giant had panned out extremely profitably for the founders, though not so well for the employees who'd worked tireless hours toward precisely this goal — his task for the day was doing the rounds of online recruitment sites and forums and networks in search of someone who needed his skills in CSS and PHP. As more white folks around Silicon Valley know how to write these languages than can speak Spanish, he knew it wasn't going to be a walk in the park, but he was relatively unbowed by the prospect.

As he neared the corner with 14th he noticed a man squatted down by the entrance steps in front of a building on the other side of East Cliff Drive. The man was dressed in buff-colored shorts and a white short-sleeved shirt and was peering in a this-needs-fixing kind of way at something that lay within a panel on one side. He reached into the space beyond and adjusted something, but was evidently not satisfied with the result.

It wasn't an exceptional scene, merely the kind of non-event that forms the texture of small towns on sunny mornings, like the guy wheeling a trolley of water into the mercado or the woman from the taqueria hefting bags of trash to the dumpster. As Tony slowed his pace, however, it struck him that — despite having rented a house near this junction for nearly two years — he'd never seen anyone enter or leave the building. Also that, even though he walked past it every day, he'd never noticed anything about it whatsoever.

He took a moment to notice it now. It too was unexceptional. Quite large, two storeys high and about as wide as the small motel that stood opposite, on the side where Tony was walking. It was clad in pale grey siding. It had a lot of windows on both floors, but all were obscured by vertically hanging plastic slats within. There was a parking lot on the right-hand side, holding a handful of cars. The building consisted of two wings joined by a longer chunk, which included the entrance beside which the man in shorts was crouching. This entrance had a kind of portico, leading to double glass doors. At the bottom of the stairs, Tony now noticed, was a stumpy concrete pillar. On this, presented without fanfare in dark blue Helvetica, were the words SYSTEMS SERVICE.

Huh, he thought. *Hard to come up with a more anonymous name than that.*

He hadn't come to a complete halt — there was little reason to in any of the above — but he had slowed down. The man by the entrance stairs stood, still looking down at whatever lay within the service panel, and then turned his head to look at Tony.

Tony nodded, and was surprised when the man didn't nod back. The giving and receiving of affable salutations comes as standard in Live Oak, and most of Santa Cruz in general. It's a neighborly place.

The man had dark, somewhat curly short hair, a moustache, and was wearing — Tony now noticed — dark glasses.

Tony continued on his way, picking his pace back up to normal strolling speed. He took the turn into 14th, and then after a few yards, he glanced back.

The man was still looking at him.

That night, he and Klara having decided that while they were hungry neither felt inspired to cook, Tony found himself wandering back down the fifty yards to the taqueria on the corner. As was his custom, he came back outside to smoke and watch the street for the ten or so minutes it would take the busy women in the back to whip up his order of fish tacos and the shrimp burrito. He found himself looking once more at the building that stood kitty corner. It struck him that in fact he'd walked close by it many more times than he'd realized. When he took his first cup of tea of the day to drink looking over the ocean each morning, he walked along its side. Still, somehow, without ever really noticing it.

He waited for a couple of cars to pass and trotted over to where the mercado stood. He looked across 14th at the side of the building.

Yes, of course: he semi-remembered it now. More grey siding, further windows, all dark. And behind…

He crossed the street. There was another car park behind the building here, much smaller than the one around the other side, big enough for maybe three vehicles at most. Then there was a wooden fence, and on the other side of this a garden area holding a few wooden chairs and a couple of tables with umbrellas. Tony had seen this kind of thing before, over the hill — forward-thinking tech companies providing alfresco meeting space to show how new-business and employee-friendly they were (though in Tony's experience a meeting was still a meeting, whether you're sitting outside or not).

After peering through the slats at the back of the building — which looked very similar to the front, with its bands of obscured windows — he walked back out onto the sidewalk and around to East Cliff Drive and along the front. He wondered what kind of business would construct a building with so many windows, then obscure them all with hanging slats. Some kind of document storage facility, perhaps, where it was important things not fade due to sunlight? Maybe…but then why have so many windows in the first place? And would such a business have much need for meetings outdoors? What kind of discussions would take place there? "So, guys — let's carry on keeping these documents really safe, okay?"

Tony stood in front of the steps leading to the portico. He knew his food would be ready by now, but he didn't feel he was done yet. He walked up the stairs. The parking lot was empty, the windows were all dark, and it was after eight o'clock. It doesn't matter if you know you're only approaching in a spirit of idle inquiry, you can feel that you look suspicious walking up to a building that is closed for the night. He wasn't even sure why he was doing it. Pure curiosity, he guessed.

The first thing he saw was an open space on the other side of the double glass doors. On the right was a reception desk. As he got closer and his relationship to the streetlight reflections on the glass changed, he noticed something else.

There was a car in there.

Not a small car, either. It was huge. And old.

He put his face close to the glass. The car was the size of a big SUV, but antique. It was mainly red, with gold and chrome highlights on the headlamps and running boards and along the sides and top of the windscreen. There was no roof. It looked like some glamorous touring vehicle from the 1930s, but in immaculate condition. Either someone had spent a long time lovingly restoring it or this car had been mothballed from the day it rolled out of the factory. Though it couldn't have been stored here, of course, as the building, which now housed it, could only have dated from the 1980s at the earliest.

Also…it was hard to see how someone could have gotten it in there. The lobby wasn't large — there was only about four feet of clearance around the car on all sides, which must have been notably inconvenient for the people who worked there and who presumably had to cross the space from time to time — but the main problem with the idea was the doors Tony now stood in front of.

He took a couple of steps back and assessed. You could *maybe* have got the car through them, just, if you removed the doors and were a driver capable of very, very precise steering. But then there was the matter of the stairs.

Tony glanced back. Four concrete steps. Could you drive a car like that up those, and through those doors? He sure as hell couldn't have done, and he wasn't convinced anyone else could, either. Maybe…okay, maybe the car had been put in place earlier in the build, and they'd used a temporary wooden ramp before putting the steps in place, but that merely reinforced an idea he realized had already been growing in the back of his mind.

The car looked like it had been there first, and the building constructed around it.

A silly idea, of course — but even if it had merely been a matter of the ramp (and the more he considered it, the harder he found it to believe that the car could have been got in there up steps), it'd clearly been hella important to someone that the car be inside the building. Why? The business called itself SYSTEMS SERVICE, not "Cool Old Cars Restoration and Storage, Inc." Having worked in Silicon startups for the previous ten years, Tony was wearily familiar with excessively "characterful" company founders, the kind that believed turning up to work on a boat-sized Harley or wearing rock-climbing gear in meetings might yield some kind of competitive advantage or at least put about the idea that they were *really* cool. But…putting a vintage car in a reception area barely large enough to take it? That'd take someone very determined to make their mark — and that kind of guy probably wouldn't be running such an anonymous-looking business here at the quiet end of Live Oak.

Tony went back to the doors. The more he looked at it, the more it struck him that, rather than looking like a touring car designed to ferry the wealthy of yesteryear from national park to fashionable watering hole, it brought to mind some kind of utility vehicle. Like a mini fire-engine or something. Though...maybe that was just the color. Who the hell knew?

It was weird.

Suddenly remembering he had an order of food which would already be cooling on the counter in the taqueria, Tony took a last look and walked away.

He spent the next two days sending out further CVs and tweaking his brag site, which was supposed to showcase his coding skills but had developed an annoying bug — creating an intermittent rendering fault that had been pointed out (rather smugly) by the only two companies who'd responded to his first tranche of submissions. The problem with code is, once it's been written, it's very hard to see past the way it presents. If it *looks* okay, and runs by the syntax checker without falling over, then you assume it must work. And in fact, it *does* work, on one level — but it won't do what you wanted it to. "What is the sound of one hand clapping?" is a grammatical utterance. It just doesn't mean anything. Tony's site was clapping one-handed, and so nobody was hearing it.

Eventually he tracked down an error in a quick-and-dirty function he'd bolted on to massage user experience on IE9 — surprise, surprise — and fixed it. Then waited. His in-box failed to flood with job offers as a result.

In the meantime, he fetched coffees from the Windmill on both mornings, and slowed his pace when walking past the building on the other side of East Cliff Drive. Now he knew about the car in the lobby, it was relatively easy to spot during the daytime, too. So how come he hadn't before? On the hundreds of occasions he'd strolled by to get a latte from Mary or Michael, or to head around the corner and down past the lagoon on a longer walk to the harbor (the gift shop there was the nearest place in the neighborhood to buy cigarettes), he'd never noticed it. Sitting at his desk, eyes closed, he'd found he could conjure up very accurate mental pictures of the taqueria, the mercado, the Last Resort Hair Salon, the Southwestern restaurant and the two motels that stood between the corner and the Windmill Cafe — right down to the color and typography of all of their signs.

Yet he'd never noticed the building on the other side, or even glanced at it long enough to clock the fact there was a *car* inside, for god's sake.

Tony was well aware this was a trivial matter expanding to fill the mind of someone who wasn't sufficiently busy in real life, but it still bugged him. Was it just that it was an exceptionally dull-looking building, and that trees and clouds or passing traffic had always proved more of a draw on his attention?

The second time he walked by, he noticed something else. He waited for the traffic to clear, and then jogged across the road to see.

Something had changed about the panel on the side of the steps that the man had been inspecting. It was closed but there was a sticker on it, a six-inch-long strip of tape. The tape was yellow, about an inch and a half wide, and had the word CAUTION on it in very small letters. It had been placed neatly so as to lay half on the panel and half on the area outside, sealing it.

And yet the word on the tape was really not large. Almost as if the person who'd put it there — the guy in the shorts, presumably — had wanted to recognize that there was a problem within, but in such a way that didn't broadcast the news to anyone who wasn't standing close up. Another technician, perhaps.

Abruptly irritated with himself, Tony stepped back. Who cared? Klara would be home in a few hours, expecting a more productive day from him than having sent out a few emails and fixing a brag site that shouldn't have been broken in the first place.

He crossed over and walked up 14th, firmly putting the building out of his mind.

Klara got back home later than she said she would. He fixed a pasta meal; they watched a little television and went to bed. She fell asleep quickly. She was busy at work — hence the lateness. He lay awake for a while, eyes closed, then gave up and opened them. Lying in the dark staring at the ceiling didn't help, nor periods lying on both sides and his stomach. Mind not tired enough, he supposed. After years of working too hard, coasting for day after day wasn't getting him to where he was ready to check out. He assumed that's what it was, anyway.

He gave it another half-hour and then quietly got out of bed. He wandered along the corridor to the kitchen, gently closed the door to avoid making any noise, and made himself a cup of tea. He took this into the sitting room. It had always been his favorite room, partly because of the big, U-shaped sofa that went around one end. The house had been built in the 1940s by someone who looked like he'd learned his trade on boats. There was a lot of wood, many strange angles, and storage nooks and crannies everywhere. The entire ground floor was given over to a double garage and storage space, all under the control of their landlord. Everything else was on the second floor, including an expansive deck, the corner of which pointed off toward the junction between East Cliff and 14th and further reinforced the sensation of being on some kind of land-locked ship. Tony liked the elevation of the living space, which was rare in Live Oak. It conferred the feeling of being raised above the neighborhood, and not just in literal ways.

Now, standing with his drink in front of the long window, he realized it did something else. He opened the sliding door and stepped out onto the deck.

Yes.

You could see the top of the building from here.

How had he never noticed that before? The house was the fourth up from East Cliff Drive. The two houses in between were single storey, and the motel on the corner only two storey on the right-hand side. This meant that, above the trees, you could see the upper story of the SYSTEM SERVICES building.

There was a light on.

Tony knew there was something different about the building before realizing what it was. By the time his brain had processed the information, the light had gone out. Just like that. It was as if…it was *almost* as though someone had been watching, seen him notice the light, and extinguished it. Immediately.

But that made no sense. From this distance — it had to be eighty yards — he would have been nothing more than a blurry shape on the deck. His face *might* have been visible as a pale spot, but if someone had been indoors with the light on, they'd never have been able to make that out through the glass. Why would they do it, anyhow?

Though, while he was asking questions, why would someone be in the building at gone midnight anyway?

A cleaner? Maybe.

Seized by a sudden impulse, Tony hurried back indoors. He slipped his feet into the beach shoes by the door and pulled on his zip-up fleece. His PJs were dark blue. From a distance, no one was going to know the difference, or care. In Live Oak people walked around looking more casual than this in the mid-afternoon.

He grabbed his keys and hurried down the stairs to the front door.

He stood at the corner for ten minutes, starting to feel both cold and foolish. The taqueria and mercado were long-closed, all the lights in the motel extinguished too. A few cars drifted by, but otherwise the corner was dead. Nobody came out of the building. No light went on. Nothing, basically, happened. At all.

He gave it a few more minutes and admitted to himself it was a bust. He was about to turn for home when he stopped, and thought what the heck.

Instead he walked down the block to the end of the ocean-side stretch of 14th. He'd discovered a half-empty pack of forgotten cigarettes and a book of matches in the side pocket of the fleece. He could sit on one of the benches on the low cliff that overlooked the cove. He'd done that any number of times in the mornings, but never in the middle of the night.

It was something different, and he still didn't feel remotely like going to sleep.

He ambled down the block. All the lights in the houses he passed were off. It was like he was the only person awake in the whole town. At the end of the street he went through the gate that marked the back off as state park land, and walked down over the slope.

The beach below was deserted, of course. Because of parking restrictions it was locals-only most of the time, and this was, of course, the middle of the night. Tony headed to the nearer of the two benches, and sat. He looked right, toward the lighthouse at the harbor, the boardwalk, and the few lights that lined West Cliff a mile or two away. It was very quiet.

When he'd finished his cigarette he stayed a few minutes longer, finally starting to feel a little tired. He walked home, barely glancing at the building on the corner as he passed. There was nothing to see.

As he walked up the driveway toward the house, he was startled to see a figure up on the deck.

"Hey," he said, quietly, not wanting to disturb the neighbors. He raised his hand. Klara didn't wave back, but turned and disappeared from view.

Not very friendly, Tony thought.

He let himself into the house and went upstairs, half-expecting to find her in the kitchen. She wasn't. He headed into the sitting room, but that was empty, too. He took a mouthful of the tea he'd left, but it was cold.

He went through into the bedroom. The lights were off. Slightly irritated by now — so he'd got up in the night and gone for a walk, that wasn't a crime, and shouldn't she maybe have some kind of considerate inquiry to make about how her husband was? — he wasn't very subtle about climbing back into bed.

Klara made a noise. It was a distinctive noise. The sound of a person who'd been fast asleep, disturbed, and gone straight back to the depths again.

Tony went still. "Klara?"

She grunted, barely, and turned on her side away from him. As she did, the counterpane moved enough to release a little waft of warm air, the kind of air that accretes around a sleeping body and holds it comfortable.

She was asleep. Genuinely asleep.

It could not have been her.

Tony was out on the deck when Klara left for work the next morning. He hadn't asked about what happened. He hadn't needed to. Over breakfast she'd said what a great night's sleep she'd had, and how refreshed she felt. You don't say that — at least, not without heavy irony, which hadn't seemed present — if you've got up in the night to check where your husband is and then waited for him out in the cold, before huffily going back to bed.

Klara saw him up on the deck and waved as she climbed into her car. Tony watched her turn out onto the street and went back to his real reason for being there.

He had fallen asleep, eventually — but it had taken a long time.

Certainly longer than it had taken to work out that it was hard to imagine how someone could have got out of the house without Tony seeing them. He — Tony assumed it had to be a "he" — hadn't vaulted down off the deck. The only other way out of the house, raised as it was, would be via the stairs Tony had entered by. Maybe, maybe, the person could have hidden in one of the other rooms, waited until Tony had gone through to the bedroom, and then slipped out. Hell of a high-risk strategy, however. If he hadn't been so convinced it was Klara out on the deck, he could have gone rampaging through the house, checking everywhere.

There was no way of knowing how he'd done it. There was no way of telling why the other thing was beating in Tony's mind, either: a strange, dark certainty that the figure had something to do with the building he could see from the deck. The building on the corner.

There was no reason to think this except that he'd seen the figure right after going out in the night, after witnessing a light in one of the building's upstairs rooms. That wasn't a tight connection, he knew, but he had no other explanation for it. If one thing happens and then another thing happens…you draw lines. The question is whether the second thing was intended.

He stood on the deck another ten minutes, watching. From this angle he couldn't see as far down as the portico or entrance, so had no way of knowing if anyone went in or out. The sun was up, too, so he couldn't tell if any of the lights on the first storey were on.

No way of knowing or telling anything.

He eventually went indoors and opened the laptop on the kitchen table. No replies to his CVs of yesterday, or the days before. He opened up another blank email and prepared to send a fifth or seventh tranche…he'd lost count.

But then he closed the machine instead, snatched up his keys, and left the house.

* * *

The owner of the Windmill Café was surprised to see him at half-past nine in the morning. "You're early today," she said. Tony explained he was tiring of his schedule and mixing it up a little. Mary nodded sagely, and made his coffee. Mary knew it was not the place of a coffee-shop proprietor to make judgments about how much free time some of her customers seemed to have on their hands.

Tony took his drink out onto the small terrace area by the road. This was screened from traffic, more or less, by a row of bushes. From a standing position you could look over them, however, and across to the building on the corner. You couldn't see much from this angle, though. Along the front and both sides ran a neat and very well-tended strip of earth holding little plants and succulents and shrubs, not to mention a number of fairly large and recently-trimmed cypress trees. Needless to say, he had never seen anyone tending or trimming any of them. He hadn't even noticed they were there.

He decided he was done looking from afar. He left the terrace, crossed the road, and headed quickly along to the building. Walked up the steps without hesitating and up to the glass doors. Realizing he felt short of breath, he took a deep one, and then entered.

The lobby was very cool, almost chill. The car/mini-truck/whatever was right there, looking even larger at close quarters. Tony knew they built such things bigger back then, when the technology was new and standard stylings and dimensions had yet to be determined, but still: it was massive. Intimidatingly so. The combination of colors and materials and contours should have been striking and attractive, and theoretically they were...but it also looked like the kind of vehicle that, many decades ago, might have been used to come up slowly behind someone in the night. Or to chase them down.

There was a man behind the reception desk. He was wearing a charcoal-colored suit and tie, with a white shirt. His hair was dark and curly.

"We're aware of the problem," he said.

Tony blinked at him. "Huh?"

The man nodded. "We're aware. Thank you." He looked back down at a piece of paper on his desk.

"What do you…do here?"

The man did not answer. Tony felt uneasy, but not to the point of being incapacitated. He took a couple of steps away from the desk and toward a door halfway along the wall. It had a glass panel in its upper half. Presumably this led to the wing on that side. Perhaps he'd get a glimpse of what it was like through there, some sense of what people might be working at. He got just far enough to see a fluorescent-lit corridor, with a standard office-style cubicle off it.

The man at reception coughed.

When Tony looked around at him, the man shook his head, barely. A tiny movement, to one side and then back. Tony realized the man was wearing dark glasses. Had he been wearing them before? He wasn't sure.

How could he not be sure?

"The repairman will be back this evening," the man said. "He has the part now."

"What…are you talking about?"

"Thank you," the man said.

Tony just stood there.

"Goodbye."

Tony found himself back out on the sidewalk. He remembered getting there well enough — reaching out to the door, opening it, walking under the portico and down the steps. He just didn't recall choosing to. He supposed it made sense, though. The man behind the desk clearly didn't have anything else to say. Tony had no more questions to ask.

As he started up the sidewalk toward the corner he glanced at the panel on the side of the stairs.

The strip of tape was still there.

CAUTION

He tried to work, in the sense of dispatching yet more emails. He even re-sent his CV to one of the companies who'd commented on the error on his site, pointing out that it was now fixed. The only reply he received that entire morning came from this person, saying yes, he could see that, but had such an error been committed on a site for one of their clients it could have cost tens of thousands of dollars in lost revenue. The email did not go on to say that they would keep Tony's details on file.

At mid-day he went to the fridge and looked inside. There was food, but nothing that he wanted. He kept looking, convinced there must be something he couldn't see: he'd *bought* most of the stuff, for God's sake.

In the end he got so frustrated that he decided to get methodical on it. He wedged the fridge door open with a quart of milk and took every single thing out of the fridge and lay or stood it in rows. Bacon. Cheese, three types. Beer. Coconut water. Lettuce. Ranch dressing. Some kind of dumb low-fat sausage — that was Klara's. Beets. Chard. Blah. Celery. Carrots. Blah. Onion. Garlic. Mayo. Cream cheese. Strawberries. Pine nuts.

It made sense. It was all stuff he ate, every day and all the time. So why didn't it work? Why didn't it do what it was supposed to? Why didn't he want to eat it?

Why couldn't he hear the other hand clapping?

He spent the afternoon on one of the benches that stood on the cliff overlooking Twin Lakes beach. There was nothing much to see. The weather was cool and it was a weekday. Every now and then a jogger would huff along the waterline, living the dream. Over the course of four hours, eleven people walked one way or the other accompanied by dogs, one of them flouting the rule that said canines on this beach had to be kept on leash. Unfortunately, they encountered someone coming from the other direction who took exception to their behavior. There was a discussion that rapidly accelerated into a shouting match. The words were not audible from a distance, only the mutual anger. It ended with the two parties storming off in different directions.

Not much happened after that.

Eventually Tony became aware that daylight was fading, and a low fog coming in off the bay.

When he next noticed, the fog had crept most of the way up the beach and it was the other side of twilight. It had also started to drizzle. He looked at his watch.

Twenty after six. Klara would be home.

As he was standing up, he saw something. Down on the beach, a couple of hundred yards away, a small group of people were standing together. Four of them. All wore dark clothing. It was impossible to tell from where Tony stood — and they were mixed up in the fog — but it looked like they were wearing suits. Odd attire for a stroll along the beach in the coming dark, but in Santa Cruz stranger things have happened, and doubtless will again.

Tony walked up 14th to the junction. He had to wait several minutes to cross East Cliff Drive. There was an unusual amount of traffic, many of them dark cars of similar size, none of which seemed inclined to let him cross, despite his standing right up on the curb.

He eventually made it to the other side. He glanced across at the taqueria as he started up his block, vaguely thinking that maybe tacos would be good again tonight, and saw it was slammed in there, too. Usually a busy night for the Taqueria Michoacan meant two or at most three people ahead of you in line. Right now he couldn't even see the counter or soda fridge in there, the space was so crammed full of people. One of them was facing out and looking through the window.

His pale, expressionless face didn't move, but his eyes swiveled to follow Tony's progress. This so unnerved Tony that he forgot to glance back and check the building on the corner. It didn't matter. He was done caring about that place.

Klara's car was in the driveway. Tony realized his absence would provoke comment. He rubbed his face quickly with his hands, trying to warm it.

He let himself in and trotted up the stairs. The sitting room was sporadically lit by dim lamps around the walls. Klara was sitting on the sofa, in the middle of the right arm, as was her custom.

There were two men, one in a suit, sitting in the middle of the other. They were in conversation. Another man was sitting in the middle of the U. He was looking at the screen of something that looked like a very thin iPad. The other two men stopped talking and looked over at him, as if waiting for information.

"Where have you been?" Klara asked.

"Walking," Tony said. "Who the hell are these guys?"

"Um, what?"

Tony indicated the men on the sofa. Klara turned to look, then back at him with a quizzical look on her face. "Are you talking about the lamps?"

"No," Tony said. "The guys. The *men*."

He was distracted by a movement on the right, and turned to see a woman walking along the hallway toward the main bedroom. She vanished around the corner into the darkness, as if on the way to perform an errand.

"Seriously, Klara — what the fuck?"

"I don't know," she said, very calmly. "I was hoping you were going to explain it to me."

"Explain what?"

"The fridge."

"The fridge? What about it?"

"I tell you what, Tony. You go into the kitchen, then come back, and tell me what about it."

Tony could feel he was being pulled off course, and that whatever had happened to the fridge couldn't be anywhere near as important as the question of what these people were doing in their house, but he could tell also that Klara was in one of her quietly combative moods. Fine. Play it her way.

He strode into the kitchen. Three men sat around the table, having what appeared to be a meeting. None of their faces looked quite right.

He saw immediately what Klara meant about the fridge, though. All the food was still laid out in neat rows on the floor in front of it. Christ. When he'd left the house, he'd evidently just stood up and walked out. He'd forgotten to put it all back.

Okay, that had been dumb. But she could have put it back when she found it.

He went back into the sitting room. "Fine," he said. "I'm sorry. I was…clearing it out. I got distracted, forgot about it. I'll put it back now."

"That would be good," she said, very calmly.

"Yeah, okay. I'll do it just as soon as…"

Tony stopped talking. Up until the moment he'd started saying the word "soon," the three men had still been sitting on the sofa. Now…they weren't.

They'd gone. Just blinked out of sight.

"Now what?" Klara asked. She sounded tired.

Tony hurried back into the kitchen. There was no one at the table in there now. Just the lines of food, leading out from the fridge.

The doorbell rang.

The sound of this always caused Tony to flinch. It was an old doorbell and it didn't work well. What had been designed as a musical sequence of bell sounds had degraded over the years into a discordant and drawn-out cacophony. This time it sounded worse than usual.

He stepped back into the sitting room. Klara was sitting looking at him, making no move to stand. Clearly she felt he was going to answer it.

"Aren't you going to?"

"What?" she said. She didn't look like she'd even *heard* the bell.

He opened the door and clomped down the stairs. When he got to the bottom he could see three men standing outside. He opened the door. Cold air came in.

"It's working again now," the man in front said. He, like the others, was wearing dark glasses. All had short, curly hair.

"What do you mean?"

"You won't see anything like that again," the man said. "We apologize for the inconvenience."

Tony wasn't sure what he was talking about. Whether it was the building down on the corner, or the men and woman up in their house. Or maybe even the people who'd been crowding out the taqueria, or the unusual number of cars driving along the road. The feeling the world had this evening, of being much fuller than he'd realized, as if there were always people there whose presence he'd previously been unaware of. Who'd always been there, and very close by. He realized that none of the men in front of him were wearing dark glasses after all. There was merely something about their eyes that performed the same function. That hid them. That clouded their effects, muffled or negated the sound of the impact they had on the world. These people were single hands, silently not-clapping, but still present for hundreds of years.

"Are you…always around?"

"In a way," the man said. "But not one that should concern you. It really would be better just to accept that the problem has gone away."

He stepped to the side. The motion revealed a vehicle out on the street, its engine running. Even in the darkness it was easy to see it was the car that had been inside the building on the corner. Curdled yellow light leaked from its headlamps, sparkling in the drizzle. Two further men sat in the back, but it was a very big car. The inference was clear. There was plenty of room for them, the men at the door... and Tony.

"I'll tell," Tony said, impotently.

"I wouldn't," the man said. "It won't go well. She won't believe you. Nobody will."

The men turned as one and walked down the drive to the waiting car. Tony watched as they got in. The car reversed back up the road, far too quickly and smoothly.

When he was sure it wasn't coming back, he shut the door and ran upstairs. Klara was sitting with her arms folded. She was alone in the house and it no longer looked or felt as if there was anybody else there, or ever had been.

"We need to talk," Tony said.

"Yes we do," she said, looking relieved.

She did not believe him. He did, however, eventually believe what she went on to tell him about her and one of her male colleagues, and all the late meetings that had turned into something else.

For a time he clung on, emailing, rewriting. The bug that existed between them, hidden somewhere in the lines that looked so grammatical, resisted detection. He kept watch on the building on the corner meanwhile, but there was no car inside now, no tape over the panel on the stairs, and nothing interesting ever happened.

After a while he found it harder to see, not least as there were more pressing things to worry about. Structures collapse remarkably quickly.

Job, wife, house, life. It crashes fast when it crashes. Soon he left Live Oak.

Now he lives around downtown.

* * *

By the end of the second coffee, Tony had become incoherent. I left him to it. I've seen him on the streets since, several times, but he has made no attempt to talk to me again. He thinks I'm not really listening, and he's right.

I said this was his story. I didn't say I believed it. I don't. You shouldn't either.

That would be best.

The Good Listener

I GOT INTO SANTA CRUZ JUST AFTER NOON, an easy three-hour drive up from Big Sur. My mood was murky and I found Santa Cruz's road system difficult to parse once I got off the highway, so I asked the rental car to negotiate the last few miles by itself. The nav was so accustomed to me feeding it very specific route instructions — gleaned from the itinerary, reconstructed from location services data off my father's phone — that it asked if I was sure about this. I said I was, and it told me that it would guide me to the Dream Inn by the most efficient means it could determine. I said that would be fine. In the meantime it spooled my notes up onto the windshield because that's what I'd asked for every day at this point. I knew what they held for this evening so I just turned the wheel and pressed the gas and tapped the brake and watched out the window as the car piloted me smoothly toward the ocean, the last stop on my journey, and its one small mystery.

* * *

I remember the first truly adult thing my father said to me. I would have been around fifteen and we were on the deck after an evening meal at home. I asked him why he didn't say much at such family events — except, because I was fifteen, what I actually said was along the lines of why was he so quiet and why didn't he join in the conversation like other people's more fun and engaged dads but instead sat there looking like he was thinking about something else the whole damned time. He was leaning against the rail smoking a cigarette and looking out into the woods and after a moment he turned and looked at me, coolly, but with something I later came to understand was a measured and long-game kind of love.

He said: "There came a point when you and your sister had started talking, and I realized that, with the two of you and your mom, there was just never going to be that much dead air in the family, and I could either fight to get every damned sentence out…or not."

I don't remember my reply. I'm sure it was smart and would have earned a high five from my school buddies for getting off a good one against the older generation, but I doubt it was thoughtful or polite. This would have been around late 2011, early 2012.

Six years later my parents split after my mom hooked up with a colleague. In 2020 the divorce went through. I remember my mom making a joke at the party that evening — her arm around said colleague — about how finally she'd got 20/20 vision of reality back. I didn't laugh. By then I was at college and had started to dimly appreciate that the world was a little more complicated than I'd thought. It just also seemed mean-spirited.

On November 14 of 2025, my dad was killed in a car accident.

The Dream Inn stands on a cliff above Cowell Beach, somewhere you've heard of if you're a surfer. It and Steamer Lane just up the road are meccas for those who are into the sport, which does not include me. The hotel stands upon the cliff and hangs over it, in fact:

a draping 1960s-styled structure regooded into boutique hotel status twenty years ago, and still doing well.

I put my car in the lot opposite — there was no entry for valet parking on my dad's bill for his stay, so I assumed that was what he'd done too — and carried my bag across the road. I checked into the room next to the one he'd had, for three nights. I put the suitcase on the bed and went out onto the balcony to look at the sea. It was sunny and clear, and I could see all the way across the bay to Monterey. From the eighth floor, all you could hear was the sound of waves and the barking of sea lions.

I took my dad's phone out of my pocket and held it in my hand. It had been in my possession for five months, from the day when we all visited his place in the week after his death. As we stood in his little apartment wondering what we were supposed to be feeling and how on earth to articulate it, I noticed the phone on the table by the window. It was part of the collection of belongings that had been salvaged from his car after the wreck, and it caught my eye because it was the same one he'd had the first time I'd come to visit him in the city, after the divorce became final. He'd moved back to New York three months before and we'd gone walking around Greenwich Village and then sat drinking coffees outside some place he'd evidently become familiar with.

He took me by surprise in two ways. First, by talking. It wasn't like he said so much, but he said *something*. I'd undertaken the trip out of a feeling of duty and because the party my mom had held made me feel uncomfortable. I had not expected much of the visit. I certainly hadn't expected him to sit asking me questions and apparently engaging with the answers.

I was also struck by the fact the phone he'd put on the table was brand spanking new, in fact the same model that I had myself. I commented on this.

"Well, yeah," he said, looking sheepish. "I don't have communication on tap like I did in the old days. Have to make more effort myself."

After that the conversation dried up and it felt more like business as usual.

The phone on the table by the window in his apartment was the exact same one, looking a little battered and bordering on retro, what with it being five years old now. I slipped it in my pocket without asking my mom or sister if that was okay. I figured they wouldn't care. I'm sure I was right.

I spent the first day in Santa Cruz following the itinerary as closely as possible, as I had throughout the trip. I went to the two coffee shops he'd stopped at and also the restaurant where he'd taken lunch. I matched the times as best I could, though I ate and drank what I wanted. The second-hand bookstore he'd visited was closed for the day. I couldn't be sure exactly what period he'd spent in it, but I walked away a couple of minutes after four, the time at which his accounts logged that he'd paid $26.14 (including tax) for a book on local history.

Early evening I ate a burger in a place called Betty's on Pacific, the main drag. Again I ate what I wanted, which is what he would have done. Then I went back to the hotel. It was still early but it appeared he'd done that too, according to a Speke logged at 9:34 which told the world — or the portion of it listening on that social network — that he was about to turn in. Tired, I guess. He'd been nearly thirty years older than I was now, of course.

I don't know how it went for him, but it took me a while to get to sleep. Tomorrow was the last-but-one day of the trip, and also the big one.

Not the last day, but the day with the hole.

I gradually started to visit him more often in NYC. On one of these trips about a year and a half ago he mentioned how he'd always wanted to make the drive up the Pacific Coast Highway from L.A. to

San Francisco, and now he was going to go ahead and do it. I asked him whether most people didn't make the journey the other way, heading south. Aha, he said, but if you drove *north* then the driver got the best view of the sea all the way. Of course if you shared the driving you'd have to share that too, but there'd be other advantages.

It was too subtle for me. I didn't get it.

By the time I realized he'd been issuing a low-key invitation, he was already dead. I was real busy at work and even if I'd got it then I would have said I didn't have the time. Things were sufficiently affable enough between us by that point that I would have gone ahead and made the mistake of thinking it'd be no big deal if I didn't go.

I would have assumed there would be some other time.

My dad's phone lay in a drawer in my house for five months after he died. Then one night, for some reason, it occurred to me to take it out. I guess I was missing him or something, maybe regretting all the silences there had been, now that there was no way of ever filling them.

As I held the phone in my hands, a thought occurred to me. I dug in another of my drawers and, sure enough, found the charger I'd owned for the same model of phone. The stores may be full of new tech but there's an awful lot of the old stuff still knocking around in people's homes. I slotted the charger in the wall and plugged the other end in the phone, savoring the old-school vibe of having to connect power to a device by wires, rather than just dropping it on an inductance pad.

Seconds later the screen blinked into life. I pressed the virtual home button. It pinged and the OS locked onto the free neighborhood Wi-Fi and started bleating about the million software updates that had happened in the intervening months. I paused them all, not wanting to change the state of the phone as it had been on the day he died.

I had a look around it. I was surprised. There were a *lot* of apps on the phone, and not just what I would have expected. Sure, there were productivity apps and business reference material and travel guides, but also Twitter and Speke and BinThere and TellMeStuff and TripBuddies and even GodPOV. For a guy I remembered as being extremely challenged in the communicating department, he had a lot of hooks into the outside world.

I tried kicking up Speke — my own social network of choice — but hit a login screen. After so long dead, the phone needed everything to be logged into again.

Feeling sad, and as if this was symbolic of something or other, I put the phone down.

But then I picked it up again and after a few minutes found what I was looking for: his password database app. I assumed I'd be screwed there too, that he'd have used eyecog or a voice gesture like any normal person, but when I ran my thumb over the virtual keyboard a dialog swiveled into view saying I'd got the password wrong. This came close enough to implying he'd used a typed sequence of letters and/or numbers that I spent the next two hours — with the help of a few beers — trying to work it out. I got there in the end.

HelenaNoelleScott.

The names of his children and his ex-wife, run together. Had he chosen this password before the divorce, or afterward? I didn't know. It didn't matter. It was still hard to think about.

I spent the morning and afternoon of my second day in Santa Cruz walking. There was a breakfast check-in at the Ideal Grille, a quickie lunch at the Sputty's concession on the Boardwalk, and a transaction at the Starbucks up on the West Side. The last had recently closed down and been turned into a student-oriented lentil-and-chai outfit, but I stuck it out. There was an ATM outside, as I'd known there would be. I got some money from it.

I dawdled on the way back to the hotel, trying to ensure I got back at around the same time I believed he had. I was a few minutes early — getting to the room at 4:56, ten minutes before he'd rung down for a room-service pot of tea, as logged on his online receipt — but close enough. I took a shower, changed my clothes (Dad had always been a stickler for marking a difference between day and evening in exactly these ways), and sat at the end of the bed.

A few minutes later it was 5:27.

And I was in the hole.

Once I'd gained entry to the password database I unlocked and logged in to everything on his phone. And I was stunned. He'd had over six hundred followers on Speke, and had been following around the same number. Not movie-star level, of course. Far less than some mouthy blogger. But for an unsociable guy in his late fifties, pretty solid.

Even more surprising to me were the check-in apps. He'd logged everything in the last few years. Each time he went to a cafe, restaurant, bar, or store, there it was. Then the travel apps — hotels, flights, even car rentals, all logged and rated. I'd drunk enough beer by this point that I was open to the maudlin, and it struck me maybe he'd done this because he didn't have a wife to share with anymore. Maybe, maybe not. Maybe he actually liked using all this social stuff. Maybe it was a game.

Maybe he'd just been really bored.

Either way, that's when I got the idea. I tapped my own phone to wake the TVPC. My friends think I'm a throwback for sleeping the thing when I'm not using it, but if you have the occasional tendency to talk to yourself when you're alone, the ever-listening ear of voicecog can lead to unexpected and unhelpful results. I told the TV to expect a list, and then read out all my dad's sites, their login passwords, gave it the dates, and asked it to triangulate with all available APIs.

Forty seconds later a rough outline appeared on the screen. I finally allowed my dad's phone to download all the software updates it had stacked, then got the TV to mix in the results from onboard location services together with cached records from his bank accounts.

In five minutes I had it, chapter and verse.

A week later I flew into L.A.

The itinerary, as I took to calling it, was the summation of everything my father's phone and Web services had to tell me about his trip up the Pacific Coast Highway. The Web is very, very good at this stuff now. If you let it hook into the outlets of all the sites you belong to, all the status updates and logins you've made (consciously or otherwise), each occasion you've waved your phone over an NFT terminal to pay for goods or services, every time you've asked a question of a Net-linked satnav or a sponsored street-corner AskMe post, every time your phone sends up a blip to establish the nearest radio mast…it knows a *lot*. It listens to everything that we say and do and it remembers it all. The past doesn't fall away like it used to, disappearing behind as you keep moving forward. Experience is saved. Recalled.

Somewhere in the cloud is everything you've done. If you want, you can get it back.

I couldn't get *him* back, of course. But now I had the itinerary. I should have gone with him. I decided to do the best I could, five months too late.

The hole is a period of fourteen hours. It stretches from early evening on the second-last day of his trip until 9:26 the following morning, when he bought (and rated, highly) a coffee at an indie cafe downtown. It's not such a big or inexplicable hole. He was staying in the Dream Inn, of course — I wasn't suspecting he'd suddenly gone to the moon and back. There was no record of an evening meal, however, which was unique in the entire trip and thus mildly intriguing. No record of anything being bought or done during that entire period, in fact, though there'd been an ATM withdrawal of a hundred dollars in the afternoon (which was why I'd done the same). There was no way of filling in the missing time. I'd even had the software re-triangulate again, in the hope it'd missed something before, but nothing came.

It was blank. Dead air.

I needed to fill it somehow. I'd been hoping an idea would come to me, a way of spending the evening that might seem an appropriate means of honoring him. It did not. I wasn't feeling in an inspired mood. Tomorrow would be the last day of my trip. Of his trip. The day after, he'd left the hotel just before eleven in the morning and drove through town (buying $152.50 of gas and some bottled water on the outskirts) before heading onto Highway 17 to start the journey to San Francisco airport. At 1:47 a poorly maintained truck lost its load across both lanes, resulting in the random and pointless death of my father and five other road-users. His death was logged at 2:22.

Superstitiously, perhaps, I was intending to drive to the airport via another route. I wanted to replicate the trip, but I'm not a total nutcase.

I sat in the hotel room for an hour getting bored and sad. Then I realized this was dumb.

I left the hotel intending to simply go for a walk. My dad liked walking. That could well have been what he did that night — missing out on his supper by accident and figuring he could stand it for once, before winding up back in the room and munching the free cookies they provided, before going to bed early again. Traveling by yourself can be interesting and is good for the soul, but there comes a point where you've read as much as you can read for one day. None of the e-readers on his phone showed a log of having been used that evening.

As I stood outside the hotel I remembered seeing it had a bar somewhere, and decided I'd go for a beer first. The bar turned out not to be in the main building, which was how I'd missed it so far, but in a meeting facility attached to it by a corridor. When I walked in I wished I'd come the night before, whether it was on the itinerary or not. It was quiet and calm and empty, with dimly lit tables in front of huge plate glass windows giving a great view onto the wharf and the ocean.

I sat up at the bar, for the moment deserted. A few minutes later a woman came from out back. She was in her mid-forties, I'd guess, blond hair pulled back in a ponytail. She looked like she ran, or hiked.

When she saw me she frowned, and seemed to hesitate, before coming over. I ordered a beer and turned to look out over the sea.

As sometimes happens, the first beer made me decide a second would be a good idea. The bar had started to fill up in the meantime, people in suits, and I had to wait a while because the woman seemed to be running the place single-handedly. As she eventually pulled my second Sierra Nevada, I caught her looking at me again.

"Everything okay?" I asked.

She smiled hurriedly, shook her head. Then evidently decided to say what was on her mind. "You look familiar," she said. "Been here before?"

I shook my head. "My dad came here once, though. About five months ago. We look alike."

"What was his name?"

"Rick Motz."

Her reaction to this was hard to interpret. She went down the other end of the bar to serve a customer.

Half an hour later, I ordered another beer. In the meantime I'd watched the sun go down over the bay, eaten a lot of peanuts, and come up with a question I wanted to ask.

As she handed me the drink I asked it. "So — did you and my dad talk at all?"

"Sure."

"Just a few words, or…?"

"Oh, more than that. It was a really quiet night. Most of the evening he was the only person in here." She shrugged, as if it was all no big deal. It was not completely convincing.

"He died," I said. It was clumsy and graceless, but I didn't know how else to say it.

She looked shocked. I told her how it had happened. "That's terrible," she said. She said it in a way that seemed sincere.

I drank a mouthful to let the moment dissipate. "So, you guys chatted?"

"Quite a bit."

"What about?"

"I don't remember. Something, I guess. You know how that goes. He made me laugh. A lot."

"He *did?*"

"For sure. He was funny. He was a good listener, too."

She left to deal with a new party of raucous business people, fresh out of a brainstorming session. I drank my beer slowly and looked out through the window at the remaining hints of the view of the beach.

I thought about my dad and wondered whether all the time I'd been growing up he hadn't been not-speaking after all. I wondered if he'd been listening, instead.

I ordered and drank one more beer, and was about to autopay by TABapp when I realized that was wrong. I got out my wallet and paid with cash from the ATM instead. As, I was now guessing, he had done.

When I got up to leave the waitress came over. She was carrying a tray of dirty glasses and she looked tired, but nonetheless she came the length of the bar to say goodbye.

"I'm real sorry to hear about your dad," she said.

I nodded, not knowing what to say, and feeling — for the first time on the entire trip — completely empty, and as if I wanted to cry. "Thank you."

"You miss him?"

I nodded, and she nodded too.

She looked out of the window, into the blackness over the ocean.

"He was a nice man," she said.

Next day I followed the itinerary. Coffee shops, another bookstore, this and that. The day after I went home, driving up to SFO via the coast road rather than taking Highway 17 inland. I made it back in one piece.

I'm glad I was able to trace the trip I didn't take. I'm glad he went on the journey he'd always wanted, I'm glad he stayed at the Dream Inn, and I'm glad he decided to head down to the bar. I still don't know for sure where my father spent the missing hours after that — maybe in his hotel room, maybe not — though I suspect I know how, and with whom.

I'm happy for the hole to remain. I no longer feel the need to fill it. There have always been silences in the world, and that's the way it should be. There should be gaps. Sometimes it's in those moments of silence, of dead air, that the meaningful things happen. It's good we have things listening to all our stories now, keeping track of everything we have been and done.

It's even better if, like the best listeners, they turn a deaf ear from time to time.

Different Now

SHE WAS OUT OF THE DOOR before Chris had time to grasp what was going on. What started as a run of the mill argument had suddenly escalated out of control, bored misery giving way to alarm. Then the flat seemed very empty, and she was gone.

Until moments before, it had just been the usual depressing bickering, the holding up of past hurts for inspection, and he'd been wondering how much longer he was going to defend his corner. There had been a time when he'd been prepared to stay up all night, feeling bound to hang in there until the swapping of grievances could be steered toward a new compromise. A time when he could not have contemplated sleeping next to her unless they did so as friends.

But *so many nights.*

For a few months or weeks things would be all right, and then the familiar slow spiral toward confrontation would start. She would shout, and he would mutter: both completely in the right and both utterly in the wrong. These days he didn't have the energy to argue until dawn when he knew any truce was only temporary, or the stomach to put up with melodrama when what they needed was discussion. When the point of diminishing returns had been reached, he usually went to bed, to be joined an hour later by Jo, vicious and sniffling. The next day would be very unpleasant, the day after less so. Sooner or later both would apologize so they could start living their lie for a little longer, go on inhabiting the same fragile world.

Chris grabbed his keys and ran for the door. He tripped over the pile of newspapers stranded in the middle of the floor by leave-it-where-it-drops Jo, and almost fell, but his beat of irritation was perfunctory. This was very bad. He'd looked at her and for the first time seen that he didn't know her anymore, as if he was in the room with an utter stranger. Suddenly it hadn't been just another row, a chance for both to be flamboyantly hurt: the cord that had always somehow remained between them had lain naked and exposed, waiting for the axe.

Fumbling to lock the door, Chris dropped his keys and swore. He didn't like the note of hysteria in his voice. It wasn't like him. However loud the shouting, he always stayed distant enough to watch, even when he was center stage. Stuffing the keys in his jeans, he leapt down the steps to the hall four at a time.

The outside door was open, swaying from the strong wind outside. Rain spattered the familiar black plastic bags habitually left in the hall by the tenants of the downstairs flat, who he suspected were also responsible for the grey camper van, which had sat outside on four flat tires since before he'd moved in.

He shouted at their door with all his strength, throat rasping: "Oh what a surprise: someone's left some fucking rubbish in the hall!"

Frightened by his fury he bolted out of the door and ran to the end of the path, wildly looking up and down the street. All he could see were waving branches and wet moonlit patches. He'd hoped that she would grind to a halt just outside the house, but clearly she'd got further. Swearing desperately, he trotted back and pulled the door shut before heading out onto the pavement.

She couldn't have much more than two minutes' start on him, which made it probable she'd gone right. Though it was theoretically possible that she could have covered the two hundred yards or so to the end of the road on the left, it seemed unlikely.

Chris jogged to the nearer corner and stood at the insignificant crossroads, straining his ears for the sound of footsteps. All he heard was the sound of distant traffic on the Seven Sisters Road; the featureless cramped streets of terraced houses facing him were silent apart from the sound of rain on swaying leaves. He called her name and heard nothing more than the thin sound of his own voice.

Head down and shoulders hunched against the wind-whipped rain, he trotted out of Cornwall Road, across the small junction, and into the road that began the most direct route to the station.

After a few minutes he stopped, panting. There was still no sign of Jo, and there were now a couple of different ways she might have gone. Assuming she'd have been walking toward the station to head for home, she should have taken the left fork — but she had only walked the route a couple of times, and always with him. Chances were she wouldn't have had a clear memory of the route, and the alternative road was slightly wider than the one that led to the station. Chris had a sneaking suspicion that — faced with the choice — she might have assumed that was the best way to go. Not that there was any way of telling: he didn't even know if she'd headed for the station at all.

Shivering, simultaneously wishing he'd thought to bring a coat and realizing that going back for one would lose him any chance of catching up, Chris headed for the wider road, walking quickly.

It was impossible to see very far down the road, as it curved sharply round to the left, presenting a blank face of wall broken by occasional squares of light. From his level all Chris could see was patches of ceiling and snatches of curtain. It seemed easy to believe there was no one in any of the rooms, that they were empty and always had been. In one ground-floor room a television flickered by itself, somehow making the sight even less hospitable than the windows that were dark and reflective black. Disturbed, Chris turned his attention back to the pavement. Somewhere, a long way off, a car horn sounded.

Suddenly he glimpsed movement some way ahead, and hurried forward. It was difficult to see clearly in the steadily falling rain, and hard to see what might be there against the pocks and puddles in the pavement. A shape moved out from behind a car, but it was only a small dog, white and shivering. Wiping rain from his face, Chris trotted up to the next junction.

The streets all looked the same. All bent slightly, all had pavements torn apart through years of patching, and all looked orange and shiny black with water, the patterns of light changing as branches of grey leaves slashed in front of the streetlights. There was still no sign of Jo, no sign of anyone. Chris picked a road at random and headed down it.

He was far from sure what would happen when he found her. Nothing like this had ever happened before. If she'd headed for home, which would involve a tube to a mainline station and then an hour on a train, that was bad. If she'd not even been thinking that clearly, but had just set off, that was even worse, given her paranoia about walking any streets late at night. Either way it seemed possible that things might finally have broken down, and he realized suddenly that he didn't want them to. However bad things might be between them, she was the only person who really knew him. And more than that, he loved her.

Another turning, another road. Chris felt increasingly desperate now, felt an already bad situation getting away from him, and he was now far from sure where he was. Not having a car meant he didn't know the area very well, his movements restricted to walking to the station and the nearest shops. He thought that the station was probably still over to the left, but when he started to choose left turns, the roads bent and doglegged, bringing him back or taking him in the wrong direction, through rows and rows of three-storey brick punctuated by sheets of dark glass.

Finally he stopped and rested, hands on his knees and chest aching.

After a few moments the pain felt at once less urgent but more deep-seated, a feeling he remembered from horrific cross-country runs at school. Then, too, the rain had sheeted down, as if settled in forever. Chris raised his head, squinting into the lines of water.

Someone was standing at the top of the street.

Chris straightened, and took a pace forward. About fifty yards away, motionless and grey behind the rain, stood a woman of Jo's size and shape. It had to be Jo. Feeling a lurch of compassion, Chris walked quickly toward her, and then started to trot.

As he neared her he slowed to a walk. She was facing away from him, shoulders slumped, heedless of the rain, which coursed down her soaking hair and clothes. She made no movement as he approached and Chris felt tears welling up: Jo hated the rain, and there are always things about someone that, however trivial, make them more themselves than anyone else.

He stood at her side for a moment, then gently touched her shoulder. For a moment there was no response, and then she looked up slowly, timidly.

It wasn't Jo.

Chris took a step backward, confused. The woman continued to look at him as rain ran down her face, not staring, just including him in her gaze.

"I'm sorry, I thought..." Chris stopped, unable to finish the obvious sentence, transfixed by her face.

It wasn't Jo, but it so nearly was. The face was so similar, so *equal* to Jo's, and yet something was different. He took a few more steps back, shrugging to show his harmlessness, and started to turn away.

As he did so the woman turned too, and he caught a glimpse of her face in three-quarter view. She began slowly to step through the puddles, heading up a road he'd already tried. Chris stared after her, and knew what it was about her face.

It was the face of someone he didn't know.

The face of someone you've caught sight of across a room for the very first time, the face of a stranger you don't yet understand, a face before you've seen it thousands of times, loved and kissed every inch of it, seen its every smile and frown. It was the face Jo would always have shown had he not plucked up his courage on a night four years ago, and walked across the room to timidly make her acquaintance.

Had he not met her and loved her, had she not become his world, she would always have had that face. The woman's face was Jo's in a world where they'd never met.

Chris started up the road after the woman, just as she turned the corner. Anxious to keep sight of her, he slipped on a patch of lurid moss glistening blackly on the pavement. Narrowly avoiding a sprawling fall, he awkwardly maintained his balance, twisting his knee. Slowing to a fast lurch he painfully rounded the corner in time to see the flap of a coat disappearing from sight. He rubbed his knee and then set off in pursuit.

He hadn't tried this particular road, and didn't recognize it or the turning. Wiping water from his face, he trotted into the sheets of rain, feeling the silence behind the hissing patter of drops. He slipped once more navigating the turn at speed, but managed to keep his feet.

At the end he stopped, chest heaving again. She had disappeared.

There was no obvious direction she could have gone. The other three roads all stretched straight for many yards before curving, and it should have been possible to see her whichever way she'd taken. Chris glanced about wildly, peering into the rain. Then he noticed something.

The road opposite was Cornwall Road.

Bewildered, he took a few steps forward into the middle of the road. He turned and looked the way he'd come. The road was unfamiliar, curving a wholly different way to the road he walked down to the station. The road that cut across was different too: it was narrower and had more trees. The whole junction was different, and yet…

He walked slowly into Cornwall Road. There, about ten yards up on the left, was the familiar white gateway, the entrance to Number 7. Light fell weakly down from the upper window. Proceeding like a nervous gunfighter, casting frequent glances behind, Chris tried to marry the two views in his mind. But they wouldn't gel, couldn't.

Cornwall Road now joined with different roads, and the grey camper van was gone.

He pushed open the dark green gate and stepped up to the door. Through misted glass he saw the hallway was clear, with no sign of rubbish bags. He turned and looked at the entry-phone. The label by the topmost buzzer said "Price," which was not his name.

He wondered briefly where Jo was now, but already the name seemed unfamiliar, ordinary, like that of someone he'd met once at a party, some years ago. His key did not turn the lock, and was made for a different door.

Chris took a last look at the house and then turned and faced the rain, pausing for a moment before stepping out into it. He had no idea where he lived, whom he loved, or where he should go.

Things were different now.

Author of the Death

FINALLY I DECIDED I'D HAD ENOUGH and I wasn't going to put up with it any more and it was high time something was done the hell about it. My father was a vague character at best but there's one way in which I evidently do take after him. Once he'd decided to do something, apparently, that was it. That thing was going to happen, and it was going to happen *now*. As soon as I realized I was clinically fed up with the situation, compelling verbs were required – and there was only one immediate course of action I could think of. I grabbed my coat and looked for my gun, but I couldn't find it. Sometimes it's here, sometimes it's not, and probably it wasn't such a great idea to take it anyhow. I had a mission, a simple goal. I didn't need a weapon.

I needed focus.

I knew tracking down a writer wasn't going to be an easy task. They're everywhere but yet nowhere, too – a state of affairs I'm sure reminds some of them of one conception of deity. (Is it called "pantheism"? I can't remember. I probably shouldn't know anyway.) I have only ever been in New York, except for a couple of short chapters in a small town nearby called Westerford. It was never clear to me how I even got to Westerford, however – as I was just cut there and back on chapter breaks – so that idea was a non-starter, and to be absolutely honest I suspect he just made the place up anyhow.

Bottom line was that I was stuck with looking for him in the city.

If I'd believed he knew the place very well, then this would have been a very daunting prospect — NYC is a hell of a big patch of ground even if you stick to the island and don't start on the other boroughs. I had reason to suspect that his knowledge was limited to Manhattan, however, and far from comprehensive even there.

I made a list of locations, the places I knew well, and got out into the streets.

Six hours later my feet hurt and I was getting irritable. I'd looked everywhere. Everywhere I could remember having been, or where scenes with other characters had taken place, or that I'd heard described by other people — finally washing up at the Campbell Apartment in Grand Central Station, a bar surprisingly few people know about. I'd been there once for a meeting about a job that got derailed. The meeting had always felt to me like filler, but I'd liked the venue. Dark, subterranean-feeling, dirty light filtered through a big stained-glass window. It looked and felt exactly as described, and so I thought it likely the guy had actually been there, rather than merely having read about it. He wasn't there now, though.

I had a drink anyway and left and started to walk wearily back down 5th Avenue, cigarette in hand. It was mid-afternoon and starting to get colder. I'd had plenty of time to consider whether what I was doing was a good idea (and if it even made any kind of ontological sense), but something I evidently inherited from my mother (much better fleshed out as a character than my father, featuring in two long, bucolic memory sequences and a series of late-climax flash-backs) is that once I've embarked on a project, it does tend to get done.

So I walked, and I walked some more. Instead of cutting over to 3rd and down into the East Village — which is where I live, for better or worse — I went the other way, switching back and forth between 6th, 7th, and 8th, down through Chelsea, back over to Union Square, then over and down into Meatpacking, though only briefly, because

I didn't seem to know it very well.

No sign of him, anywhere. I didn't know what I was expecting, if I was hoping I'd just run into him on a street corner or something, but it didn't happen.

He evidently didn't know what was going to happen next, how to get me onto the next series of events.

The short paragraphs were a giveaway.

He was treading water.

It was a hiatus.

So I made my own choice.

I was down on the fringes of Soho when I spotted another Starbucks. I'd already been in about ten. He is forever dropping a Starbucks into the run of play — situating events there, revisiting recollections, or having people pick up a take-out to engineer a beat of "real life" texture. Each was well described, as though he'd actually been there, and so I'd taken the trouble to seek them out. This one was new to me, however.

The interior was big enough to have three separate seating areas, and looked comfortable and welcoming. It smelled like they always do. There was the harsh cough of steam being pumped through yet another portion of espresso. Quiet chatter. Anodyne music. People reading Lethem and Franzen or Derrida and Barthes.

Weird thing was, it felt familiar.

Not familiar to *me*, but still…familiar. I know that sounds strange. I knew that I didn't know the place personally, but it felt like I *could* have. I decided I might as well have yet another Americano, and was wandering over toward the line when I realized some guy was looking at me.

I turned and looked back at him. He was in an armchair by a table close to the window. Late twenties, with sharply defined and well-described facial features. Something about him said he was no stranger to criminal behavior, but that's not what struck me most about him.

He looked how I felt. He looked weary.

He looked stuck.

I took a pace in his direction. "Do I know you?"

"Don't see how."

"That's what I thought. So why are you staring at me?"

"You look familiar," he said. "Like…I dunno."

"Can't be. I've never been in here before."

"You sure?"

"Yes. I've done stuff in the Starbucks on the corner of 42nd and 6th, the one on 6th between 46th and Times Square, and another at an unspecified street address up near Columbus Circle. Also I've stuck my head in a bunch more today, uptown, and on the way down here, just in case. But I've never been in this particular one. I'm sure."

He shook his head, sat back in his chair, ready to disengage. "Sorry to have bothered you."

I was struck by a crazy thought.

"Who's your writer?"

"Michael Marshall Smith," he said, diffidently, fully expecting the name not to mean anything to me.

I stared at him. "No way."

"What?" he said. He sat forward again in his chair, looking wary. "You're…you're one of his, too?"

"Well yes, and no. Actually I'm in a Michael Marshall novel — different name, different genre, but the same guy."

"Holy shit." He looked at me, dumbfounded. "That's outside the *box*. I never met someone else before. I mean, the people in this place, obviously, but not someone from a whole other *story*."

"Me neither," I said. I pulled a chair over to the table. "You mind?"

"Go ahead," he said, and I sat.

We looked at each other for a full minute. It felt very weird. I've met other characters before, of course — but only ones from my own story, like the guy said. They had their place and were all situated in relation to the star at the center of their firmament: which would be me.

This guy wasn't like that. He was totally other. I had no idea what he was about.

"How come you're here?" he asked, eventually. "I mean, suddenly, like this. You've never been in this place before. But now here you are."

"I got tired of waiting," I said. "Bored of being in that scummy apartment in the East Village. He barely even knows the area. Spent half a morning walking around it, like, five years ago. That's all. There's a couple of streets that are pretty convincing and he nailed a few local shops — including a deli and a liquor store, thank God — but after that it's basically atmosphere and a few well-chosen adjectives."

"How long do you have?"

"About a hundred and fifteen thousand words."

He stared at me. "You're in a *novel?*"

"I'm the protagonist, dude."

"Shit."

I shrugged. He sat back in his chair, caught between envy and resentment. "Jesus, then you don't know you're born. I'm only in a short story, and even by the standards of the form, it's pretty fucking brief. Three thousand words. Whole thing takes place right here in this Starbucks. I don't even get to go *out the door*. I don't know shit about the city. I can *see* it, through that window, but that's all I get."

"Hell," I said. "That's tough."

"Tough is right. And look at what I'm wearing."

I'd already noticed his clothes were nondescript. Jeans. A shirt in some indeterminate color. Shoes that I couldn't even see. "Pretty vague."

"Exactly," he said. "I don't have a coat because I don't do anything but be in here and so he didn't bother to describe one, not even a thin jacket hanging over the back of my chair, for Christ's sake."

"That's understandable," I said. "He can't be bogging down with extraneous details, not at your kind of word length. Plus if he did mention a coat, people might assume it was going to become relevant at some point and get pissed off when it wasn't. Any good editor would pick him up on it, blue-line it out."

"Yeah, maybe so. But it gets *cold* in here, come the middle of the night."

I thought about that, and about the idea of being trapped in one location forever, pinned to one small location for eternity. It made me feel cold, too.

"I'm going to find the guy," I said. "Tell him I'm grateful for being — though some pretty harsh things happen to me, especially in back story — but I'd like some broader horizons now."

"*Find* him? How the hell do you hope to do that?"

I shrugged. Again. I shrug a lot. "By searching the city — the parts of it he knows, at least. That's what I'm doing now. It's how I ran into you. Which is something that's never happened to me before, and that makes me think that I'm achieving *something,* at least."

"But what are the odds of banging into him?"

"Not good. I know that. But weren't there any coincidences in your story?"

"Like what?"

"I don't know. Things that were kind of convenient, that helped drive the plot forward without too much hard work?"

He thought about it. "Not really."

"There were in mine. Small things, he didn't take the piss with it, but — "

"'Take the piss'? What's that supposed to mean?"

"See, that's interesting. We don't say that here, do we? It's a British expression, I think. I'm supposed to be American born and bred, yet once in a while I'll say something that's a little bit off."

"Maybe the guy *is* British, but sets his stuff here in the US. Blame the copyeditor for not picking up on it."

"Could be. But my point is that, while he didn't fall back on any whopper coincidences, he was happy to ease the way every now and then with a combination of circumstances that was a little convenient."

"I guess in a novel you have to, maybe. My thing, it happens in real time, so he didn't need to resort to that kind of kludge."

"Right. But given that I'm driving *this* story, I'm hoping that my rules apply. And so it's possible, if I keep walking, there's a small coincidence out there waiting to happen. Like meeting you."

I waited for him to think about this. It was strange, but also exciting, to be dealing with someone new, *completely* new, who wasn't subservient to my protagonist status. It felt as though doors might be opening. I didn't know where they'd lead, but I was starting to think I could find them. If I *believed* enough. Maybe I could make it back to Westerford after all, that leafy town upstate where I'd been for those brief chapters. I could start a new life, do new things. Perhaps I could even get to the beach down in Florida featured in a small flashback. That would be great, but actually *anywhere* would do. Somewhere new. A place I could stretch my wings and find some other way to be.

The guy was frowning at me. "Are you okay?"

"What do you mean?"

"You stopped talking. Just sat there looking intense."

"Sorry. I had a stretch of interior monologue. Slightly lyrical. Takes a while to get through."

"I guess you first-person guys get a lot of that. Me, I'm in third. I just *do* stuff, pretty much."

"So let's *do* stuff," I said. "Let's get out of this generic coffee house and go looking for him."

"I can't."

"Why?"

He looked sheepish. "I don't think I can leave here. I've never been through that door. My whole life, I've been in here. I think that's it for me."

"Have you ever tried? Gone up to the door and pulled on the handle and seen what happens?"

He looked down at his feet. "Well, no. I'm just supposed to do what I do, right?"

"Not necessarily," I said. "I've spent longer with the guy than you, remember. I think he kind of likes it when one of us does something off our own bat. There was a minor character in my book, he dies in the end, but he sometimes got the chance to go do his own thing, and the writer would work around it. Maybe you're the same way."

"I don't want to die in the end."

"No, of course. Not saying that's going to happen. Just…if you're like me, if you're the narrator, the audience *knows* you're going to live — unless the guy's prepared to do something tricky or flip into unreliable narrator at the end. So there's a set arc for me, and I kind of have to stick to it, because I manifest the story and vice versa and he can't screw with that. But with the more minor characters — no offense — he can let them roam free a little more, see where they end up."

"'Unreliable narrator'? What the hell is that?"

"It's a literary term. Not sure how I know it, given that I used to be a cop, but…"

The guy looked nervous. "You're a *cop?*"

"No. *Ex*-cop. That way he could short-hand me as a tough guy with certain skill sets and a troubled past, without having to do much actual research, or getting stuck with writing a police procedural."

"That's a relief. My character's not a very nice guy, I don't think. There's a pervading sense of guilt throughout, though it's never clear what for."

"Doesn't matter. I'm not going to arrest you, even if I still could. Come on. Let's go."

I stood, and waited for him to follow suit.

"I just don't think I can, dude," he muttered, looking wretched. "I look out that window and all I see is two-dimensional."

We turned and looked together. The light outside was beginning to fade. "Barely even that," he said. "It's just two sentences, to me. 'It was cold and grey and flat outside.' And 'A couple of leaves zigzagged slowly down from the tree along the sidewalk, falling brown and gold and dead.' That's it."

"Look," I said, pointing. Two leaves were doing just what he'd said, and it *did* look cold out there, and the light was grey and flat.

"Every day," he said. "Every day they do that."

"So evidently what happens out there *is* your domain, at least to a degree. You could—"

He shook his head. "I can't do it. I'm sorry."

I felt bad for him, and realized how lucky I was. "I'll come back," I said. "I have to keep looking, but I will come back."

"Really?"

"Sure. I know where you live, right? And you're in this new story now, too. That's something, at least. You branched out. You're recurring."

"Yeah, I guess. Though I'm still stuck in the same place."

"I'll come back tomorrow."

"Okay," he said, shyly. "That...that would be cool."

We shook hands. "The name's John."

"Oh," he said. "So's mine."

I laughed. "Guess we were never supposed to wind up on the same pages. Never mind. We'll cope. I'm going to find the guy, and when I do, we'll talk."

"Good luck," he smiled.

I felt jealous. I'd never been allowed to do that. I have to *say* things, or *ask* them. Shout them, once in a while. I can't "smile" them. There's tougher editing on the novels than with the short stories, I guess, or a more restrictive house style. Though...right now I was *in* a short, wasn't I?

"Thanks," I smiled, and took off my coat. "Here."

"Don't you need it?"

"I've got an apartment. There are closets. I've never looked inside, but there must be something. Worst case, I can put on a sweater or another shirt."

"Thanks, man."

When I got to the door I heard him wish me luck again. I turned back and winked.

"Thanks. And keep the faith, my friend."

When I stepped outside onto the sidewalk, however, everything changed. I knew right away that a decision had been made. It's happened to me before. I stroll aimlessly through a chapter, with lots of thinking and not much doing, and then suddenly there's a blank line break and the next event arrives.

I noticed a man on the other side of the street. He was wandering along, slowly, aimlessly, smoking a cigarette. He glanced across at the Starbucks I'd just left, and I could see him wondering if he could face yet another coffee. There wasn't so much traffic, but what there was, was moving fast enough that he'd have to go back to the corner to cross. It was enough to make him decide it wasn't worth it.

I'd never seen the man before, but I knew who he was. I knew I'd found him.

I thought it again, for emphasis.

I knew.

He looked a little like me and also a little like the guy I'd just left in the Starbucks, the other John. A bit shorter, and a little older, with a touch of grey in the temples. Less distinctive overall. He looked tired, too. Jet-lagged, was my guess. Come over from London for a meeting with his publisher and some research, doggedly using his first day in the city to walk the streets. Not for him, I knew, the hours of reading or scanning the Internet or using Google Street View™. He liked to do his research with his feet, wanted to get to know the city through the miles he moved through it.

Suddenly I realized what this could mean.

The writer *could* merely be reminding himself of these streets for the sake of it, because that's what he always did and it was better than lurking in his hotel room. Or it could merely wind up as background in another short story.

But...it *could* also be that there was a sequel in the works. A sequel to my book.

He could be *considering* doing it, at least. He didn't normally. He usually came up with a new bunch of characters for each book, which was why we ended up in such fixed and limited worlds, without a future. But maybe he was clueing in to the fact that many readers don't *want* to sit through the wheel being reinvented each time, but would prefer to settle back into a recurring set of characters like a comfortable old chair.

The more I thought about it, the more plausible it seemed. I'd always felt that there were elements in my story that hadn't been tied up as satisfyingly as they could have. I'd been left on a cautiously upbeat note, but there was a lot more to be said.

Maybe he was going to do it.

Maybe there was going to be more.

I felt myself smiling. Meanwhile the writer ground to a halt, looking up and down the street. I saw his eyes lighting on this and that — store fronts, fire escapes, passers-by — absorbing everything without noticing, passing it down to the part of his mind that stored these snippets of local color for later use.

I turned away, not wanting him to see my face. When I'd left the apartment that morning, a meeting had been exactly what I wanted. Now I didn't. I didn't want to run the risk of derailing him. I wanted whatever was going through his head to run its course, just in case there was a chance that I was right.

I heard a noise behind me.

I turned to see the guy from the Starbucks, the other John. He was standing in the doorway of the coffee shop, and the sound he'd made was a grunt of disbelief.

He'd done it. He'd tried the door, and opened it.

He stepped cautiously out onto the sidewalk. "Holy crap, John," he said, seeing me. "Look!"

"You *did* it, man."

The joy I felt was partly for him, but mainly for myself. He'd come out because of me, after all. I'd met him and I'd *changed* things. If that much was possible, then maybe everything else was too. Perhaps the writer was considering a sequel precisely because I'd started to prove myself capable of independent movement, worthy of further development.

Maybe I was even going to be a series.

The other John was staring around in wonder. He took a couple of steps up the sidewalk. He turned and looked back the other way. Another pair of leaves came zigzagging gently down from the tree, falling brown and golden.

He reached out and grabbed one, crumpling it in his hands. "I did that," he shouted. "I *did* that!"

"Way to go," I said.

He waved his hands in the air triumphantly, still shouting. He was making a lot of noise now. Enough that it reached across the street, evidently...

...because at that moment, the writer looked up.

He saw John, of course. John was the guy making all the noise, dancing around on the sidewalk, brandishing a crushed leaf in his hand.

The writer frowned, cigarette halfway to his mouth, as though something about John struck him, but he wasn't sure what. It could be that he was merely wondering if he could use the guy in something, not realizing that he already had.

But then his eyes skated past John, and landed on me. And he froze.

He knew who I was.

He was bound to, I guess. I'd recognized *him* immediately, after all, and he'd spent nearly a year with me inside his head, every day, every working hour. Could be that he'd already been thinking about me, too, moments before, if he genuinely was considering pulling me out of the backlist for another turn in the light, as I hoped.

He kept on looking at me. He blinked.

"Hey," I said. "You're Michael, right?"

He started to back away up the street.

I was confused — this was the last thing I'd expected — but then I realized. He was scared. I'd assumed he'd understand how things work, but maybe not. I guess these guys just put down the words and chase their deadlines, not realizing what comes to life between the sentences that come out of their heads in torrents or fits and starts.

He thought he was losing his mind.

"No, it's okay," I said, hurrying up my side of the street, trying to catch up with him. There were too many people and so I darted across the road instead.

"Go away," he said, between clenched teeth, hurrying backward as I got closer. His eyes were wide. "Go *away.*"

"It's *okay,*" I said, trying to sound soothing. "I got no problem with you. Not anymore. I…I think I know why you're here. And that's cool. It's *great,* in fact. I don't want to freak you out. I just wanted to say 'hi,' and, you know, wish you good luck."

"You are *not* real," he hissed, and kept backing away — but he realized he was right up against a crossroads, and had to stop. "I am *very* tired, that's all."

"Absolutely," I said. "That's all it is. And I just happen to look a little like a guy you wrote. Look, we'll go our separate ways. It's the way it should be. But let's at least shake hands, okay? No hard feelings. And, you know, obviously I love your work."

I raised my right hand. His eyes got wider still.

I realized my hand felt cold and heavy, and when I glanced down at it I remembered that actually, I *had* found my gun before I left the apartment. It seemed like he was prepared to go down the unreliable narrator route after all. I tried to throw it away, to prove I was harmless, but it wouldn't leave my hand.

"Michael," I said, trying to sound reassuring. "It's okay. You know me — I'm not a killer. I'm basically a good person. More sinned against than sinning, like all your protagonists. Just ignore the gun, okay?"

But he'd started to back away again, so scared now that he'd forgotten where he was standing, and he stepped back into the road and lost his balance and a cab came around the corner and smacked straight into him.

I haven't been back to the Starbucks in Soho. I said I would, and I will, but I haven't yet. I don't know what to say to John. I don't know how to explain what happened. I don't want to have to describe how it felt to look down at the writer's head on the street, with all the blood leaking out of it, or to watch his eyes as they went from clear to glassy to frosted. I don't want to admit to the fact that I was the author of that event.

I also don't want to see John yet because afterward I tracked down one of the writer's story collections. I found it in the discount section in a Borders. Borders may be history in the real world — more's the pity — but my novel was set back in 2006, so for me they're still around. I found the short story John's in, and I read it. It's pretty good, but it's kind of spooky and heads toward a dark, bad conclusion. I don't want to have to explain to John that he dies in the end after all, or why that may be better than being me.

Because…I do not.

I do not die. I walk these streets and these pages forever, and there will never be a sequel now.

I should have just stuck to my arc, to my own story, been satisfied with what I had. Now I'm trapped in this dead end.

Down at the bottom of this chunk of words.

It doesn't even end properly. It fades to white.

It just stops.

Sad, Dark Thing

AIMLESS. A SHORT, SIMPLE WORD. It means "without aim," where "aim" derives from the notion of calculation with a view to action. Lacking purpose or direction, therefore, without a considered goal. People mainly use the word in a blunt, softened fashion. They walk "aimlessly" down the street, unsure whether to have a coffee or check out the new magazines in the bookstore or maybe sit on that bench and watch the world go by. It's not a big deal, this form of aimlessness. It's a temporary state and often comes with a side order of ease. An hour without something hanging over you, time spent with no great duty to do or achieve anything in particular? In this world of busy lives and do-this and do-that, that sounds pretty good.

But being wholly without purpose, with no direction home? That's not such a good deal. Being truly aimless is like being dead. It may even be the same thing, or worse. It is the aimless who find the wrong roads, and drive down them, simply because they have nowhere else to go.

* * *

Miller usually found himself driving on Saturday afternoons. He could make the morning go away by staying in bed an extra half-hour, tidying away stray emails, spending time on the deck, looking out over the forest with a magazine or the iPad and a succession of coffees. He made the coffees in a machine that sat on the kitchen counter and cost nearly eight hundred dollars. It made a very good cup of coffee. It should. It had cost nearly eight hundred dollars.

By noon a combination of caffeine and other factors would mean he wasn't very hungry. He would go back indoors nonetheless, and put together a plate from the fridge. The ingredients would be things he'd gathered from delis up in San Francisco during the week or else from the New Leaf markets in Santa Cruz or Felton as he returned home on Friday afternoon. The idea was this would constitute a treat, and remind him of the good things in life. That was the idea. He would also pour some juice into one of the only two glasses in the cabinet that got any use. The other was his scotch glass, the one with the faded white logo on it, but this only came out in the evenings. He was very firm about that.

He would bring the plate and glass back out and eat at the table that stood further along the deck from the chair in which he'd spent most of the morning. By then the sun would have moved around, and the table got shade, which he preferred when he was eating. The change in position was also supposed to make it feel like he was doing something different to what he'd done all morning, though it did not, especially. He was still a man sitting in silence on a raised deck, within view of many trees, eating expensive foods that tasted like cardboard.

Afterward he took the plate back indoors and washed it in the sink. He had a dishwasher, naturally. Dishwashers are there to save time. He washed the plate and silverware by hand, watching the water swirl away and then drying everything and putting it to one side. He was down a wife, and a child, now living three hundred miles away. He was short on women and children, therefore, but in their place, from the hollows they had left behind, he had time. Time crawled in an endless parade of minutes from between those cracks, arriving like an army of little black ants, crawling up over his skin, up his face, and into his mouth, ears, and eyes.

So why not wash the plate? And the knife, and the fork, and the glass. Hold back the ants, for a few minutes at least.

He never left the house with a goal. On those afternoons he was, truly, aimless. From where the house stood, high in the Santa Cruz mountains, he could have reached a number of diverting places within an hour or two. San Jose. Saratoga. Los Gatos. Santa Cruz itself, then south to Monterey, Carmel, and Big Sur. Even way down to Los Angeles, if he felt like making a weekend of it.

And then what?

Instead he simply drove.

There are only so many major routes you can take through the area's mountains and redwood forests. Highways 17 and 9, or the road out over to Bonny Doon, Route 1 north or south. Of these, 17 is the one of any real size. In between the main thoroughfares, however, there are other options. Roads that don't do much except connect one minor two-lane highway to another. Roads that used to count for something before modern alternatives came along to supplant or supersede or negate them.

Side roads, old roads, forgotten roads.

Usually there wasn't much to see down them. Stretches of forest, maybe a stream, eventually a house, well back from the road. Rural, mountainous backwoods where the tree and poison oak reigned supreme. Chains across tracks that led down or up into the woods, some gentle inclines, others pretty steep, meandering off toward some house that stood even further from the through-lines, back in a twenty- or fifty-acre lot. Every now and then you'd pass one of the area's few tourist traps, like the Mystery Spot, an old-fashioned affair that claimed to honor a site of Unfathomable Weirdness but in fact paid cheerful homage to geometry, and to man's willingness to be deceived.

He'd seen all of these long ago. The local attractions with his wife and child, the shadowed roads and tracks on his own solitary excursions over the last few months. At least, you might have thought he would have seen them all. Every Saturday he drove, however, and every time he found a road he had never seen before.

Today the road was off Branciforte Drive, the long, old highway that heads off through largely uncolonized regions of the mountains and forests to the southeast of Scott's Valley. As he drove north along it, mind elsewhere and nowhere, he noticed a turning. A glance in the rear-view mirror showed no one behind and so he slowed to peer along the turn.

A two-lane road, overhung with tall trees, including some redwoods. It gave no indication of leading anywhere at all. Fine by him.

He made the turn and drove on. The trees were tall and thick, cutting off much of the light from above. The road passed smoothly up and down, riding the natural contours, curving abruptly once in a while to avoid the trunk of an especially big tree or to skirt a small canyon carved out over millennia by some small and bloody-minded stream. There were no houses or other signs of habitation. Could be public land, he was beginning to think, though he didn't recall there being any around here and hadn't seen any indication of a park boundary, and then he saw a sign by the road up ahead.

STOP

That's all it said. Despite himself, he found he was doing just that, pulling over toward it. When the car was stationary, he looked at the sign curiously. It had been hand-lettered, some time ago, in black felt marker on a panel cut from a cardboard box and nailed to a tree.

He looked back the way he'd come, then up the road once more. He saw no traffic in either direction, and also no indication of why the sign would be here. Sure, the road curved again about forty yards ahead, but no more markedly than it had ten or fifteen times since he'd left Branciforte Drive. There had been no warning signs on those bends. If you simply wanted people to observe the speed limit then you'd be more likely to advise them to SLOW, and anyway it didn't look like an official sign.

Then he realized that, further on, there was in fact a turning off the road.

He took his foot off the brake and let the car roll forward down the slope, crunching over twigs and gravel. A driveway, it seemed, though a long one, bending off into the trees. Single lane, roughly made up. Maybe five yards down it was another sign, evidently the work of the same craftsman as the previous one.

TOURISTS WELCOME

He grunted, in something like a laugh. If you had yourself some kind of attraction, then of course tourists were welcome. What would be the point otherwise? It was a strange way of putting it.

An odd way of advertising it, too. No indication of what was in store or why a busy family should turn off what was already a pretty minor road and head off into the woods. No lure except those two words.

They were working on him, though, he had to admit. He eased his foot gently back on the gas and carefully directed the car along the track, between the trees.

After about a quarter of a mile, he saw a building ahead. A couple of them, in fact, arranged in a loose compound. One a ramshackle two-storey farmhouse, the other a disused barn. There was also something that was or had been a garage, with a broken-down truck/tractor parked diagonally in front of it. It was parked insofar as it was not moving, at least not in the sense that whoever had last driven the thing had made any effort, when abandoning it, to align its form with anything. The surfaces of the vehicle were dusty and rusted and liberally covered in old leaves and specks of bark. A wooden crate, about four feet square, stood rotting in the back. The near front tire was flat.

The track ended in a widened parking area, big enough for four or five cars. It was empty. There was no sign of life at all, in fact, but something — he wasn't sure what — said this habitation was still a going concern, rather than collection of ruins that someone had walked away from at some point in the last few years.

Nailed to a tree in front of the main house was another cardboard sign.

WELCOME

He parked, turned off the engine, and got out. It was very quiet. It usually is in these mountains, when you're away from the road. Sometimes you'll hear the faint roar of an airplane, way up above, but apart from that it's just the occasional tweet of some winged creature or an indistinct rustle as something small and furry or scaly makes its way through the bushes.

He stood a few minutes, flapping his hand to discourage a noisy fly, which appeared from nowhere, bothered his face, and then zipped chaotically off.

Eventually he called out. "Hello?"

You'd think that — on what was evidently a very slow day for this attraction, whatever it was — the sound of an arriving vehicle would have someone bustling into sight, eager to make a few bucks, to pitch their wares. He stood a few minutes more, however, without seeing or hearing any sign of life. It figured. Aimless people find aimless things, and it didn't seem like much was going to happen here. You find what you're looking for, and he hadn't been looking for anything at all.

He turned back toward the car, aware that he wasn't even feeling disappointment. He hadn't expected much, and that's exactly what he'd got.

As he held up his hand to press the button to unlock the doors, however, he heard a creaking sound.

He turned back to see there was now a man on the tilting porch that ran along half of the front of the wooden house. He was dressed in canvas jeans and a vest that had probably once been white. The man had probably once been clean, too, though he looked now like he'd spent most of the morning trying to fix the underside of a car. Perhaps he had.

"What you want?"

His voice was flat and unwelcoming. He looked to be in his mid- to late-fifties. Hair once black was now half-grey, and also none too clean. He did not seem like he'd been either expecting or desirous of company.

"What have you got?"

The man on the porch leant on the rail and kept looking at him, but said nothing.

"It says, 'Tourists Welcome'," Miller said, when it became clear the local had nothing to offer. "I'm not feeling especially welcome, to be honest."

The man on the porch looked weary. "Christ. The boy was supposed to take down those damned signs. They still up?"

"Yes."

"Even the one out on the road, says 'Stop'?"

"Yes," Miller said. "Otherwise I wouldn't have stopped."

The other man swore and shook his head. "Told the boy weeks ago. Told him I don't know how many times."

Miller frowned. "You don't notice, when you drive in and out? That the signs are still there?"

"Haven't been to town in a while."

"Well, look. I turned down your road because it looked like there was something to see."

"Nope. Doesn't say anything like that."

"It's implied, though, wouldn't you say?"

The man lifted his chin a little. "You a lawyer?"

"No. I'm a businessman. With time on my hands. Is there something to see here, or not?"

After a moment the man on the porch straightened, and came walking down the steps.

"One dollar," he said. "As you're here."

"For what? The parking?"

The man stared at him as if he was crazy. "No. To see."

"One dollar?" It seemed inconceivable that in this day and age there would be anything under the sun for a dollar, especially if it was trying to present as something worth experiencing. "Really?"

"That's cheap," the man said, misunderstanding.

"It is what it is," Miller said, getting his wallet out and pulling a dollar bill from it.

The other man laughed, a short, sour sound. "You got that right."

After he'd taken the dollar and stuffed it into one of the pockets of his jeans, the man walked away. Miller took this to mean that he should follow, and so he did. It looked for a moment as if they were headed toward the house, but then the path — such as it was — took an abrupt right onto a course that led them between the house and the tilting barn. The house was large and gabled and must have once been quite something. Lord knows what it was doing out here, lost by itself in a patch of forest that had never been near a major road or town or anyplace else that people with money might wish to be. Its glory days were long behind it, anyway. Looking up at it, you'd give it about another five years standing, unless someone got onto rebuilding or at least shoring it right away.

The man led the way through slender trunks into an area around the back of the barn. Though the land in front of the house and around the side had barely been what you'd think of as tamed, here the forest abruptly came into its own. Trees of significant size shot up all around, looking – as redwoods do – like they'd been there since the dawn of time. A sharp, rocky incline led down toward a stream about thirty yards away. The stream was perhaps eight feet across, with steep sides. A rickety bridge of old, grey wood lay across it. The man led him to the near side of this, and then stopped.

"What?"

"This is it."

Miller looked again at the bridge. "A dollar, to look at a bridge some guy threw up fifty years ago?" Suddenly it wasn't seeming so dumb a pricing system after all.

The man handed him a small, tarnished key, and raised his other arm to point. Between the trees on the other side of the creek was a small hut.

"It's in there."

"What is?"

The man shrugged. "A sad, dark thing."

The water that trickled below the bridge smelled fresh and clean. Miller got a better look at the hut, shed, whatever, when he reached the other side. It was about half the size of a log cabin, but made of grey, battered planks instead of logs. The patterns of lichen over the sides and the moss-covered roof said it been here, and in this form, for a good long time – far longer than the house, most likely. Could be an original settler's cabin, the home of whichever long-ago pioneer had first arrived here, driven west by hope or desperation. It looked about contemporary with the rickety bridge, certainly.

There was a small padlock on the door.

He looked back.

The other man was still standing at the far end of the bridge, looking at the canopy of leaves above. It wasn't clear what he'd be looking at, but it didn't seem like he was waiting for the right moment to rush over, bang the other guy on the head, and steal his wallet.

If he'd wanted to do that he could have done it back up at the house. There was no sign of anyone else around – this boy he'd mentioned, for example – and he looked like he was waiting patiently for the conclusion of whatever needed to happen for him to have earned his dollar.

Miller turned back and fitted the key in the lock. It was stiff, but it turned. He opened the door. Inside was total dark. He hesitated, looked back across the bridge, but the man had gone.

He opened the door further, and stepped inside.

The interior of the cabin was cooler than it had been outside, but also stuffy. There was a faint smell. Not a bad smell, particularly. It was like old, damp leaves. It was like the back of a closet where you store things you do not need. It was like a corner of the attic of a house not much loved, in the night, after rain.

The only light was that which managed to get past him from the door behind. The cabin had no windows, or if it had, they had been covered over. The door he'd entered by was right at one end of the building, which meant the rest of the interior led ahead. It could only have been ten, twelve feet. It seemed longer, because it was so dark. The man stood there, not sure what happened next.

The door slowly swung closed behind him, not all the way but leaving a gap of a couple of inches. No one came and shut it on him or turned the lock or started hollering about he'd have to pay a thousand bucks to get back out again. The man waited.

In a while, there was a quiet sound.

It was a rustling. Not quite a shuffling. A sense of something moving a little at the far end, turning away from the wall, perhaps. Just after the sound, there was a low waft of a new odor, as if the movement had caused something to change its relationship to the environment, as if a body long held curled or crouched in a particular shape or position had realigned enough for hidden sweat to be released into the unmoving air.

Miller froze.

In all his life, he'd never felt the hairs on the back of his neck rise. You read about it, hear about it. You knew they were supposed to do it, but he'd never felt it, not his own hairs, on his own neck. They did it then, though, and the peculiar thing was that he was not afraid, or not only that.

He was in there with something, that was for certain. It was not a known thing, either. It was…he didn't know. He wasn't sure. He just knew that there was *something* over there in the darkness. Something about the size of a man, he thought, maybe a little smaller.

He wasn't sure it was male, though. Something told him otherwise. He couldn't imagine what that might be, as he couldn't see it and he couldn't hear anything, either — after the initial movement, it had been still. Nonetheless something in the air told him it understood despair, bitter madness, and melancholy better than even he did. He somehow also knew that beneath the shadows it wrapped around itself — like a pair of dark angel's wings — it was naked, and not male.

He knew also that it was this, and not fear, that was making his breathing come ragged and forced.

He stayed in there with it for half an hour, doing nothing, just listening, staring into the darkness but not seeing anything. That's how long it seemed like it had been, anyway, when he eventually emerged back into the forest. It was hard to tell.

He closed the cabin door behind him but he did not lock it, because he saw that the man was back, standing once more at the far end of the bridge. Miller clasped the key firmly in his fist and walked over toward him.

"How much?" he said.

"For what? You already paid."

"No," Miller said. "I want to buy it."

It was eight by the time Miller got back to his house. He didn't know how that could be unless he'd spent longer in the cabin than he realized. It didn't matter a whole lot, and in fact there were good things about it. The light had begun to fade. In twenty minutes it would be gone entirely. He spent those minutes sitting in the front seat of the car, waiting for darkness, his mind as close to a comfortable blank as it had been in a long time.

When it was finally dark he got out the car and went over to the house. He dealt with the security system, opened the front door and left it hanging open.

He walked back to the vehicle and went around to the trunk. He rested his hand on the metal there for a moment, and it felt cold. He unlocked the back and turned away, not fast but naturally, and walked toward the wooden steps, which led to the smaller of the two raised decks. He walked up them and stood there for a few minutes, looking out into the dark stand of trees, and then turned and headed back down the steps toward the car.

The trunk was empty now, and so he shut it, and walked slowly toward the open door of his house, and went inside, and shut and locked that door behind him too.

It was night, and it was dark, and they were both inside, and that felt right.

He poured a small scotch into a large glass. He took it out through the sliding glass doors to the chair on the main deck where he'd spent the morning, and sat cradling the drink, taking a sip once in a while. He found himself remembering, as he often did at this time of day, the first time he'd met his wife. He'd been living down on East Cliff then, in a house that was much smaller than this one but only a couple of minutes' walk from the beach. Late one Saturday afternoon, bored and restless, he'd taken a walk to the Crow's Nest, the big restaurant that was the only place to eat or drink along that stretch. He'd bought a similar scotch at the upstairs bar and taken it out onto the balcony to watch the sun go down over the harbor. After a while he noticed that, amongst the family groups of sunburned tourists and knots of tattooed locals, there was a woman at a table by herself. She had a tall glass of beer and seemed to be doing the same thing he was, and he wondered why. Not why she was doing it, but why he was — why they both were. He did not know then, and he did not know now, why people sit and look out into the distance by themselves, or what they hope to see.

After a couple more drinks he went over and introduced himself. Her name was Catherine, and she worked at the university. They got married eighteen months later, and though by then — his business having taken off in the meantime — he could have afforded anywhere in town, they hired out the Crow's Nest and had the wedding party there. A year after that, their daughter was born and they called her Matilde after Catherine's mother, who was French. Business was still good and they moved out of his place on East Cliff and into the big house he had built in the mountains and for seven years all was good, and then, for some reason, it was no longer good anymore. He didn't think it had been his fault, though it could have been. He didn't think it was her fault, either, though that, too, was possible. It had simply stopped working. They'd been two people, and then one, but then two again, facing different ways. There had been a view to share together, then there was not, and if you look with only one eye then there is no depth of field. There had been no infidelity. In some ways that might have been easier. It would have been something to react to, to blame, to hide behind. Far worse, in fact, to sit on opposite sides of the breakfast table and wonder whom the other person was, and why they were there, and when they would go.

Six months later, she did. Matilde went with her, of course. He didn't think there was much more that could be said or understood on the subject. When first he'd sat out on this deck alone, trying to work it all through in his head, the recounting could take hours. As time went on, the story seemed to get shorter and shorter. As they said around these parts, it is what it is.

Or it was what it was.

Time passed and then it was late. The scotch was long gone but he didn't feel the desire for more. He took the glass indoors and washed it at the sink, putting it on the draining board next to the plate and the knife and the fork from lunch. No lights were on. He hadn't bothered to flick any switches when he came in, and — having sat for so long out on the deck — his eyes were accustomed, and he felt no need to turn any on now.

He dried his hands on a cloth and walked around the house, aimlessly at first. He had done this many times in the last few months, hearing echoes. When he got to the area that had been Catherine's study, he stopped. There was nothing left in the space now, bar the empty desk and the empty bookshelves. He could tell that the chair had been moved, however. He didn't recall precisely how it had been, or when he'd last listlessly walked this way, but he knew that it had been moved, somehow.

He went back to walking, and eventually found himself hesitating outside the room that had been Matilde's. The door was slightly ajar. The space beyond was dark.

He could feel a warmth coming out of it, though, and heard a sound in there, something quiet, and he turned and walked slowly away.

* * *

He took a shower in the dark. Afterward he padded back to the kitchen in his bare feet and a gown and picked his scotch glass up from the draining board. Even after many, many trips through the dishwasher you could see the ghost of the restaurant logo that had once been stamped on it, the remains of a mast and a crow's nest. Catherine had slipped it into her purse one long-ago night, without his knowing about it, and then given the glass to him as an anniversary present. How did a person who would do that change into the person now living half the state away? He didn't know, any more than he knew why he had so little to say on the phone to his daughter, or why people sat and looked at views, or why they drove to nowhere on Saturday afternoons. Our heads turn and point at things. Light comes into our eyes. Words come out of our mouths.

And then? And so?

Carefully, he brought the edge of the glass down upon the edge of the counter. It broke pretty much as he'd hoped it would, the base remaining in one piece, the sides shattering into several jagged points.

He padded back through into the bedroom, put the glass on the night stand, took off the robe, and lay back on the bed. That's how they'd always done it, when they'd wanted to signal that tonight didn't have to just be about going to sleep. Under the covers with a book, then probably not tonight, Josephine.

Naked and on top, on the other hand…

A shorthand. A shared language. There is little sadder than a tongue for which only one speaker remains. He closed his eyes, and after a while, for the first time since he'd stood stunned in the driveway and watched his family drive away, he cried.

Afterward he lay and waited.

She came in the night.

* * *

Three days later, in the late afternoon, a battered truck pulled down into the driveway and parked alongside the car that was there. It was the first time the truck had been on the road in nearly two years, and the driver left the engine running when he got out because he wasn't sure it would start up again. The patched front tire was holding up, though, for now.

He went around the back and opened up the wooden crate, propping the flap with a stick. Then he walked over to the big front door and rang on the bell. Waited a while, and did it again. No answer. Of course.

He rubbed his face in his hands, wearily, took a step back. The door looked solid. No way a kick would get it open. He looked around and saw the steps up to the side deck.

When he got to the back of the house, he picked up the chair that sat by itself, hefted it to judge the weight, and threw it through the big glass door. When he'd satisfied himself that the hole in the smashed glass was big enough, he walked back along the deck and around the front and then up the driveway to stand on the road for a while, out of view of the house.

He smoked a cigarette, and then another to be sure, and when he came back down the driveway he was relieved to see that the flap on the crate on the back of his truck was now closed.

He climbed into the cab and sat a moment, looking at the big house. Then he put the truck into reverse, got back up to the highway, and drove slowly home.

When he made the turn into his own drive later, he saw the STOP sign was still there. Didn't matter how many times he told the boy, the sign was still there.

He drove along the track to the house, parked the truck. He opened the crate without looking at it, and went inside.

* * *

Later, sitting on his porch in the darkness, he listened to the sound of the wind moving through the tops of the trees. He drank a warm beer, and then another. He looked at the grime on his hands. He wondered what it was that made some people catch sight of the sign, what it was in their eyes, what it was in the way they looked, that made them see. He wondered how the man in the big house had done it, and hoped he had not suffered much. He wondered why he had never attempted the same thing. He wondered why it was only on nights like these that he was able to remember that his boy had been dead twenty years.

Finally he went indoors and lay in bed staring at the ceiling. He did this every night, even though there was never anything there to see: nothing unless it is that sad, dark thing that eventually takes us in its arms and makes us sleep.

What Happens When You Wake Up in the Night

THE FIRST THING I WAS UNHAPPY ABOUT was the dark. I do not like the dark very much. It is not the worst thing in the world but it is not the best thing in the world, either. When I was very smaller I used to wake up sometimes in the middle of the night and be scared when I woke up because it was so dark. I went to bed with my light on, the light that turns round and round on the drawers by the side of my bed. It has animals on it and it turns around and it makes shapes and patterns on the ceiling and it is pretty and my mummy's friend Jeanette gave it to me. It is not too bright but it is bright enough and you can see what is what. But then it started that when I woke up in the middle of the night the light would not be on anymore and it would be completely dark instead and it would make me sad. I didn't understand this but one night when I'd woken up and cried a lot my mummy told me that she came in every night and turned off the light after I was asleep, so it didn't wake me up. But I said that wasn't any good, because if I *did* wake up in the night and the light wasn't on, then I might be scared, and cry. She said it seemed that I was waking up every night at the moment, and she and Daddy had worked out that it might be the light that woke me, and after I was awake I'd get up and go into their room and see what was up with them, which meant she got no sleep any night ever and it was driving her completely nuts.

So we made a deal, and the deal said I could have the light on all night *but* I promised that I would not go into their room in the night unless it was *really* important, and it is a good deal and so I'm allowed to have my light on again now, which is why the first thing I noticed when I woke up was that it was dark. The light was off.

Mummy had broken the deal.

I was cross about this but I was also very sleepy and so wasn't sure if I was going to shout about it or not.

Then I noticed it was cold.

Before I go to bed, Mummy puts a heater on while I am having my bath, and also I have two blankets on top of my duvet, and so I am a warm little bunny and it is fine. Sometimes if I wake in the middle of the night it feels a bit cold but if I snuggle down again it's okay.

But this felt really cold.

My light was not on and I was cold.

I put my hand out to put my light on, which was the first thing to do. There is a switch on a white wire that comes from the light and I can turn it on myself — I can even find it in the dark when there is no light.

I tried to do that but I could not find the wire with my hand. So I sat up and tried again, but still I could not find it, and I wondered if Mummy had moved it, and I thought I might go and ask her, but I could not see the door. It had been so long since I had been in my room in the night without my light being on that I had forgotten how dark it gets. It's *really* dark.

I knew it would be hard to find the door if I could not see it, so I did it a clever way.

I used my imagination.

I sat still for a moment and remembered what my bedroom is like. It is like a rectangle and has some drawers by the top of my bed where my head goes. My light is on the drawers, usually. My room also has a table where my coloring books go and some small toys, and two more sets of drawers, and windows down the other end. They have curtains so the street lights do not keep me awake, and because in summer it gets bright too early in the morning and so I wake everybody up when they should still be asleep because they have work to do and they need some sleep. And there is a big chair but it is always covered in toys and it is not important.

I turned to the side so my legs hung off the bed and down onto the floor. In my imagination I could see that if I stood up and walked straight in front of me, I would nearly be at my bedroom door, but that I would have to go a little way... left, too.

So I stood up and did the walking.

It was funny doing it in the dark. I stepped on something soft with one of my feet, I think it was a toy that had fallen off the chair. Then I touched one of the other drawers with my hand, and I knew I was close to the door, so I turned left and walked that way a bit.

I reached out with my hands then and tried to find my dressing gown. I was trying to find it because I was cold, but also because it hangs off the back of my bedroom door on a little hook and so when I found the dressing gown I would know I had got to the right place to open the door.

But I could not find the dressing gown. Sometimes my mummy takes things downstairs and washes them in the washing machine in the kitchen and then dries them in another machine that makes them dry, so maybe that was where it was. I was quite awake now and very cold so I decided not to keep trying to find the gown and just go wake Mummy and Daddy and tell them that I was awake.

But I couldn't find my doorknob.

I knew I must be where the door is, because it is in the corner where the two walls of my room come together. I reached out with my hands and could feel the two sides of the corner, but I could not find the doorknob, even though I moved my hands all over where it should be. When I was smaller, the doorknob came off once, and Mummy was very scared because she thought if it happened again I would be trapped in my bedroom and I wouldn't be able to get out, so she shouted at Daddy until he fixed it with a different screw. But it had never come off again so I did not know where it could be now. I wondered if I had got off my bed in the wrong way because it was dark and I had got it mixed up in my imagination, and maybe I should go back to my bed and start again.

Then a voice said: "Maddy, what are you *doing?*"

I was so surprised I made a scared sound, and jumped. I trod on something, and the same voice said, "Ow!" I heard someone moving and sitting up. Even though it was in the dark I knew it was my mummy.

"Mummy?" I said. "Where are you?"

"Maddy, I've *told* you about coming into our room."

"I'm not."

"It's just not *fair*. Mummy has to go to work and Daddy has to go to work and you have to go to school and we *all* need our sleep. We made a *deal*, remember?"

"But *you* broke the deal. You took away my light."

"I haven't touched your light."

"You did!"

"Maddy, don't *lie*. We've talked about lying."

"You took my light!"

"I haven't taken your light and I didn't turn it off."

"But it's not turned on."

She made a sighing sound. "Maybe the bulb went."

"Went to where?"

"I mean, got broken."

"No, my whole *light* is not there."

"Maddy..."

"It's not! I put my hand out and I couldn't find it!"

My mummy made a sound like she was very cross or very tired, I don't know which. Sometimes they sound the same. She didn't say anything for a little minute.

"Look," she said then, and she did not sound very cross now, just very sleepy and as if she loved me, but wished I was still asleep. "It's the middle of the night and everyone should be in bed. Their *own* bed."

"I'm sorry, Mummy."

"That's okay." I heard her standing up. "Come on. Let's go back to your room."

"What do you mean?" I said.

"Back to your room. Now. I'll tuck you in, and then we can all go back to sleep."

"I *am* in my room."

"Maddy — don't start."

"I *am* in my room!"

"Maddy, this is just silly. Why would you...why is it so dark in here?"

"Because my light is off. I told you."

"Maddy, your light is in *your* room. Don't — "

She stopped talking suddenly. I heard her fingers moving against something, the wall, maybe. "What the hell?"

Her voice sounded different.

"'Hell' is a naughty word," I told her.

"Shush."

I heard her fingers swishing over the wall again. She had been asleep on the floor, right next to the wall. I heard her feet moving on the carpet and then there was a banging sound and she said a naughty word again, but she did not sound angry but like she did not understand something. It was like a question mark sound.

"For the love of *Christ*."

That was not my mummy talking. She said: "Dan?"

"Who the hell else? Any chance you'll just take her back to bed? Or I can do it. I don't mind. But let's one of us do it. It's the middle of the fucking night."

"Dan!"

"'Fucking' is a *very* naughty — "

"Yes, yes, I'm terribly sorry," my daddy said. He sounded as if he was only half not in a dream. "But we have *talked* about you coming into our room in the middle of the night, Maddy. Talked about it endlessly. And — "

"Dan," my mummy said, starting to talk when he was still talking, which is not good and can be rude. "Where *are* you?"

"I'm right *here,*" he said. "For god's *sake*. I'm…did you put up new curtains or something?"

"No," Mummy said.

"It's not normally this dark in here, is it?"

"My light has gone," I said. "That's why it is so dark."

"Your light is in *your* room," Daddy said.

I could hear him sitting up. I could hear his hands, too. They were not right next to Mummy, but at the other end of my room. I could hear them moving around on the carpet.

"Am I on the floor?" he asked. "What the hell am I doing *on the floor?*"

I heard him stand up. I did not tell him "hell" is a naughty word. I did not think that he would like it.

I heard him move around a little more, his hands knocking into things.

"Maddy," Mummy said, "where do you think you are?"

"I'm in my *room,*" I said.

"Dan?" she said to Daddy. My daddy's other name is "Dan." It is like "dad" but has a *nuh*-sound at the end instead of a *duh*-sound. "*Is* this Maddy's room?"

I heard him moving around again, as if he was checking things with his hands.

"What are we doing in here?" he said, sounding as if was not certain. "Is this her room?"

"Yes, it's *my room*," I said.

I was beginning to think Daddy or Mummy could not hear properly because I kept saying things over and over but they did not listen. I told them again. "I woke up, and my light was off, and this is my room."

"Have you tried the switch by the door?" Daddy asked Mummy.

I heard Mummy move to the door, and her fingers swishing on the wall, swishing and patting. "It's not there."

"What do you mean it's not there?"

"What do you think I mean?"

"For Christ's sake."

I heard Daddy walking carefully across the room to where Mummy was.

Mummy said: "Satisfied?"

"How *can* it not be there? Maddy — can you turn the light by your bed on, please?" Daddy sounded cross now.

"She says it isn't there."

"What do you mean, not there?"

"It's not *there*," I said. "I already told Mummy, fourteen times. I was coming into your room to tell you, and then Mummy woke up and she was on the floor."

"Are the street lamps out?"

This was Mummy asking. I heard Daddy go away from the door and go back to the other end of the room, where he had woken up from. He knocked into the table as he was moving and made a cross sound but kept on moving again.

"Dan? Is that why it's so dark? Is it a power cut?"

"I don't know," he said. "I…can't find the curtains."

"Can't find the gap, you mean?"

"No. Can't find the *curtains*. They're not here."

"You're sure you're in the right — "

"Of course I'm in the right place. They're not here. I can't feel them. It's just wall."

"It is just wall where my door is, too," I said. I was happy that Daddy had found the same thing as me, because if he had found it, too, then it could not be wrong.

I heard Mummy check the wall near us with her hands. She was breathing a little quickly.

"She's right. It's just wall," she said, so now we all knew the same thing. "It's just wall, everywhere."

But Mummy's voice sounded quiet and a bit scared and so it did not make me so happy when she said it.

"Okay, this is ridiculous," Daddy said. "Stay where you are. Don't move."

I could hear what he was doing. He was going along the sides of the room, with his fingers on the walls. He went around the drawers near the window, then past where my calendar hangs, where I put what day it is in the mornings, then along my bed.

"She's right," he said. "The lamp isn't here."

"I'm really cold," Mummy said.

Daddy went past me and into the corner where Mummy had been sleeping, where I had trod on her when I was trying to find the door.

But he couldn't find the door either.

He said the door had gone, and the windows, and all the walls felt like they were made of stone. Mummy tried to find the curtains but she couldn't. They tried to find the door and the window for a long time but they still couldn't find them and then my mummy started crying.

Daddy said crying would not help, which he says to me sometimes, and he kept on looking in the dark for some more time, trying to find the door.

But in the end he stopped, and he came and sat down with us. I don't know how long ago that was. It's hard to remember in the dark. But I think it was quite long ago.

Sometimes we sleep, but later we wake up and everything is still the same. I do not get hungry but it is always dark and it is always very cold.

Mummy and Daddy had ideas and used their imaginations. Mummy thought there was maybe a fire, and it burned all our house down. Daddy says we think we are in my room because I woke up first, but he says really we are in a small place made of stone, near a church somewhere.

I don't know but we have been here a very long time now and still it is not morning yet. It is quiet and I do not like it. Mummy and Daddy do not talk much anymore, and this is why if you wake up in the night you should never ever get up out of bed.

The Things He Said

MY FATHER SAID SOMETHING to me one time. In fact he said a lot of things to me, over the years, and many of them weren't what you'd call helpful, or polite – or loving, come to that. But in the last couple months I've found myself thinking back over a lot of them and often find they had a grain of truth. I consider what he said in the new light of things, and move on, and then they're done. This one thing, though, has kept coming back to me. It's not very original, but I can't help that. He was not a very original man.

What he said was that you had to take care of yourself, first and foremost and always, because there wasn't no one else in the world who was going to do it for you. Look after Number One, was how he put it.

About this he was absolutely right. Of that I have no doubt.

* * *

I start every day to a schedule. Live the whole day by it, actually. I don't know if it makes much difference in the wider scheme of things, but having a set of tasks certainly helps the day kick off more positively. It gets you over that hump.

I wake around 6:00 A.M., or a little earlier. So far, that has meant the dawn has either been here, or coming. As the weeks go by it will mean a period of darkness after waking, a time spent waiting in the cabin. It will not make a great deal of difference apart from that.

I wash with the can of water I set aside the night before, and eat whatever I put next to it. The washing is not strictly necessary but, again, I have always found it a good way to greet the day. You wash after a period of work, after all, and what else is a night of sleep, if not work, or a journey at least? You wash, and the day starts, a day marked off from what has gone before.

In the meantime I have another can of water heating over a fire. The chimney is blocked up and the doors and windows are sealed overnight against the cold, so the fire must of necessity be small. That's fine — all I need is to make enough water for a cup of coffee.

I take this with me when I open the cabin and step outside, which will generally be at about 6:20 A.M. I live within the shade of mountains, an area that is largely forested. Though the cabin itself is obscured by trees, from my door I have a good view down over the ten or so acres between it and the next stretch of thicker woods. I tend to sit there on the stoop a couple minutes, sipping my coffee, looking around. You can't always see what you're looking for, though, which is why I do what I do next.

I leave the door open behind me and walk a distance, which is about three hundred yards in length — I measured it with strides when I set it up — made of four unequal sides. This contains the cabin and my shed, and a few trees, and is bounded by wires. I call them wires but really they're lengths of fishing line, strung between a series of trees. The fact that I'm there checking them, on schedule, means they're very likely to be in place, but I check them anyway.

First, to make sure none of them need re-fixing because of wind — but also that there's no sign something came close without actually tripping them.

I walk them all slowly, looking carefully at where they're attached to the trees, and checking the ground on the other side for signs anything got that far, and then stopped — either by accident or because they saw the wires. This is a good, slow, task for that time in the morning, wakes you up nice and easy. I once met a woman who'd been in therapy — hired a vacation cottage over near Elum for half a summer, a long time ago this was — and it seemed like the big thing she'd learned was to ignore everything she thought in the first hour of the day. That's when the negative stuff will try to bring you down, she said, and she was right about that, if not much else. You come back from the night with your head and soul empty, and bad things try to fill you up. There's a lot to get exercised about, if you let it. But if you've got a task, something to fill your head and move your limbs, by the time you've finished it, the day has begun and you're onto the next thing. You're over that hump, like I said.

When that job's finished, I go back to the cabin and have the second cup of coffee, which I keep kind of warm by laying my breakfast plate over the top of the mug while I'm outside. I'll have put the fire out before checking the wires, so there's no more hot water for the moment. I used to have one of those vacuum flasks and that was great, but it got broken. I'm on the lookout for a replacement. No luck yet. The colder it gets, the more that's going to become a real priority.

I'll drink this second cup planning what I'm going to do that day. I could do this the night before, but usually I don't. It's what I do between 7:30 and 8:00 A.M. It's in the schedule.

Most days, the next thing is going into the woods. I used to have a vegetable patch behind the cabin but the soil here isn't that great and it was always kind of hit-and-miss. After the thing, it would also be too much of a clue that someone is living here.

There's plenty to find out in the woods, if you know what to look for. Wild versions of the vegetables in stores, other plants that don't actually taste so good but give you some of the green stuff you need. Sometimes you'll even see something you can kill to eat — a rabbit or a deer, that kind of thing — but not often. With time I assume I may see more, but for now stocks are low. With winter coming on, it's going to get a little harder for all this stuff. Maybe a *lot* harder.

We'll see. No point in worrying about it now. Worry don't get nothing but worry, as my father also used to say.

Maybe a couple hours spent out in the woods, then I carry back what I've found and store it in the shed. I'll check on the things already waiting, see what stage they're at when it comes to eating. The hanging process is very important. While I'm there I'll check the walls and roof are still sound and the canvas I've layered around the inside is still watertight. As close to airtight as possible, too.

I don't know if there are bears in these parts anymore — I've lived here forty years, man and boy, and I haven't seen one in a long time, nor wolves either — but you may as well be sure. One of them catches a scent of food and they're bound to come have a look-see, blundering through the wires and screwing up all that stuff. Fixing it would throw the schedule right out! I'm joking, mainly, but you know, it really would be kind of a pain, and my stock of fishing wire is not inexhaustible.

It's important to live within your means, within what you know you can replace. A long-game way of life, as my father used to say. I had someone living here with me for a while, and it was kind of nice, but she found it hard to understand the importance of these things, of playing that long game. Her name was Ramona, and she came from over Noqualmi way. The arrangement didn't last long. Less than ten days, in fact. I did miss her a little after she walked out the door but things are simpler again now she's gone.

Time'll be about 10:30 A.M. by then, maybe 11:00, and I'm ready for a third cup of coffee. So I go back to the cabin, shut and seal up all the doors and windows again, and light the fire. Do the same as when I get up, make two cups, cover one to keep it semi-warm for later. I'll check around the inside of the cabin while the water's heating, making sure everything's in good shape. It's a simple house. No electricity — lines don't come out this far — and no running water.

I got a septic tank under the house that I put in ten years back, and I get drinking and washing water from the well. There's not much to go wrong and it doesn't need checking every day. But if something's on the schedule, then it gets done, and if it gets done, then you know it's done and it's not something you have to worry about.

I go back outside, leaving the door open behind me again, and check the exterior of the house. That does need an eye kept on it. The worse the weather gets, the more there'll be a little of this or that needs doing. That's okay. I've got tools, and I know how to use them. I was a handyman before the thing, and I am, therefore, kind of handy. I'm glad about that now. Probably a lot of people thought being computer programmers or bankers or TV stars was a better deal, the real cool beans. It's likely that, by now, they may have changed their minds. I'll check the shingles on the roof, make sure the joints between the logs are still tight. I do not mess with any of the grasses or bushes that lie in the area within the wires, or outside either. I like them the way they are.

Now, it's about midday. I'll fill half an hour with my sculpturing, then. There's a patch of ground about a hundred yards the other side of the wires on the east side of the house, where I'm arranging rocks. There's a central area where they're piled up higher, and around that they're just strewn to look natural. You might think this is a weird thing to do for someone who won't have a vegetable patch in case someone sees it, but I'm very careful with the rocks. Spent a long time studying on how the natural formations look around here.

Spent even longer walking back from distant points with just the right kind of rocks. I was born right on this hillside. I know the area better'n probably anyone. The way I'm working it, the central area is going to look like just another outcrop, and the stuff around, like it just fell off and has been lying there for years.

It passes the time, anyway.

I eat my meal around 1:00 P.M. Kind of late, but otherwise the afternoon can feel a little long. I eat what I left over from supper the night before. Saves a fire. Although leaving the door open when I'm around the property disperses most of the smoke, letting it out slowly, a portion is always going to linger in the cabin, I guess. If it's been a still day, when I wake up the next morning my chest can feel kind of clotted. Better than having it all shoot up the chimney, but it's not a perfect system. It could be improved. I'm thinking about it, in my spare time, which occurs between 1:30 and 2:00 P.M.

The afternoons are where the schedule becomes a tad more free-form. It depends what my needs are. At first, after the thing, I would walk out to stock up on whatever I could find in the local towns. There's two within reasonable foot distance — Elum, which is about six miles away, and Noqualmi, a little further in the other direction. But those were both real small towns, and there's really nothing left there now. Stores, houses, they're all empty and stripped even if not actually burned down. This left me in a bit of a spot for a while but then, when I was walking back through the woods from Noqualmi empty-handed one afternoon, I spied a little gully I didn't think I knew. Walked up it, and realized there might be other sources I hadn't yet explored. Felt dumb for not thinking of it before, in fact.

So that's what I do some afternoons. This area wasn't ever home to so many vacation cabins or cottages, on account of the skiing never really took off and the winter here is really just bitter cold, instead of picturesque cold — but there are a few. I've found nine, so far. First half-dozen were ones where I'd done some handiwork at some point — like for the therapy woman — so they were easier to find. Others I've come upon while out wandering. They've kept me going on tinned vegetables, extra blankets. I even had a little gas stove for a while, which was great. Got right around the whole smoke problem, and so I had hot coffee all day long. Ran out of gas pretty soon, of course. Finding some more is a way up my wish list, I'll tell you, just below a new vacuum flask.

Problem is, those places were never year-round dwellings, and the owners didn't leave much stuff on site, and I haven't even found a new one in a couple weeks. But I live in hope. I'm searching in a semi-organized grid pattern. Could be more rigorous about it, but something tells me it's a good idea to leave open the possibility you might have missed a place earlier, that when you're finished you're not actually finished — that's it and it's all done and so what now?

Living in hope takes work, and thinking ahead. A schedule does no harm, either, of course. The lessons you learn at a parent's knee — or bent over it — have a way of coming back, even if you thought you weren't listening.

What I'm focusing on most of all right now, though, is building my stocks of food. The winter is upon us, there is no doubt, and the sky and the trees and the way the wind's coming down off the mountain say it's going to land hard and bed itself down for the duration. This area is going to be very isolated. It was that way before the thing, and sure as hell no one's going to be going out of their way to head out here now.

There's not a whole lot you can do to increase the chance of finding stuff. At first I would go to the towns, and I had some success there. It made sense that they'd come to sniff around the houses and bins. Towns were a draw, however small. But that doesn't seem to happen so much now. Stocks have got depleted in general and — like

I say — it's cold and getting colder and that's not the time of year when you think *hey, I'll head into the mountains.*

So what I mainly do now is head out back into the woods. From the back of the cabin there's about three roads you can get to in an hour or so's walking, in various directions. One used to be the main route down to Oregon, past Yakima and such. Wasn't ever like it was a constant stream of traffic, but that was where I got lucky the last two times, and so you tend to get superstitious and head back to the same place until you realize it's just not working anymore.

The first time was just a single, middle-aged guy, staggering down the middle of the road. I don't even know where he'd come from or where he thought he was going. This was not a man who knew how to forage or find stuff, and he was thin and half-delirious. Cheered right up when he met me.

The last time was better. A young guy and girl in a car. They hadn't been an item before the thing, but they were now. He believed so, anyway. He was pretty on the button, or thought he was. They had guns and a trunk full of cans and clothes, back seat packed with plastic containers of gasoline. I stopped them by standing in the middle of the road. He was wary as hell and kept his hand on his gun the whole time, but the girl was worn out and lonely and some folks have just not yet got out of the habit of wanting to see people, mixing with other humans once in a while.

I told them Noqualmi still had some houses worth holing up in, and that there'd been no trouble there in a while on account of it had been empty in months, and so the tide had drifted on. I know he thought I was going to ask to come in the car, too, but after I'd talked with them a while I just stepped back and wished them luck. I watched them drive on up the road, then walked off in a different direction.

Middle of that evening — in a marked diversion from the usual schedule, but I judged it to be worth it — I went down through the woods and came into Noqualmi via a back way. Didn't take too long to find their car, parked up behind one of the houses. They weren't ever going to last that long, I'm afraid. They had a candle burning, for heaven's sake. You could see it from out in the backyard, and that is the one thing that you really *can't* do. Three nights out of five, I could have got there and been too late already. I got lucky, I guess. I waited until they put the light out, and then a little longer.

The guy looked like he'd have just enough wits about him to trick the doors, so I went in by one of the windows. They were asleep. Worse things could have happened to them, to be honest, much worse. There should have been one of them keeping watch. He should have known that. He could have done better by her, I think.

Getting them back to the cabin took most of the next day, one trip for each. I left their car right where it was. I don't need a car. They're too conspicuous. He was kind of skinny, but she has a little bulk. Right now they're the reason why the winter isn't worrying me as much as it probably should. Them, plus a few others I've been lucky enough to come across — and yes, I do thank my luck. Sure, there's method in what I've done, and most people wouldn't have enjoyed the success rate I've had. But in the end, like my father used to say, any time you're out looking for deer, it's really luck that's driving the day. A string of chances and decisions that are out of your hands, that will put you in the right place at the right time, and brings what you're looking for rambling your way.

If I don't go out hunting in the afternoon then I'll either nap a while or go do a bit more sculpting. It only occurred to me to start that project a few weeks ago, and I'd like to get some more done before it starts to snow.

At first, after the thing, it looked like everything just fell apart at once, that the change was done and dusted. Then it started to become clear it didn't work that way, that there were waves. So, if you'd started to assume maybe something wasn't going to happen, that wasn't necessarily correct. Further precautions seemed like a good idea.

Either way, by 5:00 P.M. the light's starting to go and it's time to close up the day. I'll go out to the shed and cut a portion of something down for dinner, grab something of a plant or vegetable nature to go with it, or — every third day — open a can of corn. Got a whole lot of corn still, which figures, because I don't really like it that much.

I'll cook the meat over the day's third fire, straight away, before it gets dark, next to a final can of water — I really need to find myself another of those vacuum flasks, because not having warm coffee in the evening is what gets me closest to feeling down — and have that whole process finished as quick as I can.

I've gotten used to the regime as a whole, but that portion of the day is where you can find your heart beating, just a little. I grew up used to the idea that the dark wasn't anything to fear, that nothing was going to come and do anything bad to you — from outside your house, anyway. Night meant quietness outside and nothing but forest sounds, which — if you understood what was causing them — were no real cause for alarm. It's not that way now, after the thing, and so that point in the schedule where you seal up the property and trust that your preparations, and the wires, are going to do their job, is where it all comes home to you all over again. You recall the situation.

Otherwise, apart from a few things like the nature of the food I eat, it's really not so different to the way life was before. I understand the food thing might seem like a big deal, but really it isn't. Waste not, want not — and yes, he said that, too. Plenty other animals do it, and now isn't the time for beggars to be choosers. That's what we've become, bottom line — animals, doing what's required to get by, and there isn't any shame in that. It's all we ever were, if we'd stopped to think about it. We believed we had the whole deal nailed out pretty good, were shooting in some pre-ordained arc up to the sky.

Then someone, somewhere, fucked up. I never heard an explanation that made much sense. People talked a lot about a variety of things, but people always talked a lot, didn't they? Either way, you go past Noqualmi cemetery now, or the one in Elum, and the ground there looks like Swiss cheese. A lot of empty holes, though there are some sites yet to burst out, later waves in waiting.

Few of them didn't get far past the gates, of course. I took down a handful myself, in the early days.

I remember the first one I saw up here, too, a couple weeks after the thing. It came by itself, blundering slowly up the rise. It was night-time, of course, so I heard it coming rather than seeing anything. At first I thought it was someone real, was even dumb enough to go outside, shine a light, try to see who it was. I soon realized my error, I can tell you that. It was warmer then, and the smell coming off up the hill was what gave it away. I went back indoors, got the gun. Only thing I use it for now, as shells are at a premium. Everything else, I use a knife.

Afterward I had a good look, though I didn't touch it. Poked it with a stick, turned it over. It really did smell awful bad, and they're not something you're going to consider eating — even if there wasn't a possibility you could catch something off the flesh. I don't know if there's some disease *to* be caught, if that's how it even works, but it's a risk I'm not taking now or likely ever.

I wrapped the body up in a sheet and dragged it a long, long way from the property. Do the same with any others that make it up here from time to time. Dump them in different directions, too, just in case. I don't know what level of intelligence is at work, but they're going to have to try harder at it if they ever hope to get to me — especially since I put in the wires.

I have never seen any of them abroad during the day, but that doesn't mean they aren't, or won't in the future. So wherever I go, I'm very careful. I don't let smoke come out of my chimney, instead dispersing it out the doors and window — and only during the day.

The wires go through to trips with bells inside the cabin. Not loud bells — no sense in broadcasting to one of them that they just shambled through something significant.

The biggest danger is the shed, naturally — hence trying to make it airtight. Unlike just about everything else, however, that problem's going to get easier as it gets colder. There's going to come a point where I'll be chipping dinner off with a chisel, but at least the danger of smell leaking out the cracks will drop right down to nothing.

Once everything's secured for the night, I eat my meal in the last of the daylight, with the last hot cup of coffee of the day. I set aside a little food for the morning. I do not stay up late.

The windows are all covered with blackout material, naturally, but I still don't like to take the risk. So I sit there in the dark for a spell, thinking things over. I get some of my best ideas under those conditions, in fact — there's something about the lack of distraction that makes it like a waking dream, lets you think laterally. My latest notion is a sign. I'm considering putting one up, somewhere along one of the roads, that just says THIS WAY, and points. I'm thinking if someone came along and saw a sign like that, they'd hope maybe there was a little group of people along there, some folks getting organized, safety in numbers and that, and so they'd go along to see what's what.

And find me, waiting for them, a little way into the woods.

I'll not catch all of them — the smart guy in the car would have driven straight by, for example, though his girl might have had something to say on the subject — but a few would find my web. I have to think the idea through properly — don't know for sure that the dead ones can't read, for example, though at night they wouldn't be able to see the sign anyway, if I carve it the right way — but I have hopes for it as a plan. We'll see.

It's hard not to listen out, when you've climbed in bed, but I've been doing that all my life. Listening for the wind, or for bears snuffling around, back when you saw them up here. Listening for the sound of footsteps coming slowly toward the door of the room I used to sleep in when I was a kid.

I know the wires will warn me, though, and you can bet I've got my response to such a thing rigorously worked out.

I generally do not have much trouble getting off to sleep, and that's on account of the schedule. It keeps me active, so the body's ready for some rest come the end of day. It also gives me a structure, stops me getting het up about the general situation.

Sure, this life is not ideal. But, you know, it's not that different on the day-to-day. I don't miss the television because I never had one. Listening to the radio these days would only freak you out. Don't hanker after company because there was never much of that after my father died. Might have been nice if the Ramona thing had worked out, but she didn't understand the importance of the schedule, of thinking things through, of sticking to a set of rules that have been proven to work.

She was kind of husky and lasted a good long time, though, so it's not like there wasn't advantages to the way things panned out. I caught her halfway down the hill, making a big old fuss about what she'd found in the shed. She was not an athletic person. Wasn't any real possibility she was going to get away, or that she would have lasted long out there, without me to guide her. What happened was for the best, except I broke the vacuum flask smacking it down on the back of her head, which I have since come to regret.

Otherwise I'm at peace with what occurred, and most other things. The real important thing is when you wake up, you know what's what — that you've got something to do, a task to get you over the hump of remembering, yet again, what the world's come to. I'm lucky that way.

The sculpting's the one area I'd like to get ahead of. The central part is pretty much done — it's coming up for three feet high, and I believe it would be hard to get up through that. But sometimes, when I'm lying in the dark waiting for sleep to come, I wonder if I shouldn't extend that higher portion; just in case there's a degree of tunnelling possible, sideways and then up. I want to be sure there's enough weight, and that it's spread widely enough over his grave.

I owe my father a lot, when I think over it. In his way, through the things he said, he taught me a great deal of what it turned out I needed to know. I am grateful to him for that, I guess.

But I still don't want to see him again.

Substitutions

HALFWAY THROUGH UNPACKING the second red bag I turned to my wife — who was busily engaged in pecking out an email on her BlackBerry — and said something encouraging about the bag's contents.

"Well, you know," she said, not really paying attention, "I do try."

I went back to taking items out and laying them on the counter, which is my way. Because I work from home it's always me who unpacks the grocery shopping when it's delivered: Helen's presence this morning was unusual, courtesy of a meeting that had been put back an hour (the subject of the terse email currently being hammered out). Rather than standing with the fridge door open and putting items directly into it, I put everything on the counter first, so I can sort through it and get a sense of what's there, then stow everything neatly in the fridge organized by type/nature/potential meal groupings, as a kind of Phase Two of the unloading operation.

The content of the bags — red ones for stuff that needs refrigeration, purple for freezer goods, green for everything else — is never entirely predictable. My wife has control of the online ordering process, which she conducts either from her laptop or, in extremis, her phone. While I've not personally constructed the order, its contents are however seldom much of a surprise. There's an established pattern. We have cats, so there'll be two large bags of litter — it's precisely being able to avoid hoicking that kind of thing off supermarket shelves, into a trolley and across a busy car park which makes online grocery shopping such a boon. There will be a few green bags containing bottled water, sacks for the rubbish bins, toilet rolls and paper towel, cleaning materials, tins of store cupboard staples (baked beans, tuna, tinned tomatoes), a box of Diet Coke for me (which Helen tolerates on the condition that I never let it anywhere near our son), that kind of thing. There will be one, or at the most two, purple bags of frozen goods, holding frozen peas, frozen organic fish cakes for the kid, and so on. We never buy enough frozen food to fill more than one purple carrier but sometimes they split it between a couple, presumably for some logistical reason. Helen views this as both a waste of resources and a threat to the environment, and has sent at least two emails to the company on the subject. I don't mind much as we use the bags for clearing out the cats' litter tray, and I'd rather have spares on hand than risk running out.

Then there are the red bags, the main event. The red bags represent the daily news of food consumption — in contrast to the contextual magazine articles of the green bags, or the long-term forecasts of the purple. In the red bags will be the Greek yogurt, blueberries, and strawberries Helen uses to make her morning smoothie; a variety of vegetables and salad materials; some free-range and organic chicken fillets (I never used to be clear on the difference between the non-identical twin joys of organic and free range, but eleven years of marriage has made me better informed); some extra-sharp cheddar (Helen favors cheese that tastes as though it wants your tongue to be sad), and a few other bits and pieces.

The individual items may vary a little from week to week, but basically, that's what gets brought to our door most Wednesday mornings. Once in a while there may be substitutions in the delivery (when the supermarket has run out of a specified item, and one judged to be of near equivalence is provided instead): these have to be carefully checked, as Helen's idea of similarity differs somewhat from the supermarket's. Otherwise, you could set your watch by our shopping, if you'll pardon the mixed metaphor — and this continuity of content is why I'd turned to Helen when I was halfway through the second red bag.

Yes, there'd been spring onions and a set of red, green, and yellow peppers — standard weekly fare. But there were also two packs of brightly colored and fun-filled children's yogurts, and a block of much milder cheddar of the kind Oscar and I tend to prefer, plus a family pack of deadly-looking chocolate desserts. Not to mention a six-pack of thick and juicy-looking steaks, and a large variety pack of further Italian cured meats holding five different types of salami.

"Yum," I said.

I was genuinely pleased, and a little touched. Normally I source this kind of stuff — on the few occasions when I treat myself — from the deli or mini-market, which are both about ten minutes' walk away from the house (in opposite directions, sadly). Seeing it come into the house via the more socially condoned route of the super-market delivery was strangely affecting.

"Hmm?" Helen said. She was nearing the end of her email. I could tell because the speed of her typing increases markedly as she approaches the point when she can fire her missive off into space.

She jabbed SEND and finally looked up properly. "What's that you said?"

"Good shop. Unusual. But I like it."

She smiled, glad that I was happy, but then frowned. "What the hell's that?"

I looked where she was pointing. "Yogurts."

She grabbed the pack and stared with evident distaste at the ingredient list. "I didn't order those. Obviously. Or *that*." Now she was pointing at the pile of salamis and meats. "And the cheese is wrong. Oh, bloody *hell*."

And with that, she was gone.

I waited, becalmed in the kitchen, to see what would unfold. A quick look in the other bags — the greens and purples — didn't explain much. They all contained exactly the kind of thing we tended to order.

Five minutes later I heard the sound of two pairs of footsteps coming down the stairs. Helen re-entered the kitchen followed by the man who'd delivered the shopping. He was carrying three red bags and looked mildly cowed.

"What it is, right," he muttered, defensively, "is the checking system. I've told management about it before. There are flaws. In the checking system."

"I'm sure it can't be helped," Helen said, cheerfully, and turned to me. "Bottom line is that all the bags are correct except for the red ones, which belong to someone else."

When I'd put all the items from the counter back into the bags I'd taken them out of, an exchange took place. Their red bags for ours. The delivery guy apologized five more times — somehow making it clear, without recourse to words, that he was apologizing for the system as a whole, rather than any failure on his part — and trudged off back up the stairs.

"I'll let him out," Helen said, darting forward to give me a peck on the cheek. "Got to go anyway. You're all right unpacking all this, yes?"

"Of course," I said. "I always manage somehow."

And off she went. It only took a few minutes to unpack the low-fat yogurts, sharp cheese, salad materials, and free-range and organic chicken breasts.

* * *

A funny thing happened, however. When I broke off from work late morning to go down to the kitchen to make a cup of tea, I lingered at the fridge for a moment after getting the milk out, and I found myself thinking:

What if that had *been our food?*

I wasn't expressing discontent. We eat well. I personally don't have much of a fix on what eating healthily involves (beyond the fact it evidently requires ingesting more fruit and vegetables per day than feels entirely natural), and so it's a good thing that Helen does. If there's anything I want that doesn't arrive at our door through the effortless magic of supermarket delivery, there's nothing to stop me going out and buying it myself. It's not as if the fridge or cupboards have been programmed to reject non-acceptable items, or to set off a siren and contact the diet police when confronted with off-topic foodstuffs.

It was more that I got a sudden and strangely wistful glimpse of another life — and of another woman.

I was being assumptive, of course. It was entirely possible that the contents of the red bags I'd originally unpacked had been selected by the male of some nearby household. It didn't feel that way, however. It seemed easier to believe that somewhere nearby was another household rather like ours. A man, a woman, and a child (or perhaps two, we're unusual in having stopped at one). All the people in this family would be different to us, of course, but for the moment it was the idea of the woman which stuck in my head.

I wondered what she'd look like. What kind of things made her laugh. How, too, she'd managed to miss out on the health propaganda constantly pushed at the middle-classes (she *had* to be middle class, most people in our neighborhood are, and *everyone* who orders online from our particular supermarket has to be, it's the law) — or what had empowered her to ignore it.

We get steak every now and then, of course — but it would never be in the company of all the other meats and rich foods. One dose of weapons-grade animal fats per week is quite risky enough for this household, thank you. We live a moderate, evenly balanced life when it comes to food (and, really, when it comes to everything else). The shopping I'd seen conjured the idea of a household which sailed a different sea — and of a different kind of woman steering the ship.

I was a little intrigued, that's all.

A couple of days later, I was still intrigued. You'd be right in suspecting this speaks of a life in which excitement levels are low. I edit, from home. Technical manuals are my bread and butter, leavened with the occasional longer piece of IT journalism. I'm good at it, fast and accurate, and for the most part enjoy my work. Perhaps "enjoy" isn't quite the right word (putting my editing hat on for a moment): let's say instead that I'm content that it's my profession, am well-paid and always busy, and feel no strong desire to be doing anything else, either in general or particular.

But nobody's going to be making a movie of my life any day soon. Not even a French director would touch it.

And that's perhaps why, sometimes, little ideas will get into my head and stick around for longer than they might in the mind of someone who has more pressing or varied (or compelling) things to deal with on a day-to-day basis.

I was still thinking about this other woman.

This different girl.

Not in a salacious way — how could I be? I had no idea what she looked like, or what kind of person she was (beyond that indicated by her supermarket choices). That's the key word, I think — *difference*. Like any man who's been in a relationship for a long time (and doubtless a lot of women too, I've never asked), once in a while you beguile a few minutes in fantasy. Sometimes these are sexual, of course, but often it's something more subtle that catches your internal eye. I've never felt the urge to be unfaithful to Helen — even now our sex life has dropped to the distant background hum of the long-term married — and that's partly because, having thought it through, I've come to believe that fantasies are generally not about other people, but about yourself. What's *really* going on, if you spend a few minutes dreaming about living in a scuzzy urban bedsit with a (much younger) tattooed barmaid/suicide doll, or cruising some sunny, fuzzy life with a languid French female chef? These women aren't real, of course, and so the attraction cannot be bedded in them. They don't exist. Doubtless these and all other alternate lifestyles would come to feel everyday and stale after a while, too, and so I suspect the appeal of such daydreams actually lies in the shifted perception of yourself that these nebulous lives would enshrine.

You'd see yourself differently, and so would other people, and *that's* what your mind is really playing with: a different you, in a different now.

Perhaps that insight speaks merely of a lack of courage (or testosterone); nonetheless, the idea of this nearby woman kept cropping up in my mind. Perhaps there was also a creative part of my mind seeking voice. I don't edit fiction, and have never tried to write any either. I enjoy working with words, helping to corral them into neat and meaningful pens like so many conceptual sheep, but I've discovered in myself neither the ability nor the urge to seek to make them evoke people or situations which are not "true." With this imaginary woman, however — not actually imaginary of course, unless it was a *man*, it was more a case of her being "unknown" — I found myself trying to picture her, her house, and her life. I guess it's that thing which happens sometimes in airports and on trains, when you're confronted with evidence of other real people leading presumably real lives, and you wonder where everyone's going, and why: wonder why the person in the seat opposite is reading that particular book, and who they'll be meeting at the other end of the journey you're, for the moment, sharing.

With so little to go on, my mind was trying to fill in the gaps, tell me a story. It was a bit of fun, I suppose, a way of going beyond the walls of the home office in which I spend all my days. I'm sure I wouldn't have tried to take it further, if it hadn't been for the man from the supermarket.

A week to the day after the first delivery, he appeared on our doorstep again. This was a little unusual. Not there being another order — Helen considerately books the deliveries into the same time slot every week, so they don't disrupt my working patterns — but it being the same man. In the several years we've been getting our groceries in this way, I'm not sure I've ever encountered the same person twice, or at least not soon enough that I've recognized them from a previous delivery.

But here he was again.

"Morning," he said, standing there like a scruffy Christmas tree, laden with bags of things to eat or clean or wipe surfaces or bottoms with. "Downstairs, right?"

I stood aside to let him pass, and saw there were a couple more crates full of bags on the path outside. That meant I had a few minutes to think, which I suddenly found I was doing.

I held the door open while he came up, re-ladened himself, and tramped back downstairs again. By the time he trudged up the stairs once more, I had a plan.

"Right then," he said, digging into a pocket and pulling out a piece of paper. He glanced at it, then thrust it in my direction. "That's your lot. Everything's there. No substitutions."

Before he could go, however, I held up my hand. "Hang on," I said, brightly. "You remember last week? The thing with the red bags?"

He frowned, and then his face cleared. "Oh yeah. That was you, right? Got the wrong red bags, I know. I've spoken to Head Office about it, don't worry."

"It's not that," I said. "Hang on here a sec, if you don't mind?"

I quickly trotted downstairs, opened one of the kitchen cupboards and pulled out something more-or-less at random. A tin of corned beef – perfect.

Back up in the hallway, I held it out to the delivery guy. "I think this should have gone back into the other person's bags," I said. "I'm not sure, but my wife says she didn't order it."

The man took the can and peered at it unhappily. "Hmm," he said. "Thought most of the delivery goods was company branded. But it could be. Could be."

"Sorry about this," I said. "Didn't notice until you were gone. I… I don't suppose you remember where the other customer lived?"

"Oh yeah," he said. "As it happens, I do. Vans in this area only cover a square mile each day, if that. And I had to go through the bags with her, see, in case there was a problem with it, what with you already unpacking it here."

"Great," I said. His use of the word "her" had not been lost on me.

"She didn't say nothing about something missing, though," he said, doubtfully. He looked down at the tin again without enthusiasm, sensing that it represented a major diversion from standard practices that could only bring problems into his life. I looked at it too.

"Hang on," he said, as a thought struck him. He gave the tin to me. "Be right back."

I waited on the doorstep as he picked up the crates on the path and carried them back to his van. A couple of minutes later he reappeared, looking more optimistic.

"Sorted," he said. "As it happens, she's next but one on my list. I'll take it, see if it's hers."

I handed the corned beef back to him again, thinking quickly. I was going to need my house keys. Oh, and some shoes.

"Don't worry about bringing it back, if it's not," I said, to hold him there while I levered my feet into the pair of slip-ons which always live in the hallway.

This confused him, however. "But if it's *not* hers, then…I can't…"

"It's just I've got to go out for a while," I said. "Tell you what — if it's not hers, then just bring it back, leave it on the step, okay?"

I could see his thinking this was a bit of a pain in the neck — especially over a single tin of canned meat — but then realizing my solution meant less disruption and paperwork than the alternatives.

"Done," he said, and walked off down the path.

I ran to my study, grabbed the house keys from my shelf, and then back to the front door. I slipped out onto the step and locked up, listening hard.

When I heard the sliding slam of a van door, I walked cautiously down the path — making it to the pavement in time to see the delivery vehicle pull away.

There followed half an hour of slightly ludicrous cloak and daggery as I tried to keep up with the supermarket van without being seen. The streets in our neighborhood are full of houses exactly like ours — slightly bigger-than-usual Victorian terraces. Many of the streets curve, however, and two intersections out of three are blocked with wide metal gates, to stop people using the area as a rat route between the bigger thoroughfares that border it. The delivery driver had to take very circuitous routes to go relatively short distances, and bends in the streets meant that — were I not careful — it would have been easy for him to spot me in his side mirrors. Assuming he'd been looking, of course, which he wouldn't be — but it's hard to remind yourself of that when you're engaged in quite so silly an enterprise.

Keeping as far back as I could without risking losing him, I followed the vehicle as it traced a route that eventually led to it pulling up outside a house six or seven streets away from our house. Once he'd parked I faded back forty yards, and leaned on a tree. He'd said the stop I was interested in was not this one, but the next, and I judged him to be a person who'd use language in a precise (albeit not especially educated) way. He wouldn't have said "next but one" if he meant this house, so all I had to do was wait it out.

Whoever lived here was either catering for a party, or simply ate a lot, all the time. It took the guy nearly fifteen minutes to drag all the red, green, and purple bags up the path and into the house — where a plump grey-haired man imperiously directed their distribution indoors.

This gave me plenty of time to realize I was being absolutely ridiculous. At one point I even decided to just walk away, but my feet evidently didn't get the message, and when he eventually climbed back into the van and started the engine, I felt my heart given a strange double-thump.

She would be next.

I don't know if the delivery driver had suddenly realized he was behind schedule or something, but the next section of following was a lot tougher. The van lurched from the curb as though he'd stamped on the pedal, and he steered through the streets at a far brisker pace than before. I was soon having to trot to keep up — all the while trying not to get *too* close on his tail. I don't exercise very often (something I take recurrent low-level flak from Helen over), and before long I was panting hard.

Thankfully, it was only a few more minutes before I saw the van indicating, and then saw it abruptly swerve over to the curb again. The funny thing was, we were now only about three streets from my house. We were on, in fact, the very road I walked every morning when I strolled out to the deli to buy a latté to carry back to my desk — a key pillar in my attempts to develop something approaching a "lifestyle."

I waited (again, taking cover behind a handy tree) while the delivery man got out, slid open the van's side door, and got inside. He emerged a few minutes later carrying only three bags. They were all red, which I found interesting. No frozen food. No household materials. Just stuff to go straight in the fridge — and probably meats and charcuterie and cheeses that were a pleasure to eat, rather than foods that came on as if they were part of a gym workout.

There were only two front paths that made sense from where he'd parked, and I banked on the one on the right — sidling up the street to the next tree, in the hope of getting a better view.

I was right. The man plodded up the right-most path toward a house which, in almost every particular, was identical to the one in which Helen and Oscar and I lived. A three-storey Victorian house, the lowest a half-basement slightly below the level of the street, behind a very small and sloping "garden." I was confident this lower floor would hold a kitchen and family room and small utility area, just as ours did — though of course I couldn't see from my position across the street.

The man had the bags looped around his wrist, enabling him to reach up and ring the doorbell with that hand. After perhaps a minute, I saw the door open. I caught a glimpse of long, brown hair...

And then a sodding truck trundled into view, completely obscuring the other side of the street.

I'd been so focused on watching the house that I hadn't seen or even heard the vehicle's approach. It ground to a halt right in front of me, and the driver turned the engine off. A gangly youth hopped down out of it, busily consulting a delivery note and scanning the numbers of the houses on the side of the street where I was standing.

I moved quickly to the left, but I was too late. The supermarket delivery man was coming back down the path, and the door to the house was shut again.

"*Bollocks,*" I said, without meaning to.

I said it loudly enough that the delivery man looked up, however. It took a second for him to recognize me, but then he grinned.

"You was right," he called across the street. "Was hers after all. Cheers, mate. Job done."

And with that he climbed back into his van. I turned and walked quickly in the other direction, thinking I might as well go to the deli and get a coffee.

Maybe they could put something in it that stopped middle-aged men being utter, *utter* morons.

That evening Helen had an assignation with two old university friends. This is one of the few occasions these days when she tends to let her hair down and drink too much wine, so I made her a snack before she went out. After she'd gone, and Oscar had been encouraged up to bed (or at least to hang out in his bedroom, rather than lurking downstairs watching reality television), I found myself becalmed in the kitchen.

I'd got almost none of my work done that afternoon. Once the feelings of toe-curling embarrassment had faded — okay, so the supermarket guy had seen me on the street, but he'd had no way of knowing what I was doing there, no reason to suspect I was up to anything untoward — I'd found myself all the more intrigued.

There was the matter of the corned beef, for a start.

I knew damn well that there had been no error over it. I'd bought it myself, a month or two back, from the mini-market. I like some corned beef in a sandwich every now and then, with lettuce and a good slather of horseradish. I'd fully assumed the tin would make its way back to me. And yet, when presented with it, the woman had decided to claim it as her own.

I found this curious, even a little exciting. I knew that, had Helen been in a similar situation, she would have done nothing of the sort, even if the item in question had been totally healthy and certified GM-negative. This other woman had been given the chance to scoop up a freebie, however, and had said, "Yes, please."

Then there was her hair. It was infuriating I hadn't been given the chance to get a proper look at her, but in a way, the hair had been enough. Helen is blond, you see. Really it's a kind of very light brown, of course, but the diligent attentions of stylists keep it mid-blond. A trivial difference, but a difference all the same.

Trivial, too, was the geographical distance. The woman lived just three streets away. She paid the same rates, received cheery missives from the same local council, and would use — probably on a far more frequent basis than us — the services of the same take-away food emporiums. If she went into the center of London she'd use the same tube station. If it rained on our back garden, it would be raining on hers. The air I exhaled stood at least a chance of making it, some time later, into her lungs.

This realization did nothing to puncture the bubble which had started to grow in my head. I can't stress strongly enough that this was not a matter of desire, however nebulous. It was just interesting to me. Fascinating, perhaps.

Difference doesn't have to be very great to hold the imagination, after all. Much is made of men who run off with secretaries twenty years younger than their wives, or women who ditch their City-stalwart husbands to get funky with their dreadlocked Yoga teacher. Most affairs and marital breakages, however, do not follow this pattern. Helen and I knew four couples whose relationships had clattered into the wall of mid-life crisis, and all amounted to basically the same thing. Two men and two women had (in each case temporarily) set aside their partner for someone who was remark-ably similar. In one case — that of my old friend Paul — the woman he'd been having a semi-passionate liaison with for nine months turned out to be *so* similar to his wife that I'd been baffled on the sole occasion I'd met her (Paul soon had the sense to go back to Angela and the children, tail between his legs). Even Paul had once referred to the other woman by the wrong name during the evening, which went down about as well as you'd expect.

And this makes sense. Difference is difference, whether it be big or small, and it may even be that the smaller differences feel the most enticing. Most people do not want (and would not be capable of) throwing aside a lifetime of preference and predilection and taste. You are who you are, and you like what you like. Short of being able to have their partner manifest a different body once in a while, many seem to opt for a very similar body that just happens to have a slightly different person inside. A person of the same class and general type, but just different enough to trigger feelings of newness, to enable the sensation of experiencing something novel — to wake up, for a spell, the slumbering person inside.

Difference fades quickly, however, whereas love and the warmth of long association do not, which is why so many end up trudging right back to where they started out. Most people don't end up in liaisons with barmaids or artists or other exotics. They get busy with friends and co-workers, people living in the same tree. They don't actually want difference from the outside world.

They want it within themselves.

I realized, after mulling it over in the quiet, tidy kitchen for nearly an hour, that I wanted to be someone different too, however briefly.

So I went upstairs, told my son that I was popping out to post a letter, and went out into the night.

It was after nine by then, and dark. Autumnal, too, which I've always found the most invigorating time of year. I suppose it's distant memories of changes in the school or university year, falling leaves as an augur of moving to new levels and states of being within one's life.

I didn't walk the most direct route to the house, instead taking a long way around, strolling as casually as I could along the deserted mid-evening pavements, between lamps shedding yellow light. I was feeling…something. Feeling silly, yes, but engaged, too. This wasn't editing. This wasn't ferrying Oscar to and from school. This wasn't listening to Helen talk about her work.

The only person involved in this was me.

Eventually I found myself approaching the street in question, via one that met it at right angles. When I emerged from this I glanced up and down the road. It ended — or was interrupted — by one of the traffic-calming gates, and so was extremely quiet. There'd be little reason for anyone to use it unless they lived in one of the houses I could see.

I stood on the opposite side of the street and looked at the house where the woman lived, about twenty yards away now. A single light shone in its upper storey, doubtless a bedroom. A wider glow from the level beneath the street, however, suggested life going on down there.

My heart was beating rapidly now, and far more heavily than usual. My body as well as my mind seemed aware of this break in usual patterns of behavior, that its owner was jumping the tracks, doing something new.

I crossed the street. When I reached the other side I kept going, slowly, walking right past the house. As I did so I glanced down and to my right.

A single window was visible in the wall of the basement level, an open blind partially obscuring the top half. In the four seconds or so that it took me to walk past the house, I saw a large green rug on dark floorboards, and caught a glimpse of a painting on one wall. No people, and most specifically, not her.

I continued walking, right the way up to the gate across the road. Waited there a few moments, and then walked back the same way.

This time — emboldened by the continued lack of human

occupancy — I got a better look at the painting. It showed a small fishing village, or something of the sort, on a rocky coast. The style was rough, even from that distance, and I got the sense the artist had not been trying to evoke the joys of waterfront living. The village did not look like somewhere you'd go on holiday, that's for sure.

Then I was past the house again.

I couldn't keep doing this, I realized. Sooner or later someone in one of the other houses would spot a man pacing up and down this section of street, and decide to be neighborly — which in this day and age means calling the police.

I had an idea, and took my mobile out of my trouser pocket. I flipped it open, put it to my ear, and wandered a little way further down the street.

If anyone saw me I'd just be one of those other people you notice once in a while — some man engaged in some other, different life, talking to someone whose identity they'd never know, about matters which would remain similarly oblique. It would be enough cover for a few minutes, I thought.

I arranged it so that my meandering path — I even stepped off into the empty road for a spell, just to accentuate how little my surroundings meant to me, so engaged was I with my telephone call — gradually took me back toward the house. After about five minutes of this I stepped back up onto the curb, about level with the house's front path.

I stopped then, taken aback.

Someone had been in the lower room I could see through the window. She'd only been visible for a second — and I knew it was her, because I'd glimpsed the same long, brown hair from that morning — starting out in the middle of the room, and then walking out the door.

Was she going to return? Why would she have come into what was presumably a living room, then left again? Was she fetching something from the room — a book or magazine — and now settling down in a kitchen I couldn't see? Or was she intending to spend the evening in the living room instead, and returning to the kitchen for something she'd forgotten, to bring back with her?

I kept the phone to my ear, and turned in a slow circle. Walked a few yards up the street, with a slow, casual, leg-swinging gait, and then back again.

I'd gone past the point of feeling stupid now. I just wanted to see. When I got back to the pavement, I caught my breath.

The woman was back. More than that, she was sitting down. Not on the sofa — one corner of which I could just make out in the corner of the window — but right in the middle of the rug. She had her back to me. Her hair was thick, and hung to the middle of her back. It was very different in more than color to Helen's, who'd switched to a shorter and more-convenient-for-the-mornings style a few years back.

The woman seemed to be bent over, as if reading something laid out on the floor in front of her. I really, really wanted to know what it was. Was it *The Guardian,* choice of all right-thinking people (and knee-jerk liberals) in this part of North London? Or might it be something else, some periodical I'd never read, or even heard of? A book I might come to love?

I took another cautious step forward, barely remembering to keep up the pretense with the mobile phone still in my hand.

With my slightly-changed angle I could now see her elbows, one poking out from either side of her chest. They seemed in a rather high position for someone managing reading matter, but it was hard to tell.

My scalp and the back of my neck was itching with nervousness. I cast a glance either way up the street, just to check no one was coming. The pavements on both sides remained empty, distanced pools of lamplight falling on silence and emptiness.

When I looked back the woman had altered her position slightly, and I saw something new. I thought at first it must be whatever she was reading, but then realized first that it couldn't be, and soon after, what I was actually seeing. A plastic bag.

A red plastic bag.

Who unpacks their shopping in the living room? Other people do, I guess — and perhaps it was this connection to the very first inkling I'd had of this woman's existence (the temporary arrival of her food in the kitchen of my own house, in the very same kind of bag) that caused me to walk forward another step.

I should have looked where I was going, but I did not. My foot collided with an empty Coke can lying near the low wall at the front of the woman's property. It careered across the remaining space with a harsh scraping noise, before clattering into the wall with a smack.

I froze, staring down at her window.

The woman wrenched around, turning about the waist to glare up through her window.

I saw the red plastic bag lying on the rug in front of her, its contents spread in a semi-circle. She was not holding a newspaper or magazine or book. In one hand she held half of a thick, red steak. The other hand was up to her mouth, and had evidently been engaged in pushing raw minced beef into it when she turned.

The lower half of her face was smeared with blood. Her eyes were wide, and either her pupils were unusually large or her irises were also pitch black. Her hair started perhaps an inch or two further back than anyone's I had ever seen, and there was something about her temples that was wrong, misshapen, excessive.

We stared at each other for perhaps two seconds. A gobbet of partially chewed meat fell out of her mouth, onto her dress. I heard her say something, or snarl it. I have no idea what it might have been, and this was not merely because of the distance or muting caused by the glass of the window. It simply did not sound like any language I've ever heard. Her mouth opened far too wide in the process, too, further accentuating the strange, bulged shape of her temples.

I took a couple of huge, jerky steps backward, nearly falling over in the process. I caught one last glimpse of her face, howling something at me. There were too many vowels in what she said, and they were in an unkind order.

I heard another sound, from up the street, and turned jerkily and saw two people approaching, from the next corner, perhaps fifty yards away. They were passing underneath one of the lamps. One was taller than the other. The shorter of the two seemed to be wearing a long dress, almost Edwardian in style. The man — assuming that's what he was — had a pronounced stoop. In silhouette against the lamp light, both their heads were obviously too wide across the top.

I ran.

I ran away home.

I have not seen that supermarket man again. I'm sure I will eventually, but he'll doubtless have forgotten the corned-beef incident. Out there in the real world, it was hardly that big a deal.

Otherwise, everything is the same. Helen and I continue to enjoy a friendly, affectionate relationship, sharing our lives with a son who shows no real sign yet of turning into an adolescent monster. I work in my study, taking the collections of words that people send me and making small adjustments to them, changing something here and there, checking everything is in order and putting a part of myself into the text by introducing just a little bit of difference.

The only real alteration in my patterns is that I no longer walk down a certain street to get my habitual morning latté. Instead I head in the other direction and buy one from the mini-market instead. It's nowhere near as good, and I guess I'll soon go back to the deli, though I shall take a different route from the one that had previously been my custom.

A couple of weeks ago I was unpacking the bags from our weekly shop, and discovered a large variety pack of sliced meats. I let out a strangled sound, dropping the package to the floor. Helen happened to be in the kitchen at the time, and took this to be a joke — my expressing mock surprise at her having (on a whim) clicked a button online and thus causing all these naughty meats to arrive as a treat for the husband who, in her own and many ways, she loves.

I found a smile for her, and the next day when she was at work I wrapped the package in a plastic bag and disposed of it in a bin half a mile from our house. There's a lot you can do with chicken, and even more with vegetables.

Meanwhile, we seem to be making love a little more often. I'm not really sure why.

The Woodcutter

IT WAS A MISTAKE. Not his first mistake, but a big one. Spike knew it was. He could think of no other way of generating cash, however, and London — as he'd discovered soon after he arrived — was *not* a cheap place to live. It wasn't like he was even making so much. A couple of handfuls of pound coins in each pub, maybe thirty quid per venue. A hundred and fifty pounds a night, if he was lucky. Not chicken feed, but hardly easy money either — especially as he tried not to work the same patch night after night and so had to keep finding new areas and different pubs. Not to mention that, one evening in five, he would leave a place and find a couple of guys waiting for him outside, men who'd either threaten to beat him up unless he handed over his earnings (and then beat him up once they had the cash) or else get straight to beating him up while taking the money, as if to save time. Regardless of the methodology, being beaten up — and financial loss — were regular features of his evenings. He'd be forced to take a couple nights off afterward, to let facial swellings go down or allow time for his hands to start working fluently again, which also cut into his earning ability.

In the two months he'd been in the city he'd been lucky to clear five hundred a week. Try living in London, finding somewhere decent to sleep, something to eat — even for someone like Spike, who consumed little of substance — never mind incidental costs like dry cleaning your jacket to get the blood off, for that much. It's hard.

It's hard and cold and lonely.

During the day he walked the streets and killed time in parks. He dawdled in bookstores. He nursed an Americano for an hour at a time, choosing a different coffee shop each day, sitting outside despite the low winter temperatures, watching the streets. If you keep yourself clean and tidy and walk with apparent purpose then cities are accommodating, especially a city like London, for two thousand years a scrappers' den that has been willing to accept — or at least tolerate — just about anyone.

Can't find a job? Come to London and do our laboring and bar work. Home country having a meltdown and people starting to kill each other the whole time? Try a spell in London town. On the hunt for adventure, larks, and high times, and think you can ignore the rules?

Ah, maybe not that last one.

That had been the first mistake.

He kept an eye for others like him. Someone who might be willing to pass back the message that he'd realized the error of his ways, and was very sorry, and could he please come home now? He saw them once in a while but they were all very superior and took him in at a glance. They refused to have anything to do with him, focusing on their missions, gone for good the next day. He didn't know any of them from before and so he didn't understand how they could have tagged him as bad news so quickly, but he came to fear he'd been away so long now that he stood out, that something was beginning to fade, that if he was stuck here much longer he'd lose what made him different. He didn't know if that was even possible, but still the idea made him afraid.

He hadn't lost The Thing yet, however. He knew that because of the way he kept himself in food and lodging and — after he'd acquired the habit — cigarettes. He liked the look of smoking, he tried it, he kept doing it. Impulse control had never been his strong suit. At the end of each long afternoon he went back to his room. He'd found small, grimy lodgings off Goodge Street, more of a guest house than a hotel, cheap because it was not at all nice. It was close to the British Museum, though, another good place to kill time. It was also just around the corner from a large YMCA, and he stopped by its bar on the way out each evening. When he found himself in conversation with one of the young travellers boarding there — German, Italian, American, Eastern European, most nationalities were represented — he'd listen out for new venues to hit in the evening, though they'd almost always be heading for noisy trend-pits someone on Facebook had recommended, where Spike's shtick wouldn't work.

After a single drink at the Y, he'd get back out onto the streets and walk until he found an area he hadn't worked before. On the way home at the end of each night he walked down the alleyway, to check the door. He did this secretly, covertly, carefully — in case anyone was watching, testing him. He went in the period between 11:01 and 12:01, the correct time. He always approached humbly and with something he'd picked up that day — a dropped coin, a paper cup of collected rainwater, a blade of grass plucked from between paving stones.

None of it made a difference. The door was always there but it was never open. It might have been easier if it disappeared. If a door isn't there, then you can't hope to go through it, but if it's there but always locked, then you're trapped. Someone is keeping the door shut. Someone won't let you come back.

So now that he'd made his mistake, what the hell else was he supposed to do?

The days started to feel even longer.

* * *

Then one morning, in his tenth week, he came across the newsagent's. It was an unremarkable place, the sort of dingy little business you find on street corners in the center of London, selling celebrity magazines and cigarettes and quick sugar fixes to office workers. It was early and he was bleary from another night of bad sleep – he seemed to be dreaming more and more in recent weeks, cloudy visions of home that left him feeling empty and panicky – and found himself inside without noticing much about the place.

"Bad for you, you know," a voice said.

Spike looked up. He'd asked for what he wanted without even clocking the guy filling the space behind the counter. He saw a man who was tall and stooped and had a craggy face, with a harsh, hooked nose and sharp grey eyes. His hair was very thick and long, and his hands were extremely large. In one of these he was holding out the pack of Marlboro that Spike had asked for.

"Yeah," Spike said. "So I hear."

"I don't mean the cigarettes." The man never took his eyes off Spike's. "I mean this place."

Frowning, Spike handed over some hard-won coins and backed out of the shop. "I'll bear it in mind."

Back on the pavement he hesitated and looked back into the newsagent's. The man was still watching him. From here he looked far too large to be behind the counter. He lifted one arm and made an odd movement with it, bringing his hand down, then back up, and down and up again.

Spike walked quickly away, too tired and too early in the morning to deal with city weirdness.

It was a long and boring day but culminated in an unexpectedly good evening in a little patch near Charing Cross train station, pubs that were full of people killing time before going home, and already too drunk to realize what they were seeing was not a meticulously practiced fake, but the real thing. After performing for a table of jolly German businessmen, Spike received a tip of a fifty-pound note. Either the guy was too drunk to realize what he'd done, or — more likely — he was trying to impress a nearby table of shop girls by handing over high value tokens of exchange. It probably worked.

At nine thirty, Spike decided to call it a night and walked back up through Soho toward his "home." Without realizing until the last minute, he took a route that took him right by the newsagent he'd seen that morning.

The door was shut, but there was a light on inside. It was probably still open but there was nothing he needed, even if he'd felt like encountering the disconcerting man behind its counter again. He was almost past when he noticed something.

As with most such places there was a large grill obscuring the whole of the front window, holding well-secured examples of the newspapers and magazines for sale inside. At the bottom of this, sitting on the pavement, was something Spike hadn't seen that morning. A large cardboard box, containing a few rough cords of wood suitable for putting on an open fire.

"Firewood," a handwritten sign said.

Spike stared at it. Had it been there earlier? He didn't think so. Did people even *have* old-fashioned wood fires in houses in the middle of London anymore? Were they allowed to throw up that kind of pollution?

He went back a couple of paces to take a closer look. The sections of wood were raggedly sawn into one-foot lengths, and had then evidently split with an axe. It looked like silver birch. The papery bark seemed fresh. There was, at least under the streetlights, a slight sparkle to it. There was no price indicated.

Troubled in a way he couldn't put his finger on, Spike walked quickly home. He wanted to be inside so much that he didn't even bother to swing by the alleyway to check whether the doorway there was still locked.

He'd come to fear, perhaps, that it always would be.

Next morning he set off in a different direction. He spent much of the day walking up and down the embankment by the Thames. It was chilly and he needed regular coffees to keep him warm, but after the previous evening's earnings he didn't mind the expense too much.

He was still down by the river as darkness came at the end of the afternoon. His bones were cold and damp from a long day close to the slack grey river, and he felt tired and out of sorts. He considered simply going home, shutting the door, and climbing into bed with a book. Taking the evening off. Starting the next day fresh.

He knew himself well enough to know this was a bad idea, however. It was this kind of impulse that had gotten him here in the first place, a tendency to grow tired of one kind of life, of its hierarchies and constraints and rituals, and to think he could flip tracks. It didn't work. It hadn't worked because he was the same person over here as he'd been over there. Changing position doesn't change you: it may simply reveal you in a harsher light. Sometimes when Spike spent afternoons killing time in bookstores he wanted to go up and tap the shoulders of the people earnestly browsing the self-help section and tell them this fact, that they should give up on the idea of change and try to make friends with who they were before they did something dumb and fucked up what they had. Sure, you can leave your boyfriend or job or move house or go work for the disadvantaged in some hellhole or go on a freaky diet…but then what? Then nothing. It'll all be the same, except you can't go back. The door to the way things used to be will be locked.

Everything you do is a one-way street.

And so he wearily decided not to go home, but instead to go straight to work — and that's where he made his penultimate mistake.

* * *

He ended up working the same area he'd been in the previous night, something he'd always avoided doing before. It was right there on his route home from the embankment, though, just south of an oddly named road called The Strand, and what with it being a Friday night he reasoned that people in the pubs there were even more likely to be drunk and relaxed than the night before, and so his job should be easier. He at least had the sense to reverse the order, starting with the last pub he'd worked the previous night. Pubs have their schedules and routines and migratory patterns. Hopefully this way he'd encounter a different shift of punters than he had the night before.

This first was called the Star of Brunswick, a nice old place with lots of paneling and wooden benches. It wasn't too crowded yet, which was good. Having people on all sides made it impossible to play the angles. The same two barmaids were on duty. They recognized him. No surprise. Spike was good-looking and had The Thing. One big, dumb error he'd so far avoided was getting entangled with a girl in the city, however — and he intended to keep it that way. There are a lot of stories about what happens in those circumstances, and none end happily.

He drank a beer to loosen up and then got to work. Forty minutes later and twenty-eight pounds richer, he left and went to the next pub along the street. Again, he couldn't see anyone he recognized apart from the staff, and again, the session went well. His hands had warmed up and he moved on from coins and foam balls and started mixing in card tricks, too, wandering from table to table, enjoying — as always, and despite himself — the looks of bafflement and pleasure on people's faces.

Most of them, anyhow. Whenever you perform magic, especially in an informal setting like a pub, there will always be a few people (and they're always men) who won't smile and laugh and clap when they see the impossible, but scowl and shake their heads instead.

Guys who pride themselves on never allowing the wool to be pulled over their eyes, who have to be in control of their reality, who pride themselves as nobody's fool.

Spike pitied these people but he knew to be wary of them, too. It would be a man of this type who'd mutter something about thumb tips — having at some point spent time on the Internet learning just enough to ruin the illusion forever, which is apparently what they want — or who'd make a point of trying to make the angles difficult, coming around the side, or behind. There seemed to be a lot of them out tonight. Spike called his routine short in the second pub, and moved on after only fifteen minutes.

The next was better, but the fourth was much worse. As soon as he entered it, he spotted potential scowlers amongst a loose group of men and women in suits, all recently sprung from office jobs, starting their weekend by drinking hard and fast. Four female friends, already pretty drunk. Three men from a different company, a tight little predatory formation, smiling thin, brittle smiles and a little too ready to leap up and get the next round of drinks in hopes of finishing the evening with a grope in a cab or club or on the train back to commutersville.

Spike started on the other side of the pub but wasn't getting any traction and so wound up near the scowlers within five minutes, even though his spider-sense told him they'd be a tricky audience.

"It's up his sleeve!" one of the men shouted, before Spike had even embarked on his first trick.

Spike made a big, slow performance of removing his jacket and hanging it over the back of a nearby chair, revealing he was wearing a tight T-shirt underneath, no sleeves, of course — his standard response to this kind of heckling. It got a giggle from the girls but he knew immediately it had only been half-smart. Two of the women started ogling his body rather obviously, and all three men (only in their late twenties, Spike guessed, but already running to seed) might as well have had the words "We hate you even more now" written across their faces.

He soldiered on, running a few basic coin routines and disappearing a handkerchief. The girls lapped it up. The men scowled. One went out front of the pub to have a cigarette and on his return made a point of standing to the side of Spike, evidently hoping to be able to catch him palming. Usually if this happened, Spike took it as a sign it was time to leave. The girls were still loving it, however — and being free with the pound coins, too, pressing a few upon him after every trick rather than waiting to given him something at the end as was usual. Spike was aware they were doing this as if he was a male stripper at a hen night, and that this was likely to antagonize the males in the group yet further, but found he didn't care. He realized he was tired of the stupid people in this city, in this entire land. He wanted to call it a night. He wanted to go home. But *really* home. Not back to his shitty room and its grey promise of doing all this again tomorrow.

"Yeah yeah, it's fabulous, mate," one of the men said, the one who'd make the first quip about Spike's sleeve. "Very fucking clever. You should go on *X Factor* or something. But we were talking, okay? Run along now."

Spike smiled. "Fair enough. Just one more, though, okay? You'll like this one."

The man rolled his eyes and looked like he wanted to enter an altercation, to get tough in the hope of impressing the womenfolk, but one of the others — the man who'd gone out for a cigarette — held up his hand.

"Go on, then," he said. "Amaze me."

I couldn't amaze you, you bastard, Spike thought, *you're too dead for that.* He had the sense not to say this out loud, but not enough sense to stop what he did next.

He got one of the girls to pick a card, write her name on it — which was Karen — and return it to the pack. He then involved the entire group in shuffling, cutting, messing the deck around, producing the card as if by accident a couple of times, as a prelude to the real trick —

and then had Karen tear it into four pieces. He put everything into the performance, being as charming as possible, turning The Thing up to the max, and even the guys were getting into it. Two of them, anyway — the guy who'd demanded to be amazed was sitting back, watching, his beady little eyes on everything Spike did.

Spike ran the routine round the houses, stretching it out, and then set up the big reveal — getting the Karen girl to close her eyes and pick a card from the pack at random.

She turned it over, clearly expecting it to be the one she'd written her name on... but it wasn't.

Everyone looked confused. One of the guys laughed harshly. "Fucked it up, haven't you mate."

Spike held up his finger for silence.

"I *may* have," he admitted, tentatively. "Magic's unpredictable. But sometimes... sometimes something else happens. Sometimes the magic does its own thing. Now usually... yeah, usually, that card you picked should be your card, madam."

"Madam?" shrieked one of the other girls, and the table laughed. "She's a *right* madam!"

"Sometimes, though," Spike said, "sometimes the card slips into the future. It shows us what it *thinks* is going to happen. Or *could* happen, maybe. And..."

He hesitated, turned to the "Amaze me" man, who was still sitting back in his chair, arms folded, still unimpressed. "You feeling comfortable, mate?"

"What?"

"Just wondered. You're sitting a bit awkwardly."

The man opened his mouth to make fun, but then seemed to realize that he *did* feel uncomfortable. He adjusted the way he was sitting.

"Thought so," Spike said, nodding. "Feel a little tight around the... well, I don't know how to put it. Around the *private* regions? Do you? That what it is?"

The group sniggered — even the other two guys. Five or six people from other tables had joined the crowd now, too, standing in a ring around them.

"Maybe something got stuck down there," Spike said, and by now there was no humor in his voice. It was soft, considered, serious. "Maybe you should check."

"Check what?"

"That everything's okay. Go on — stick your hand down there. Down your trousers. Won't be the first time today, I'll bet."

More laughter from the girls, and a couple more people drifted over from a nearby table. Amaze Me was glaring angrily at Spike now, no longer wanting to be the center of attention but knowing that something was up.

"Twat," he muttered, but then — making a show of how jolly okay he was with doing it — he stuffed his hand down the front of his suit trousers. "Happy now?"

Then he frowned, and withdrew his hand much more slowly. It re-emerged holding a folded-up playing card.

The others around the table fell silent.

"Ah. That'll be the problem," Spike said, cheerfully. "Like to open it for me? Tell your future?"

The man unfolded the card. Stared at it for a long, pregnant moment, and then threw it down on the table.

It landed face up, the girl's signature obvious for everyone to see. "There you go," Spike said, into the stunned silence. "Looks like maybe you *will* get Karen in your pants tonight after all."

The crowd's reaction was…very big.

Spike held out his collecting bag and listened to coins raining into it. He kept his eyes on the man he'd just embarrassed, and by now Spike was smiling again.

"Amazed yet?" he said, and winked.

* * *

He left the pub immediately afterward, walking up the street and around a couple of corners to his next intended venue. As soon as he got inside, however, he realized he was done for the night. This pub was virtually empty, the atmosphere dead. That could actually be the best environment for what he did, when he had the energy to create the mood himself: right now, he did not.

He got a pint of strong beer and went and sat in the quietest corner. If he was finished for the night, he should go home. He didn't want to. Going home meant going past the alleyway with the doorway and finding he couldn't really go home. His room wasn't home.

For the first time in weeks he wondered whether there was anything else he could try. There must be places in this city where people like him collected. Meeting points. Notice boards. Ways of getting in contact. Not everyone came here on solo missions. He'd heard rumors of sleepers, too, who lived here for longer periods in case of urgent need of mobilization. Not spying, but spies all the same. The problem was that he didn't know any of them, or where they might be. If he'd thought this through properly before he came, then he could have tried to see if there was any lore on the subject, something specific to London (though of course if he'd thought it through properly before he came, he *wouldn't have come*). None of the books he'd pored over in shops and libraries here contained anything beyond old, mangled superstitions. Hampstead Heath had nothing. It was dead under all of the Thames bridges. The remaining scrap of the Stone of London — wedged into a nondescript wall in The City — no longer had any power at all.

It was like being in a dream where you can't wake up. A dream in which you've left your home, having come to despise it, but then realize — with the heart-piercing intensity you only get in dreams — that you were wrong.

The first pint was followed by another, and one more. He lost count after that, but he was still sitting in his corner in a now-empty pub when the gangly Australian barman called time. By then Spike's mood was atrocious, and half of that was knowing how stupid he'd been in the previous pub. The way he earned his living was precarious. If he blew it, he was in very serious trouble. He couldn't do anything else. He'd have no money. He'd be wholly lost.

"Finish up and piss off," the barman said, when he came by the table for the third time.

Spike looked up. The man took a hurried step back. "Seriously, it's gone time, mate," he muttered, then retreated behind the counter.

Spike finished his last half-pint in one swallow and got unsteadily to his feet. As he wove his way past the bar he saw something sparkling on the floor, and bent down to pick up a ten-pence piece.

"See a penny, pick it up," the barman said.

Spike nodded, but only to himself. He slipped the coin into his back pocket and lurched toward the door.

They were waiting for him ten feet away down the street. They must have been there a while because they looked cold and impatient. Men with real courage might have come inside the pub to find him, but these were not that kind.

"Hello, magic boy," the first one said.

Spike half-turned back toward the pub, but he'd already heard the barman locking up from the inside. The three men were walking closer to him now.

"Look," he said.

"No," one of the other men replied. "We've done enough looking, thanks very much. Completely manked our evening, you did. Any one of us could be screwing any one of those birds by now, if you hadn't fucked it up."

"It was just a little magic," Spike said.

"No," said one of the others.

It was the man who'd gone out for a cigarette, the man who'd told Spike to amaze him. He'd gone around behind while Spike was concentrating on the pair in front.

"My uncle used to piss about with magic," he said. "Boring cunt, he was, but he wasn't bad at the tricks. Tried to teach me, too, so I know how it works. I know the tricks. But what you were doing *wasn't* tricks, was it?"

Spike eyed him cautiously. "I don't know what you mean." He could see the other two men didn't understand either. "Of course it was tricks. I'm a magician."

"I don't know what you are," the man said, thoughtfully. "But you're clever. I caught you using a thumb tip early on, but I didn't say anything because the way you used it was... weird. It was like you didn't actually need it. Couple of the things with the coins looked dodgy too."

"What's a thumb tip?" one of the others asked. The man ignored him.

"But then that last trick," he said. "That's when I knew for sure. That was impossible."

Spike tried to laugh it off. "It's just practice, mate, that's all."

Amaze Me shook his head. "No. There's no misdirection in the world could have pulled that off. You never came anywhere near me. You fucked up. That was actual magic."

"I have no idea what you're talking about," Spike said, trying to laugh it off, "but it's time for me to go home."

He started backing away but he was too drunk, and the men had missed out on what they'd believed was a trio of easy shags, and had no intention of going home without a fight as recompense.

Suddenly all three were in fast movement.

Just before he passed out, his head in the road, gasping from another kick in the stomach, Spike saw a black cat sitting in the shadows on the other side of the street. For a moment its eyes looked a sharp grey, and then something stranger seemed to happen. It raised one of its paws off the ground and dropped it, raised it once more and dropped it again, in a chopping motion.

Spike lost consciousness a split second later, however, so this could just have been his imagination.

He made it to the alleyway. The door was locked, of course. He knelt down in front of it, resting his bruised cheek against the coldness of its battered surface. It was soothing. For a moment he thought he could smell something through the keyhole, the scent of fresh new grass warming in spring sunlight.

He fumbled in his pocket, wincing against the pain in his fingers, and found the ten pence he'd picked up earlier. He wedged it into a crack in the old brickwork.

"I found a penny," he whispered, "and picked it up. All I want is a little luck. I'm sorry. I messed up. Don't leave me here. Let me come home. Please."

Nothing happened. Eventually he hauled himself laboriously to his feet and went home.

He couldn't work the next day, or the one after that. He spent the weekend in bed, staring at the wall. He didn't eat. Late on Sunday afternoon he walked far enough to get a coffee. It made him feel sick. He returned to his room and went back to bed. He dreamed of forest clearings and hills covered in clover. He dreamed of mountains sparkling in harsh moonlight. He woke in the middle of the night to find his face wet with tears.

When he woke on Monday morning, however, and experimentally waggled his fingers, he found that — while painful — they moved well enough. Probably he should take another day off, but he didn't want to. It wasn't even about the money. It was about a dumb and stupid plan that had grown in his mind over the weekend.

Unlike most of his mistakes, he acknowledged this one was dumb and stupid right from the start. He didn't care.

He got dressed. He went out onto the streets. He walked to the nearest café and ate what he could. He'd long ago found that most things here disagreed with him, and so he did not order eggs or bacon or sausage, though all smelled good. He had a piece of toast, no butter — which also made him feel nauseous — and a stewed tomato. The tomato tasted like hot water. The bread like old leaves.

He walked into Soho, not thinking much. He walked past the newsagent's and noticed that the box of firewood outside was much fuller now. The new logs looked fatter than the first lot he'd seen, as if chopped from a different tree.

Spike's arms and legs felt stiff, but he kept walking, and walking, focusing his thoughts, until the light began to fade and the night rolled into the streets like a thick, dark fog coming up off the river.

Then he changed direction and headed down toward the little nest of pubs down by Charing Cross.

It was a long-shot, he knew that. Not a total one — people tend to be habitual, when it comes to pubs — but the kind of men who go to the pub after work on Friday won't necessarily be there on a Monday, too. He had no other lead, however, and he'd come to understand the culture of London workers well enough (and seen the beginnings of a beer gut on each of the men) for it to be worth a try.

He didn't go to that particular pub first. He'd be too early. It was only five o'clock. He went to the last one, the pub where he'd been drinking at the end by himself. It was fuller than it had been then, and the same man was behind the bar. Spike walked up to the counter and waited his turn. When the barman got to him, he paused a moment, looking at the bruises on Spike's face.

"That coin didn't bring much luck, by the look of it."

"Not yet," Spike said. "Did you know what was happening to

me? On the street outside your pub?"

The barman shook his head.

"Really? Didn't hear raised voices?"

"No, mate," he said, and turned away. He was lying, and Spike knew it, and for a moment wanted to reach out and touch him. But he did not. He'd spent the day charging up. He wasn't going to waste it.

He knew four drinks were too many, but they went down so quickly. It didn't matter. He felt totally in control as he left the pub and walked up the street.

Long shot or not, when he glanced in through the window of the next pub he saw two of the men inside. They were at a table in the corner, deep in conversation. Reliving the glories of their Friday night, perhaps.

Spike smoked a cigarette as he watched. Beer and cigarettes and coffee. Maybe he was adapting to this environment after all. Perhaps the only thing holding him back was a feeling of control. He'd been very good, never once stepped out of line. Never broken any of the rules except for the way in which he earned a living.

Maybe *that* was a mistake.

It was too cold to stay out there. Spike went in the pub, keeping out of the men's line of sight. It was easy, as this pub was very full. People moved out of his way, unconsciously, aware of something passing by them that they wanted to avoid, without having the least idea what it might be.

He stood to one side of a pillar, watching. Both men had only a couple of swallows left in their pints. Hopefully they'd stand to leave and he could follow them outside. If not, he'd wait. They'd waited for him on Friday. He'd do the same for them tonight.

That's what he'd thought, anyway, but when the Amaze Me man knocked back the rest of his beer and got up and came over toward the bar, Spike felt his resolve disappear.

He stepped back out of sight, monitoring the man's progress at the counter, trying to keep his breathing even. His hands were trembling so much that he had to keep them down by his side. When the man turned from the bar with a pint in each hand, Spike altered position so that he couldn't see his face as he passed by. The man moved quickly, in his element, keen to get back to his table and whatever bullshit he and his friend were merrily spouting back and forth, but he left a trail nonetheless, a stench that Spike had grown weary — so incredibly weary — of trying to ignore. These horrific creatures, their skins so sallow and without sparkle, none of them even touched with The Thing, pieces of perambulating meat, endlessly procreating as if in a futile spell against the stinking death coming toward each and every one of them. It was as if Spike had trapped himself in a vast abattoir.

He waited for the man to get seated and then walked over. He stood to one side of the table, saying nothing. Just waiting.

The men jabbered on to each other, voices raised against the hubbub, their eyes glittering not with magic but superficial cheer. Spike noticed both had scrapes on their knuckles, marks of contact with his face and body. They were in a much better state than Spike's hands, however: Amaze Me had made a point of stamping on both. Only the man's haste had allowed Spike to escape without fists full of broken bones — that and the fact that Spike's limbs were made of strong stuff, firm trunks and twigs that were too vital and subtle to be snapped so easily.

At that moment the man glanced up. He saw Spike standing there looking down at him, head cocked a little to one side like a bird of prey.

There was a flicker in the man's eyes.

The other man caught the frisson, and looked up too. "Fuck you doing here?" he said. Spike didn't say anything. "Seriously — did you not get the fucking message?"

"I'm sure he did," Amaze Me said, in a more judicious tone.

Either he was smarter than his friend or just more cautious. He evidently realized that if you and your friends beat the shit out of a man, and he then makes the effort to come track you down a couple of nights later, you've got a situation on your hands.

"Probably just working this pub again, right? Earning a few quid to keep him in beer money."

Spike said nothing.

"Thing is, like I told you," the man went on, "I don't like magic. So here." He reached into his pocket and pulled out a five-pound note. He held it toward Spike. "Let's just take the silly tricks as read, and you can fuck off, eh?"

Spike took the note and altered his position so he had his back to the rest of the pub, which was becoming yet more crowded. "Five quid," he said. "That's very generous. But I've got to do a trick for you, okay? Magician's code — where I come from, anyway. If you're paid, you play."

"Look, mate, just fuck off," said the other guy.

Amaze Me kept looking up at Spike. It seemed as though he realized this was an encounter that was going to need defusing in a measured way. He and his colleague were both still seated, for a start, with Spike looming over them. If the pretty boy with the magic tricks decided to start a fight, he had a clear advantage.

"Go on then," he said, magnanimous and tough at the same time. "But remember — I've got good eyes."

"You do," Spike said. "So watch carefully."

He held out his right hand. His fingers ached, but they were fluent enough to roll the five-pound note into a perfect tube. He took his time over it, getting it tight.

"So?" the other man said.

"So," Spike said. He squatted by the table and held his hands up so he was gripping the two-inch tube of rolled bank note horizontally between the thumb and index fingers of both hands, other fingers held out high.

"I want you both to be able to see this very clearly," Spike said. "I want there to be no doubt. You've got to watch the note very carefully now, okay? You've got to be eagle-eyed."

Amaze Me was intent on being just that. His gaze was locked on the note.

"That's it," Spike said. "Perfect."

He left a long, long beat…and then made the note disappear. Both men were in a position to clearly see that neither of his hands moved at all. The note simply vanished into thin air.

"Fuck," one of them said, despite himself.

"Did you see that?" Spike asked. "Did you really, really see it?"

"We saw it, you freak," Amaze Me said.

"Good," Spike said, and then, with sudden grace, he turned both his hands palm out and wiped one gently down across the eyes of each man, at the same time, as if closing the eyes of sitting corpses.

Amaze Me's mouth dropped open, as he realized that he couldn't see. That, though his eyes were open and staring, he was wholly blind.

The other man lurched to his feet, flailing around with his fists. "What have you done?" he shouted. "I can't fucking see. I can't fucking see *anything!*"

Amaze Me was blinking frantically now, rubbing his eyes with his fists, craning his head around, trying to do anything that might make a difference.

"Stop it," he said, to Spike. "Turn it off. Look, I'm sorry, all right? But turn it off."

"Can't," Spike said. "The big problem with life, I've come to see, is there's never any going back."

"Please," the man said. "I'm sorry."

He looked afraid but not afraid enough, and Spike decided he might as well go for broke. A lot of people were watching now.

He held both his hands to chest height, and then quickly snapped them into fists.

There were four quiet but irrevocable little popping sounds as two pairs of eyeballs burst, spurting glops of viscous liquid, and blood, out onto the table.

Spike turned and walked quickly out of the pub, to the sound of a lot of people screaming.

He wasn't entirely surprised to see the black cat sitting waiting on the opposite side of the street. This time, when it ran off, he was in a position to follow.

He lost sight of the cat at the bottom end of Soho, but it didn't matter. He knew where he was going next, and he hoped he knew what the appearance of the cat had meant. It hadn't crossed his path, after all.

As he ran into the alley he held up his hand and unvanished the five-pound note. Found money was always an appropriate offering, and now he'd finally shown he wasn't safe to be left languishing here. Maybe that'd been his error all along, he hoped. Maybe he'd been trying too hard to fit in, to keep his head down, to pretend to be like everyone else in this hellhole. What better way to punish him for leaving his own land than to strand him here? Surely what he'd just done *proved* that they had to do something else instead, to let him come home?

His heart was beating hard as he approached the end of the alleyway, money held out.

Then it gave a harsh double-thud.

The door was gone.

He blinked at the space in the wall where it had been for night after night after night, utterly confused, wondering if he'd somehow come down the wrong street.

But no, there was the old, ragged poster for a gay dance night at a venue that he knew had recently been torn down. And there, where he'd left it wedged into a crack in the brickwork, was the ten-pence coin from Friday night. And there was a faint smear of what he knew to be his own dried blood, from when he'd rested his face against the door. No door there now, though. Just wall.

Was there still a handle on the other side? Over where the air was sweet and fresh and the blades of grass sang songs every morning? Where the food did not make you feel sick, but whole? Where his kind went about their business and lived their endless lives, only slipping over into this hollow world when the King or Queen commanded it, to make little interventions into people's lives, keeping the universe spinning and the spheres aligned?

"There are other doors," a voice said.

Spike turned to see that a figure now stood at the entrance of the alleyway. Tall but stooped, with long, shaggy hair and beard and a big, hooked nose.

The man from the newsagent's.

He held up his hand. Dangling off one huge finger, Spike saw, was a large bunch of keys. The edges of the big, silver keys glinted in cold moonlight.

"Come," the man said. "It's time."

Believing that at last his fate had been reversed, and not realizing that in his other hand, the one behind his back, the tall man held an axe, Spike hesitated but then walked up the alley toward him.

That was his final mistake.

The big man with the grey, sad eyes waited until Spike was within a couple of yards. Then he was in sudden, terrible motion, raising the old, notched axe high above his head — and then with a chop, chop, chop, the magician was dead.

Dead and afterward meticulously dismembered, his limbs severed one from another in the quiet of the newsagent's, and then left out in the tiny yard behind it — a scrap of space lost and invisible in the shadowed depths of high, old buildings around — so that cold moonlight might fall on them, after the old methods, turning Spike's body into lengths of dry wood which the woodcutter tied into neat bundles and added to the pile in the box out in front of his shop the following morning.

If you ever see such wood for sale, do not buy it. The bundles look pretty, but do not burn well. They look a lot like short sections of silver birch.

Everything You Need

SHEILA SUPPOSED THEIR MARRIAGE had been old-fashioned right from the start. They met in 1961 and married in 1963, a year which now sounded — and felt, sometimes, though not always — an awfully long time ago; but even back in those dim and distant days the world had been changing. Women had begun to quietly reassess and realign their roles in the home and the workplace. "Quietly" was how women had most often done things in those days. It worked, too. Nobody likes being shouted at. Sometimes a soft voice gets heard far more clearly.

She and John had been perfectly well aware of the changes in society, and paid due attention. On the other hand...their way worked. He was cheerfully useless in the kitchen. Sheila was a decent cook and a whizz at keeping the place clean and tidy. He pitched in with both from time to time, but it was a chore for him and a pleasure for her, so what was the point of reversing roles for the sake of it?

Likewise with the children, and the washing and ironing. Yes, you could insist these household tasks be shared evenly — just as he could have insisted that, once the children were old enough, she go out and get a job — but neither felt the need, any more than Sheila fancied going without a bra.

Doing what the new people tell you, for the sake of it, is surely no more sensible than doing what the old people had said, for the sake of that. The traditional division of labor worked for them, and once both had realized this, they let it be, with some relief.

Not that she'd been the little wife indoors — far from it. She drove, of course (though he kept track of the car's service records, and when it needed an MOT). She was the one who dealt face-to-face with plumbers or electricians when something in the house needed fixing (though it was John who filed the maintenance contracts, and could lay his hand on them when required). He knew where the bank statements were, the mortgage agreement, receipts for major household expenses like furniture and white goods; he knew whom the car was insured with, who held their medical insurance, what it covered and what it did not, and how much they were paying each month for any number of other things and services, and to whom, and which were on direct debit, and how on earth that worked.

She fretted from time to time that it was ridiculous she didn't know any of these details, but just handed it all over to him. Usually this concern stayed within her own head but sometimes she would articulate it. He'd shrug and say it was all boring stuff and he had a system and there was no point both of them wasting time and energy over it when there were more interesting discussions to be had and cups of tea to make and long walks down country lanes to enjoy together.

Whenever some household matter required clarification or resolving, he'd quickly and easily find whatever document was needed. Afterward he'd put it back in its designated drop file and push the drawer shut. If she happened to be nearby, he'd smile at her.

"Remember," he'd say, "everything you need — it's in here."

* * *

"Here" was the three-drawer filing cabinet that stood in the middle of the wall of the upstairs room John used as an occasional office. In the days after he died, this was the room Sheila found most difficult to traverse. It had nothing to do with her. It had been his, just as the kitchen had been hers. She felt like a tourist in his office, with neither local currency nor any understanding of the language. When they'd gone on holidays to France as a family, it was her schoolgirl French that got them fed and into hotel rooms: John limited his input to standing in the background looking affable. In the office, however, she couldn't even say her name.

She found it particularly hard when confronted with some aspect of the process of death that required documentary evidence. "John dealt with all that," she'd say, feeling old and small and stupid. Fiona didn't actually roll her eyes, but you could tell she wanted to. Fiona had been climbing the corporate ladder — with some success — since the age of eighteen. She had a spreadsheet for everything and backed them up to the "cloud," whatever that was. She didn't understand that a way of being had existed between her parents, a tacit agreement, or that her mother's lack of engagement with ten thousand pieces of household management over the decades demonstrated neither lack of will nor intelligence, nor a failure of fealty to the sisterhood — but had just been the way things worked.

John would have known what the cloud was. He wouldn't have used it — he believed in bits of paper, documents you could touch and hold (and wave imperiously at someone, if required) — but he would have at least brought it within his ken. Sheila was slowly starting to realize that, when it came to the administration of the life she'd lived and now had to keep on living, her ken was entirely empty.

Each time this happened Fiona would dart up to the little office and open the filing cabinet and quickly track down whatever document was needed.

"Say what you like," she'd say, returning in triumph. "Dad's systems worked. It's all in there."

"Everything I need," her mother muttered, quietly.

"What?"

"Nothing," she said, and put the kettle on again.

The funeral came and went, a somber train arriving out of darkness to pause in a station for a couple of hours before pulling smoothly back out into the fog, never to return. Sometime during the following night a team of invisible workers came and removed all the track, abandoning Sheila on a platform from which there was no way forward or back.

Friends came to visit. So did Fiona, every day. Sometimes with her husband, occasionally with her children. Neither of these seemed to know how to deal with a grandma who was now no longer always smiling as she bustled around a kitchen filled with steam; and Mark — whom Sheila privately thought was okay, though no John — stood around looking as if he could hear unanswered emails mounting up on his phone.

After the second week their visits tailed off, but Fiona kept popping in. She was a good daughter. She had a little of both parents in her, of course, and was unconsciously compensating for her father's absence.

Sheila didn't miss her husband's efficiency, however. She missed him.

She missed the man.

After ten days Fiona brought up the idea of going to Brighton. "You always liked it there, Mum," she said. "I'll come with you. I could do with a break and it'll do you good to get out of this house. We could have tea at The Grand."

She must have seen how horrified the idea made her mother. "I know it'll be weird, without Dad," she added, quickly. "But you have to start making new memories. He wouldn't have wanted you to just stop living."

But Sheila didn't want new memories. The idea of them made her furiously sad. What possible use could they be, if she couldn't share them with John? What would she do with such memories? What would they be *for?*

Fiona dropped the subject, but three days later mentioned it again, in passing, careful to move the conversation on quickly afterward. Her mother knew she was being "managed" now, that the tactic was to drip-feed her until the idea became lodged, and came to seem reasonable, less of a denial of how the world had once stood. John had tried something similar with Sheila a few times, back in the early days. She had firmly put him right over it. He'd never tried it again. Fiona had yet to learn, evidently, that people aren't as dim as you think they are, and that taking over her father's role wasn't as simple as downloading a backup of him from the cloud.

After Fiona had left, Sheila went and sat in her chair in the living room.

She had never realized how loudly the clock ticked.

The next morning a man called from the mobile phone company. He had an Indian accent but said his name was Bob. He had great news about their phone contract.

"My husband deals with all that," Sheila said, before she had time to realize what she was saying.

Bob cheerfully asked if he could talk to her husband, then. Sheila said that would not be possible, and put the phone down.

When Fiona popped in later she could tell something was wrong, but her mother wouldn't tell her what it was. She stayed a little longer than usual, as if hoping that would wear her mother down.

It did not. Sheila felt sad, yes: today she felt wretched. That did not mean she had reverted to being a child. Dimly she sensed it was important that her daughter understand this, too, and before it was too late — that the road to role reversal between the generations was far more of a one-way street than it ever had been between the sexes.

Just before she went, Fiona mentioned that she'd heard a new bistro had opened down on the sea front in Brighton. Locally sourced food, all organic.

"Hmm," her mother said. She had not felt hungry for several days.

That night there didn't seemed to be anything on television. Sheila had adopted a temporary policy of not watching the shows she and John used to enjoy together. Not forever, just for now. Settling down in front of *University Challenge* or that cook they liked, Rick Stein, was simply not a tolerable prospect.

Unfortunately all of the other television seemed to have been made with someone different to Sheila in mind. She watched almost a whole episode of what was evidently supposed to be a comedy without feeling moved to smile. This wasn't because she was grieving. It was because it wasn't funny. When something wasn't funny and you were watching it with someone, you could enjoy not finding it funny together. By yourself, it simply wasn't funny.

Although everyone in the audience seemed to be laughing.

For a moment Sheila felt very afraid, wondering if the show was funny after all but she was unable to see it. She'd always known what funny was. She and John used to make each other laugh all the time. Even in bed. But what if that hadn't been her?

She used to say things that would make John laugh, but what if it was his laughter that made them funny, rather than what she said? What if — without realizing it — she'd left all of that to him, too?

* * *

Half an hour later she found herself upstairs, outside the little office. The door was open and the filing cabinet was visible. It was a murky green color, with beige drawers. John bought it from a catalogue and for years afterward they got a laugh out of an occasional update arriving at their door, addressed to "The Office Furniture Buyer." John would open up the kitchen waste bin, bend down and call "More post for you, Cyril…" and drop the catalog in.

Their mobile phone contract would be in the cabinet somewhere. Sheila knew she didn't have to look for it. She understood that any news "Bob" might have had for her would have been nothing more than a covert means of getting her to upgrade, or committing herself to a longer contract with the same provider. A history of leaving things to someone else didn't make her a complete dimwit.

It seemed important, however. It felt symbolic of something. It was a useful test case, too. If Bob or one of his familiars called back, she could hear him out — armed with the relevant documentation — and simply say, "No, thank you," if she so chose. There was nothing to lose.

She walked into the office and up to the cabinet. She put her hand on it. The metal felt cool to the touch. It was strange. Despite the fact that John would have had far more contact with other objects in the room — the desk, the chair, his biros on the little pot — the cabinet felt like the essence of the space.

She opened the top drawer. It was easier than she'd thought it would be. Not just that she was able to reach out and do it, but also because it slid out faster and more smoothly than she'd anticipated.

Ka-thunk, it went. It was a capable sound.

The smell of old papers wafted out. Each drop file had a neat plastic tag at the top, arranged so as to progress from left to right, all visible at once. Each one held a tiny rectangle of paper in John's extremely legible capitals, saying things like CAR, KITCHEN, and MEDICAL. Big nouns, concrete and abstract. The building blocks, tangible or otherwise, of a life lived.

Sheila ran her hand over the top of the files, causing some to open a little. Many pieces of paper lay within. Letters, receipts, contracts. Even though a lot of them presumably related to things she was still using, she had never seen anything that looked so dead. Deader even than John. He at least still lived – to some degree – in her mind. These things…they were just dead.

She closed the drawer, not having been able to spot a tag that related to mobile phones, and feeling neither inclined nor strong enough to work through the contents of all the drop files one by one.

She opened the second drawer. This didn't come so easily. Perhaps the mechanism had rusted, or a piece of paper inside had become caught. She pulled harder, and it eventually withdrew.

It wasn't just a mechanical problem, however. She was crying now. Crying hard enough that all of the energy in her body seemed focused on yanking muscles tightly in the wrong directions, stretching the tendons in her throat. There was little power left for anything else.

She dragged her sleeve across her eyes and forced herself to read the tags in this drawer.

GAS & ELECTRICITY. BROADBAND. TAX. She couldn't imagine why she would ever, ever want to open drop files labeled thus. There were more, but still not the one she was looking for.

She pushed the drawer. It suddenly slammed shut, far more easily than it had opened. The noise scared and unnerved her.

She reached down and took hold of the handle on the lowest drawer. She pulled, but nothing happened. She tugged, with all her might, but it would not open.

It wasn't locked – it gave a little – but there was evidently something jammed in it, stopping the drawer from sliding out more than about half an inch. A few more half-hearted yanks at it achieved nothing. She stopped.

She'd tried. Evidently the drawer was broken.

She left the room and went back downstairs. Later she went to bed and lay there, sleepless, for several hours. What if he'd been wrong?

What if everything she needed wasn't in there?

What then?

Fiona's visit next day was a fly-by, mid-morning, on her way to some meeting or other. She seemed distracted at first, as if these daily visits to her mother — never part of their routine before John's death — were beginning to feel a little like…not a chore, exactly, but an errand secondary to the main order of business.

Sheila caught herself thinking this and felt depressed and sad. Not at the thought, but at herself for entertaining it. That wasn't how Fiona would be feeling, and Sheila knew it. Fiona was busy. Her life went on, as all lives must. The dead die in order to remind us how non-dead are the lives of those who remain; we have children to provide us with role models to remind us the way we think now is not the only way to think. Fiona was not "distracted," merely a woman leading her own life, one that currently involved the death of her father and dealing with a grieving mother, but that also still held commitments to the living and to the future.

Sheila understood this. But still, when Fiona dropped a mention of how The Grand in Brighton was doing out-of-season deals, it was all she could do to turn away, and remain silent, rather than saying something she would have regretted.

Mid-afternoon, Bob rang again. Actually he said his name was Kevin this time but he appeared to be fundamentally the same man. He also wanted to talk to her about her mobile phone contract. Sheila did not say that John dealt with those things. She told him instead that she was unable to find their phone contract. The man assured her that this was not a problem, not in the slightest, and that the great offers he wished to make available to her were not dependent upon it.

Sheila listened for a few moments but then gently put the phone down. Of course it mattered whether she could find the contract. Otherwise why would they *have* such things?

She spent the rest of the afternoon in her chair in the sitting room, in silence. She was waiting for something. What, she didn't know.

Later, she stood in front of the window onto the garden, watching twilight darken and fade. When it was properly dark, she went upstairs.

This time she looked through the top cabinet properly, searching each drop file. Although she found many, many pieces of paper — John had obviously maintained a policy of retaining absolutely everything, even for appliances she knew for a fact had gone to the great dump in the sky many years previously — there was nothing in there about their mobile phones.

She closed the drawer. She realized it was now after nine in the evening. She realized also that she hadn't eaten anything for dinner. Or lunch. She couldn't remember the last time she'd drunk anything, either.

Had she made tea again after Fiona left, late morning? She wasn't sure. She didn't think so.

She felt dry, and tired, but knew that she had to do this, and do it tonight.

The second drawer was as hard to pull out as it had been the night before. She still couldn't work out why, and tonight at least she wasn't crying. It simply didn't slide properly. She searched through all of the files, going straight to BROADBAND to begin with, as it had occurred to her that whoever was supplying them/her with that service might be in the market to sell mobile phones, too, and John might have taken advantage of some special deal or other. (He had always read direct mail diligently, rather than throwing it away, in case they were offering something worth having. Sheila had never understood how he was able to tell if something was worth having or not.)

Their Internet supplier apparently did *not* also provide their mobile phones. Neither did anyone else in any of the second drawer's drop files. By the time she was only halfway through it Sheila's back was aching. She pulled John's old chair over from the desk, but it didn't help much. For the last few files she was leaning her elbows on the sides of the drawer. Her stomach had stopped growling some while ago, as if it had lost faith. Her mouth was arid. When she blinked she could hear the lids scrape across her eyeballs, or it seemed like she could. She felt a little light-headed as she sat upright. It didn't matter. She could have a snack afterward if she felt like it. The clock on the desk said it was now well after eleven, in fact coming up for midnight. The house was silent and cold around her.

That made no difference. She was finishing this tonight. She had to find the thing, and if everything she needed was in here, then here was where it had to be.

She closed the second drawer.

Ten minutes later she was crying. She didn't know whether the tears were of grief or frustration or both and it didn't matter. What mattered was that she couldn't open the bottom drawer. As with the night before, it would slide out about a centimeter but then come no further. She'd gone down on hands and knees in front of it, holding the handle with both hands, and pulled with all her might. She'd got one of the pens from the desk and poked it through the gap at the top, running it right along the edge in the hope of dislodging anything that might be obstructing it from within. She done that one way, then the other, then back — faster and faster, until a combination of despair and fury broke the pen into three pieces.

She'd broken a pen that John had used to write things and sign things, but achieved nothing else.

She tugged at the handle some more. She hit the drawer with her fists. Her tears were constant now, and she felt dizzy and her head was aching. The room seemed to sway as she pushed herself back up to her feet.

"You said it would be in here," she shouted, catching herself unawares. She'd had no idea she was going to say anything, much less shout it. "YOU SAID THIS HAD EVERYTHING I NEED."

She kicked the drawer, hard, and then again, heedless of the pain in her toes. She relished it, in fact, bitterly triumphant at being able to make herself feel something, at breaking out of the endless grey fog. She felt even dizzier now but didn't care — she believed she'd finally understood what people feel in the moment before they end it all, a kind of frantic glee, a rich dedication to self-harm and self-destruction and to the realization that none of it mattered and you could just keep escalating the pain until it exploded into silence.

She pulled her foot back, screaming incoherently, and kicked the drawer with all her force.

There was a soft *thunk*.

Sheila froze. The sound hadn't been loud, but it cut through the haze all the same.

Something had happened inside the drawer. Something had been dislodged or freed.

She lurched back toward the cabinet and leaned down, panting. She grasped the handle. She pulled. It slid open smoothly.

John was inside. He was bent and folded and turned over on himself, like a blanket stuffed into a too-small drawer. He had been so very thin at the end. His head seemed to lie on top of the rest of him, top toward the front, face pointing upward. His eyes were open.

They swiveled to look at her. "Hello, dear," he said.

Sheila fell to her knees, reaching for him. She tried to pull him out but he was too tightly jammed into the drawer. There was no way of ever getting him out.

She gave up trying, and though her eyes were so tear-blurred she could barely see, she saw him start to smile in the same old way as she leaned over to bring her lips down toward his mouth.

* * *

She woke the following morning in her bed. When she remembered what had happened, she got up, wrapped her robe around her, and went through to the office. The bottom drawer was shut. She knelt down in front of it and pulled, gently, not expecting it to open.

But it did. It was empty inside but for ten hanging files. Each had a plastic tag at the top, but no label.

She flicked slowly through them.

In the last she found a single index card. She took it out and found something written in John's handwriting. Not as she remembered it from their first letters to each other, or on so many birthday and Christmas cards, but as it had become in the final months, in the last days. Weaker, but defiantly neat, and still characteristically his.

"For your filing," the note said. "Put everything you need in here. Love, J."

Fiona arrived at midday, this time bearing lunch from Marks & Spencer. She looked tired. Sheila helped her unwrap the sandwiches in silence, and then the two of them stood side by side for a few moments, looking out at the street outside.

"I don't want to go to The Grand for tea, not this time," Sheila said. "Let's try The Metropole instead."

Fiona turned to her and smiled, properly, for the first time since her father died.

Bob rang again, in the afternoon. This time he was called Justin. He still had a great new offer to discuss.

Sheila told him to bugger off.

Story Notes

WHEN I BEGAN TO READ TALES of horror and the dark fantastic in the late 1980s, some of the first collections I read (and to my mind some of the best ever written) were Stephen King's. I used to love his story notes at the back — partly because his prose is sufficiently habit-forming that I would have been content to read his To Do lists — but also because I was fascinated to hear where the stories had come from, and how they'd come about. I always made sure I saved them until the very end, however. While it's not as destructive as learning how a magic trick is done, pulling aside the veils on a story has similar effects: you'll never again be able to read it in quite the same way. Sometimes this adds another layer of interest, like a director's commentary track on a great movie, but it also runs the risk of popping the fragile bubble of make-believe that makes a story work in the first place.

There will be spoilers in the following notes, so be warned: either save them until you're done with the story, or — if you don't want to know how or indeed why the rabbit was put into the hat before the show — don't read them at all.

Be further warned that you will not find the meaning of life in here, nor any notably useful pointers on the writing of fiction. These are merely a few observations about how the stories in this collection came to be written, and why. Like the speech given by the father of the bride at a wedding, they're there as background information, and do not constitute a verbal guarantee that the marriage will work.

THIS IS NOW

I wrote this story for the BBC when they were putting together a website dedicated for genre or "cult" fiction. [Sidebar: it's weird how some spellcheckers insist that you spell "website" as "Web site," and want to capitalize the 'internet' as if it's a place, like Germany. Our relationship to these spaces is changing faster than software can keep up with.] I can't remember whether the BBC wanted something specifically about vampires, but that's what I ended up doing — though I kept their role very low-key, and in fact took a certain amount of trouble not to even call them by that name. So much genre fiction is, of course, not about what it appears to be about — and what it's usually *really* about are the crucial turning points in people's lives, viewed in retrospect. The realest and scariest monsters are internal demons, the specters of regret and guilt and lack of fulfillment, awareness of the entropic end of love or the first shivers occasioned by the realization of our own aging, and the eventual inevitability of death. These things are, I suspect, what this story's actually about.

Sounds like a hoot, right?

UNBELIEF

You very rarely come across unthemed anthologies these days.

The idea of a group of stories *not* bonded together by some high concept, however wearisome — celebrity lesbian vampires, vacation-based science fiction tales with the word "spatula" in them — is apparently a tough sell. The problem with these themed anthologies is you often end up (to my mind) with a bunch of stories that wouldn't stand up without the structuring conceit, and that perhaps didn't really need to be written in the first place.

The challenge of an unthemed anthology is being put in the rare position of having no constraints on what you do. Writers are forever bitching and whining about being pigeon-holed or forced to meet publisher or reader expectations: being told to "do whatever you like," however, can bring you up short.

What *do* I like?

If no one was watching, what would I do?

When Neil invited me to contribute to STORIES, therefore, I was becalmed for a while. Then I wrote "Unbelief," which is a rather short, odd story. There probably aren't many editors in the world who would have taken it. But…they did. Bless them.

WALKING WOUNDED

This is a story about transitions. After spending many years lurching in and out of an important — but in its later stages rather dysfunctional — relationship, I'd finally broken free (or was I pushed?) and found the person who would become my wife. This tale's motif of sorting through baggage doubtless tells its own story.

The bit where the narrator cracks a couple of ribs was, sadly, inspired by Real Life Events. Nearly twenty years later they still give me gyp from time to time.

THE SEVENTEENTH KIND

This was inspired by us finally getting cable (quite some time ago now) and becoming briefly obsessed with QVC, the shopping channel. We used to love lurching back from the pub, settling back, and watching people giving their all trying to shift units of all manner of crap — live on TV. The two favorite quotes mentioned in the story were things we actually heard. After a while I became particularly intrigued by the presenters, wondering how they felt about the whole experience — from the superbly coiffed guy who gave it 110% every time (regardless of how banal the product) to a woman whose eyes seemed to betray, once in a while, awareness of the absurdity of it all: and who once memorably lost it during a half-hour debacle in which a whizzy new piece of salad-making equipment utterly failed to do what it was supposed to, instead pinging bits of celery and tomato all over the studio. I thought she was going to die laughing.

There was something weird, too, about the idea of the people who might be watching all this in the small hours, and calling in with their comments and questions. I pictured them sitting at home, alone, bathed in the light of the flickering screen...and wondered who they were.

From somewhere in between the two came this story.

AND A PLACE FOR EVERYTHING

An early story, this one riffing off an interest in Zen and positioning things in space. That's. About. It.

THE LAST BARBECUE

I wrote this for Stephen Jones's ZOMBIE APOCOLYPSE! FIGHT-BACK, the second in his series of shared world (or shared narrative) confections in which he expertly weaves a story out of contributions from many different writers.

Part of the massive canon of "Where I went on my holidays" fiction, my segment is set on the shore of South Lake Tahoe, where my family had recently spent a few days. Tahoe's a strange place. Beautiful, yes, but otherworldly. Waves gently lapping up on a little sandy shore, as tots dip their toes in the silky water. Snow-capped mountains all around. A hot air balloon serenely crossing the sky in the far distance. There's something about the environment that strongly puts me in mind of living on some gigantic spaceship in the far distant future, and coming to the People's Recreational Facility for my annual week-long break from toiling on the hydroponic farms.

Lake Tahoe is also, interestingly, not far from the Donner Pass. I didn't realize this when I wrote the story. I love it when that happens.

THE STUFF THAT GOES ON IN THEIR HEADS

One of the most intriguing but unnerving aspects of being a parent is watching your child's development, and in particular observing the mingling of changes in their personality caused by external influences with elements that seem hard-wired. Just as it can be a struggle to comprehend that your kid really *can't* see that 6 + 6 = 12, it's sometimes hard to remind yourself that their brains haven't had decades to wear familiar and comfortable tracks, to develop the kind of mental highways that have big, obvious signs above them and that anyone can follow and understand.

Children's minds are cloudy and unpredictable, perhaps even unknowable. The last great wilderness. The boundaries within are more permeable, too. What they believe to be the case may be true, even if it's not.

UNNOTICED

Another story with a straightforwardly real-world inspiration. When we first came to live in Santa Cruz we rented a wonderful house over on the East Side, one block from the ocean. It had been hand-built by some guy in the 1940s and featured an upper deck that afforded a rare degree of prospect for the neighborhood. It felt a little like living on a ship. That area of Live Oak is primarily made of up old, single-storey vacation rentals or small houses, but dotted amongst these on the main roads are occasional larger buildings of less discernible purpose. I became intrigued by one of these, and it gave birth to this story.

And yes, there genuinely was a large vintage car taking up most of the reception area. I could, I suppose, have gone in and asked about it, but I prefer most mysteries to persist, rather than be solved.

THE GOOD LISTENER

This story came about because I was invited to contribute a piece of fiction to an online initiative under the joint aegis of Sony and *The Guardian* newspaper, who wanted to explore how new technology would continue to be incorporated into the fabric of our lives. I wrote the story and then recorded my reading of it in a zany sound studio on the edge of Santa Cruz, which appeared to be in the middle of either being built or knocked down, I was never sure which. As the recording was then zapped over the internet to a London studio before being installed on the web as a podcast, the whole experience was pleasingly self-reflective: an example of new technology's reach.

The place where the story is set — the Dream Inn hotel — is of greater significance. We came to live in Santa Cruz because we wound up being "stranded" here for several weeks when an unpronounceable volcano in Iceland grounded European air travel. (Note: telling people over the phone that you've been "stranded" in a boutique beach hotel in California tends to piss them off). We had zero expectations of the town and only ended up there in the first place by accident. Fate gave us a chunk of time to get to know it, and we came very quickly to like the place very much. It as this that set us on course to eventually leaving London after a quarter of a century, and going to live in California instead.

And I suppose it's the little quirks of fate, and unexpected encounters, that this story is about.

DIFFERENT NOW

This is a much earlier story than most of the others in this volume. It was written soon after I'd come to live in London, and slots neatly into my Early Miserablist period. As opposed to my

Slightly Later Miserablist period, which I'm working on now. The classic Miserablist short story form involves a young, alienated man living in a small flat in an anonymous urban environment and being confronted with the breakdown of a relationship while the world goes wonky around him.

This is a classic Miserablist short story.

AUTHOR OF THE DEATH

This collection is by Michael Marshall Smith. You may or may not be aware that I also write novels under the name Michael Marshall. (If this is news to you, then go out and buy them. Buy them all. BUY THEM NOW.)

The distinction between the two writers has never been especially clear in my mind, but one afternoon I wondered: what if, out in the world, it made an actual difference which guy was doing the writing? The title is a play upon critical theory's daft notion of the death of the author, of course, and overall it's kind of a silly story, perhaps. But I had fun writing it… and if someone out there has the same reaction to reading it then that's my job done, right there.

SAD, DARK THING

There are two small facts worth noting about this story. The first is that it was the first tale I ever wrote about where I'm now living — Northern California. I wrote the story while back in London, between our second and third exploratory trips to the region, and the fact I was ready to try placing fiction here probably shows that a big part of my mind had already moved in.

The second is it's one of those stories that dropped into my head almost fully formed. My friend Stephen Jones emailed one morning, saying: "Just saw this phrase — thought you might be able to do something with it."

The phrase was "Sad, dark thing."

I sat very still for a few minutes, while an oblique, melancholy story seeped into my head, as if some odd narrative substance was dripping around the inside of my skull, outside my control.

Then I emailed Steve back, saying yes, I believed I could, and thank you very much. Hopefully I paid back the favor later, in that the story I wrote wound up going into Steve's A BOOK OF HORRORS, one of the first published by Jo Fletcher's new imprint. It was also nominated for a British Fantasy Award.

This is one of the reasons why, when Stephen Jones emails, I take care to read what he says.

WHAT HAPPENS WHEN YOU WAKE UP IN THE NIGHT

Being a parent is scary sometimes. Yes, a lot of it is day-to-day and affable and some of it's infuriating. I won't lie to you about that. But there's a simple and horribly powerful love involved, too, and with that comes the possibility of terrible things.

Ever since we met, my wife has been my first reader. Every novel or story or screenplay that I've finished gets printed out and put warily in front of her (or, these days, converted to PDF and emailed for consumption on her iPad). She's my filter. She tells me whether a story basically stands up.

She's never read this one. I didn't send it to her. I know it stands up (and was hugely honored when it won the British Fantasy Award in 2011). I know also that my wife really, really wouldn't enjoy reading it.

She puts up with enough through being married to me. Even I have limits.

THE THINGS HE SAID

Something I've noticed as I continue to write short stories (and, after a decade in which I produced almost none, the pace does seem to be picking up again, thankfully) is that the same subjects come up time and again. This isn't surprising, of course. Themes and situations and tropes are bound to reoccur. Once you've written one or two vampire stories, or a handful of zombie tales, you may come to feel that you've done the straight-ahead approach and become attracted to more oblique takes: stories that put the apparent subject in its proper place (the background, as color, or as an organizing structure like a musical key), and instead attempt to deal with the underlying meaning.

"The Things He Said" is one of these. It's a story about zombies. Kind of. It's more about how people deal with epic adversity, however, and about how much (or how little) change it may cause. Some people are good, some are bad, and there's a lot of us in that murky area in between. The end of the world won't change that.

SUBSTITUTIONS

This one had a simple genesis — and it's pretty much what happens at the beginning of the story. Often the stories that are most fun to write are these where you take an event from real life and say: "But what if something different had happened at the end? What if? What then?"

I was at home one morning trying to work, when a van arrived from Ocado, the North London default for supermarket delivery. I'd already absentmindedly unpacked half of the bags which had been deposited in our kitchen by the cheery delivery guy, before flags started to go up.

Gradually I realized... *this isn't our stuff.*

What I found interesting about this was partly the fact it took a while for me to cotton on, and thus how much commonality exists between people living in the same area (if I'd been confronted with a bumper pack of tofu in the first bag, the penny would have dropped sooner); mainly that I'd never realized how much something as simple as your shopping said about who you were, and the life you might be leading. Your own bags are full of the mundane stuff you expect to see in your fridge, and therefore seem to have no narrative.

They do, however, as you realize when you get a surprise peek into someone else's world.

I called the delivery company and they sent the guy back and it all got sorted out quickly and simply. That's the mundanity of real life.

Short stories *aren't* real life. In stories you can take an event or idea wherever you want…even if where it ends up isn't nice.

THE WOODCUTTER

This is the most recent story in this collection — the most recent I've written at all, in fact. It's also the only story I've so far written in the chair where I'm sitting right this moment, in a house I'm still not even close to being used to. I guess the story must be at least partly a reflection on having moved to a different country, therefore, though I don't feel the way the protagonist does (at least not consciously, or for more than a second, once in a while).

The idea at the core of the tale has been knocking around my head for quite some time, however, waiting for a home. I remember watching a pub magician working the tables one night in the Crown and Two Chairmen in Soho, and thinking: but what if those *aren't* tricks?

EVERYTHING YOU NEED

I suppose this is partly a reflection on married life, though in my case the relationship is reversed. My wife is the one who knows where the hell everything is. Some of the time. Despite the fact it's rounding off the collection, and is the title story, I'm not sure there's much I can say about this one. It is what it is. Often, when it comes to my own work, those are the stories I'm happiest with.

— MICHAEL MARSHALL SMITH
Santa Cruz, CA
February 2013

This Is Now was originally in BEST NEW HORROR 16, Robinson, 2005.

Unbelief was originally in STORIES, Morrow, 2010.

Walking Wounded was originally in DARK TERRORS 3, Gollancz, 1997.

The Seventeenth Kind was originally in THIS IS NOW, Earthling Publications, 2007.

A Place for Everything was originally in POSTSCRIPTS 10, WHC and Michael Marshall Smith Special issue, 2007.

The Last Barbecue was originally in ZOMBIE APOCALYPSE! FIGHTBACK, Running Press 2012.

The Stuff That Goes On in Their Heads was originally in SWALLOWED BY THE CRACKS, Dark Arts Books, 2011.

Unnoticed is original to this collection.

The Good Listener is original to this collection.

Different Now was originally in SCAREMONGERS, Tanjen, 1997.

Author of the Death is original to this collection.

Sad, Dark Thing was originally in A BOOK OF HORRORS, Jo Fletcher Books 2011.

What Happens When You Wake Up in the Night was originally published as a chapbook from Nightjar Press, 2009.

The Things He Said was originally in TRAVELLERS IN DARKNESS, the souvenir book of the 2007 World Horror Convention.

Substitutions was originally in BLACK WINGS, PS Publishing, 2010.

The Woodcutter is original to this collection.

Everything You Need is original to this collection.

Story Notes is original to this collection.